The Serpent Prince's Heart

Destinies Entwined in Shadows – Book Two

By

Everett Vale

© 2025 Everett Vale
All rights reserved.

This book is a work of fiction. Names, characters, places, and incidents are either the product of the author's imagination or used fictitiously. Any resemblance to actual persons, living or dead, events, or locales is entirely coincidental.

No part of this book may be reproduced, distributed, or transmitted in any form or by any means, including photocopying, recording, or other electronic or mechanical methods, without the prior written permission of the publisher, except in the case of brief quotations embodied in critical reviews and certain other noncommercial uses permitted by copyright law.

Table Of Contents

Introduction: The Beginning of the End

Prologue: The Curse of Iridale

Chapter One: The Shadows of Iridale

Chapter Two: The Road to Ruin

Chapter Three: Beneath the Veil

Chapter Four: The Dead Do Not Rise

Chapter Five: The Mark of the Void

Chapter Six: The Hollow Awakening

Chapter Seven: The Path of Ash and Blood

Chapter Eight: The Sins of the Past

Chapter Nine: The Hollow Crown

Chapter Ten: The Gathering Storm

Chapter Eleven: The City of the Forgotten

Chapter Twelve: The Stirring Veil

Epilogue: Echoes of the Future

A Heartfelt Thank You to the Reader

Introduction:

The Beginning of the End

Long before the Rose chose its bearer.

Before the shadows crept across the land, whispering forgotten truths and binding fates in chains of unseen magic.

Before Anira's journey began, before the battle that nearly consumed her, before the abyss clawed at the edges of existence—there was another story.

The war did not start when Anira took up the Rose. It began long before her, long before the name of the Serpent Prince became a myth, long before Iridale stood on the edge of ruin, before an ancient promise was broken and darkness was left to fester.

It began with Dorian.

The lost prince. The cursed heir. The man whose story had been swallowed by time, whose name had been erased from the histories, whose fate had been written in prophecy long before he ever took his first breath.

Before the battle for the Rose, before the war of shadows reached its peak, there was a choice made in blood and sacrifice.

And it was this choice—Dorian's choice—that set everything into motion.

Because the war did not begin with Anira.

It began with the Serpent Prince's heart.

Prologue:
The Curse of Iridale

The night was silent, but the shadows were restless.

High in the tower of the **Silver Keep**, beneath a sky thick with storm clouds, the King of Iridale stood over his firstborn son, a blade trembling in his grip. The chamber smelled of incense and burning sage, of old magics meant to ward off the thing he had brought into the world.

The boy did not cry.

Newborns were supposed to scream, to wail their defiance into the night, but this child—his child—had **golden eyes**, eyes that gleamed like coins in firelight, eyes that had seen something no infant should have ever glimpsed.

Eyes that belonged to **the Serpent Prince**.

The High Priest stood at his side, his face hidden beneath a hood woven with silver thread, his voice low, his tone unshaken. "You must do it quickly, Your Grace. Before the soul fully binds."

The King could not breathe.

He looked down at his son, at the tiny, fragile form wrapped in silk, at the slow rise and fall of his too-steady breaths. The child should not have been born like this. The curse had been sealed away generations ago—the first Serpent Prince was dead, his heart ripped from his chest, his soul cast into the abyss. The kingdom had suffered for its betrayal, but the cost had been necessary.

Iridale had been free.

And yet, as he stared down at the newborn in his arms, he knew that freedom had only ever been an illusion.

The High Priest whispered, "Your ancestors swore their bloodline would never again bear his mark. You cannot let this one live."

The words were the same ones whispered to kings long before him, spoken over the cradles of children whose lives had been stolen before they could ever take shape.

But something inside the King resisted.

He had seen the cost of this curse. He had studied the histories, had walked the ruins of Serakar, had stood in the old temple and felt the echoes of the past screaming in the stone.

He had always believed the sacrifices were necessary.

But now, standing over the child with the golden eyes, he felt something colder than duty settle into his bones.

The blade in his hand shook.

The High Priest stepped closer. "If you do not end it now, he will bring ruin upon us all. The Serpent Prince's heart still beats. And once it wakes, the shadows will return."

The King exhaled, slow and unsteady.

And then, instead of lowering the blade, he made a different choice.

He sheathed it.

The High Priest stiffened. "Your Grace—"

"I will not kill my son."

A silence fell between them, deep and final, a silence that felt like the turning of fate, the moment before a war begins.

The King turned, cradling the infant in his arms, stepping toward the window where the night stretched on in all directions. The storm had not yet come, but he could feel it on the wind.

Iridale had doomed itself long before this night.

And though he did not know it yet, the war that had been kept at bay for centuries had just begun anew.

The child in his arms—his son, Dorian—was proof of that.

The Serpent Prince's heart still beat.

And soon, the world would remember him.

Chapter One:

The Shadows of Iridale

The road to Iridale was long and cruel, winding through forests that had grown too wild, past rivers where the water ran thick and dark, past villages where the people did not speak her name but watched her with quiet suspicion. The world here felt older than the rest of the land, burdened by history, steeped in something unseen—a presence that lingered between the trees, between the whispers of wind curling through the mountains, between the echoes of a past that refused to be forgotten.

Aelina pulled her cloak tighter around her shoulders, the chill of the evening pressing in despite the layers she wore. She had been traveling for days, her body aching, her thoughts heavier with every step. The weight of her satchel dug into her shoulder, filled with the last of her herbs, the remnants of her dwindling hope. She had left her village with one desperate purpose—to find the cursed prince, to beg for the aid of a man who had long since been forgotten by his own kingdom.

It was madness.

But the sickness that spread through her home was not something natural. She had seen plagues before, had tended to wounds infected with time and rot, had felt the frailty of human life in the way flesh burned with fever and breath rattled in dying throats. But this was different.

This was something else.

The shadows that clung to the sick did not move like normal illness. They pulsed, dark veins stretching across skin, curling beneath eyelids like fingers of unseen hands. It did not spread through touch. It did not spread through air. It chose its victims, as if something unseen had reached into the world and marked them for ruin.

And there was only one name whispered in the quiet of fearful homes.

Prince Dorian.

The Serpent Prince.

The last heir of Iridale's cursed throne.

Aelina did not know what to expect. The stories varied—some called him a monster, a creature that had been allowed to live when his ancestors had been slain for the same bloodline, a beast who shed his skin at night and became something else entirely.

Others said he was nothing more than a man—a bitter, exiled noble whose father had forsaken him, locking him away in the ruins of a forgotten estate at the edge of the kingdom.

She did not know which truth was real.

But she knew one thing—he was the only one left who understood the magic that had poisoned her people.

The last light of dusk melted into the sky, the deep blues and purples bleeding into the horizon as the first stars flickered to life. The road had grown narrower now, the trees pressing in, thick and dark, their bare branches tangled like skeletal fingers overhead.

The road ended at a gate.

It was not the kind of gate that welcomed visitors.

It stood tall, iron-forged, its bars twisted into the shape of serpents, their bodies coiled, their fanged mouths open as if frozen in a silent snarl. The estate beyond it loomed, a ruin swallowed by time, its towers jagged against the sky, its stone walls cracked and veined with ivy.

Aelina exhaled, pressing a hand against the gate's cold iron.

The air was wrong here.

It did not hum with magic. It did not sting with the presence of something unseen. It was still—the kind of stillness that came with places abandoned too long, with places the world had long since left behind.

She pushed forward.

The gate creaked open under her touch, slow and reluctant, as if even the iron did not want her to enter.

The path leading to the front of the estate was overgrown, the stones beneath her boots cracked with moss, the once-pristine courtyard choked with wild grass and thorned vines. The air smelled of damp earth and something faintly metallic, like the remnants of old storms.

Her steps slowed as she approached the grand entrance—a set of massive oak doors, their edges carved with faded symbols, the remnants of protection wards that had long since lost their power.

She raised a hand to knock.

But before she could, the doors opened on their own.

Aelina's breath caught in her throat.

She was not alone.

A figure stood in the threshold, tall and unmoving, wrapped in the shadows of the dimly lit hall beyond. He did not speak. Did not move.

But she knew who he was.

The air shifted, and golden eyes burned in the dark.

She had found him.

And from the way he watched her—it was clear that he had been waiting.

The silence stretched between them, thick and heavy, an unspoken thing that curled around Aelina's ribs like a coiled serpent waiting to strike. The man before her—Prince Dorian, the Serpent Prince—stood motionless in the doorway, half in shadow, half bathed in the dim flicker of candlelight from within the ruined estate. His golden eyes, strange and sharp, reflected the light in a way that seemed almost unnatural, like the embers of a dying fire refusing to fade.

Aelina had spent days preparing herself for this moment. She had imagined him a hundred different ways—a monster with scaled flesh and fanged teeth, a wraith wrapped in darkness, a soulless creature stripped of everything human. But now, standing before him, she saw a man.

His features were sharp, his dark hair falling in tousled waves around his face, strands loose from where they had been tied back in a leather cord. His clothes were simple, not the silks and gold-threaded finery of a prince, but a dark tunic and a cloak lined with fur, its edges worn from years of use. The air around him carried the faintest trace of something earthy, like cedar and smoke, and beneath it, something colder—iron and ruin.

But it was his eyes that unsettled her the most.

They were watching, assessing, weighing. Not in the way a noble studied a commoner, or even in the way a man looked at a stranger intruding on his home. His gaze was something else entirely—something deeper, something knowing.

"You should not have come here." His voice was low, smooth, edged with something that sounded more like a warning than a greeting.

Aelina steadied her breath, tightening her grip on the strap of her satchel. The instinct to step back curled in the base of her spine, but she fought it, forcing herself to hold his gaze. She had faced worse than a cold reception. And if she ran now, if she let herself be intimidated by a voice wrapped in ice, then she would have failed before she had even begun.

"I had no other choice," she said, lifting her chin slightly, though the ache in her feet and the weight of exhaustion in her bones betrayed how far she had come to stand here. "My people are dying. A sickness is spreading through the villages beyond the valley, and none of the healers—none of the magi—can stop it. You are the only one left who understands what it is."

His expression did not change. He did not blink. Did not flinch. He simply watched her.

Aelina had treated enough patients to recognize when a person was lost inside their own thoughts. It was not vacancy. It was calculation. A mind working through all the possibilities, considering whether a person was a threat, a burden, or something worse—a liability.

Her pulse quickened, but she did not look away.

Finally, after what felt like an eternity, Dorian exhaled slowly, the sound barely audible over the distant rustling of wind through the ivy-choked courtyard.

"And what," he asked, voice quieter now, almost resigned, "makes you think I would help you?"

The words stung more than she expected, though she had anticipated some resistance. She had not expected bitterness.

Aelina squared her shoulders, letting the frustration settle beneath her skin like embers beneath a layer of cold ash. "Because this sickness isn't natural," she said, stepping forward, the scent of damp stone and old wood meeting her as she crossed the threshold. "It's spreading too fast. It moves like it has purpose. And if the stories about you are true, then you are the only one left in this kingdom who knows the kind of magic that might stop it."

Dorian's jaw tensed, his gaze flickering past her to the courtyard beyond, where the last remnants of twilight bled into darkness. He did not speak.

Aelina pressed forward.

"If you do nothing, Iridale will fall."

Something in his expression changed, so fleeting she almost missed it. A flicker of emotion—something like recognition, like memory—before his features smoothed over again, unreadable as stone.

Then, without another word, he turned and disappeared into the dim corridors of the estate, leaving the door open behind him.

Aelina exhaled sharply, letting out a breath she hadn't realized she'd been holding. She was not being turned away.

That was enough.

For now.

She stepped inside.

The estate was not dead, but it was close.

The corridors stretched long and dark, the stone walls lined with ancient sconces, their flickering candlelight barely strong enough to fight back the shadows that clung to the ceilings and the edges of the great hall beyond. The scent of dust and old parchment filled the air, laced with something faintly metallic—iron, or perhaps something older, something long buried within these walls.

She had expected ruin, and in some ways, she had
not been wrong. The place felt abandoned, forgotten,
a relic of a life no longer lived. But it was not entirely
empty. The hearth in the main hall still smoldered
with dying embers. The thick tapestries, though
faded, had been carefully kept from decay. The grand
table at the center of the hall had two places set,
though only one had been used.

Dorian had been alone for a long time.

But not so long that he had forgotten what it was to
live.

He stood now at the far end of the hall, near a shelf
lined with old tomes and scattered relics of a
kingdom that had long since turned its back on him.
His shoulders were rigid, his posture closed.

"You shouldn't have come," he said again, though
this time, there was less bite to the words.

Aelina unfastened the strap of her satchel and set it
on the edge of the table. "And yet, here I am."

Dorian finally looked at her. This time, the
assessment was different. Less like a man weighing
his options, more like a man trying to decide
whether to be angry or amused.

The firelight cast deep shadows across his face, emphasizing the sharp lines of his jaw, the slight furrow in his brow, the kind of quiet melancholy that wrapped itself around a person and never truly left.

He exhaled slowly, shaking his head. "You have no idea what you've walked into."

Aelina met his gaze, steady and unyielding. "Then tell me."

Another silence, filled with something far heavier than words.

Then, finally, with reluctant finality, Dorian gestured to the chair across from him.

"Sit."

Aelina sat.

And the past—the history that had led her here, the curse that had shaped the man before her, the prophecy that had begun to wake from its slumber—shifted, like a blade being drawn from its sheath.

This was the beginning of something far greater than either of them had yet to understand.

And neither of them would leave it unchanged.

The fire cracked in the hearth, its flickering glow casting uneven shadows against the stone walls. The air inside the great hall was thick, not with dust, but with the weight of something unspoken. A presence. It did not feel like magic, not in the way Aelina had known it—gentle spells whispered over fevered brows, runes carved into wood to keep sickness from crossing a doorstep. No, this was different. It pressed against her skin, sat heavy in her chest, a watchful thing lingering in the space between words.

Dorian leaned back against the table, arms crossed over his chest, his expression unreadable. He had not spoken since she sat, though he had not stopped looking at her either. His golden eyes were sharp beneath his dark lashes, narrowed slightly, as if weighing the moment, as if peeling back the layers of her presence and searching for whatever reason had truly led her here.

"Say what you came to say," he murmured at last, voice low, measured, almost bored.

Aelina inhaled slowly, willing herself to remain steady beneath his scrutiny. She could not let this moment slip from her grasp. If she did not convince him now, there would be no second chance.

She let her fingers trace the edge of the satchel resting on the table, feeling the rough fabric beneath her touch. "People are dying, Dorian." The words were quiet, but they carried a weight beyond their softness. "My village. Others near the border. It started with a fever. Then came the shadows." She paused, watching him, watching for even the slightest shift in his expression, anything that might betray familiarity. "It moves through them like—" she hesitated, the words catching in her throat. "—like it's choosing them."

Dorian was still. Too still. His jaw tightened, the muscle feathering beneath his skin, his fingers flexing where they rested against his forearm. He did not ask her to continue. He already knew what came next.

Aelina's breath hitched slightly, but she pressed on. "I've tried everything. Herbs, sigils, light magic from the clerics in Iridale's temple. None of it works. The sickness spreads without pattern, without cause, and when it takes hold..." She swallowed hard, remembering the way her neighbors' eyes had gone dark, the veins beneath their skin blackening like something rotten from the inside out. "They don't scream. They don't even fight. They just—fade. As if something has taken them away before their bodies even fall."

The silence that followed was thick, suffocating.

Then, Dorian turned, his gaze flickering toward the fire. "You want me to tell you what it is." It was not a question.

Aelina studied him. His posture was closed, his hands now resting on the table beside him, the tips of his fingers tapping once, absently, against the wood. It was a small thing. A barely noticeable habit. But she had spent enough years tending to the sick, to the grieving, to those who already knew the answers but refused to speak them aloud.

"You already know what it is," she said carefully.

Dorian exhaled sharply, tilting his head slightly as if amused by her boldness, but his smile—if it could be called that—did not reach his eyes. "You think I'm the keeper of all dark things?" He let the question hang between them before shaking his head slightly. "You are standing in a ruined estate, speaking to an exiled prince whose own kingdom abandoned him, and you expect me to have the answers to the suffering of others?"

Aelina straightened, the quiet frustration curling in her chest. "You were the first name they whispered when it began."

Dorian's gaze snapped back to hers. His golden eyes burned, sharper now, something dangerous simmering beneath the surface. "Do you know what happens to those who whisper my name in Iridale, little healer?" His voice was softer now, but darker, like silk drawn across a blade. "They do not whisper it for long."

Aelina did not look away. "I don't scare easily."

A slow breath. Measured. His fingers stilled against the wood.

Then, something changed. The tension in the air shifted, subtle but undeniable. Dorian leaned forward slightly, his presence closer now, the scent of smoke and something colder, something ancient, brushing against her. "Then you are either very brave," he murmured, "or very foolish."

The heat that curled in her stomach was unexpected.

It was not fear.

Not quite.

Aelina forced herself to remain still. "Tell me what you know."

Dorian studied her, his gaze searching, and for a flicker of a moment, she thought he might refuse her outright. He could send her away, he could step back into his shadows, let the kingdom rot in whatever sickness had begun creeping through its veins.

But then—he sighed.

He pushed off the table, pacing toward the hearth, his fingers dragging through his dark hair.

"You say the sickness moves with no pattern," he murmured, staring into the flames. "That it chooses its victims."

Aelina nodded slowly.

Dorian's voice dropped lower, something more unsettled curling in his tone. "Then it's not a sickness at all."

The room felt colder.

Aelina sat forward slightly. "Then what is it?"

Dorian exhaled. "It is a calling."

A chill laced her spine. "A calling to what?"

He turned back to her, golden eyes glinting beneath the firelight, and this time, there was no mockery in his voice, no sarcasm beneath his breath.

"To whatever is waking."

The words were quiet, but they pressed into her like a weight she had not been prepared to carry.

Something was waking.

And it had already begun to choose.

Aelina's grip tightened on the arms of the chair. The urgency that had driven her across miles of frozen land, through nameless forests and forgotten roads, now settled into something worse.

It was no longer about her village.

It was no longer about saving a few lives.

If Dorian was right—if this was a summoning, if something in the depths of magic was pulling people away—then this was only the beginning.

A beginning she was no longer certain she would be able to stop.

Dorian watched her carefully, as if waiting for her to understand, for the weight of what he had just said to sink in.

And it did.

Aelina forced herself to swallow against the fear creeping into her throat. "Then what do we do?"

Dorian's expression was unreadable.

Then, slowly, deliberately, he sat across from her, his posture finally shifting from avoidance to decision.

He met her gaze head-on.

"We find out who is calling," he said, voice quiet, final. "And we stop them before it's too late."

The fire cast flickering shadows along the stone walls, stretching Dorian's figure into something even taller, broader—a silhouette caught between man and something else. Aelina was no stranger to the weight of a presence, to the way a room could be claimed without a single word. She had seen it in grieving parents clutching their dying children, in men who came to her with wounds too deep to heal, in women who had learned how to mask their suffering behind steel gazes.

But Dorian's presence was different.

It did not come from sorrow.

It did not come from power.

It came from something older, something buried so deep that even he did not fully understand it.

"You don't seem surprised," Aelina said carefully.

Dorian leaned back in his chair, resting his elbow on the armrest, his fingers dragging along his jaw in idle thought. He did not answer immediately, and in the growing silence, Aelina could hear the wind pressing against the high windows, whispering against the cracks of the ruined estate.

Finally, he exhaled, slow and measured. "Because I knew it would happen sooner or later."

Aelina's pulse quickened. "What do you mean?"

Dorian tilted his head slightly, watching her as though deciding how much he wished to reveal. His golden eyes flickered, unreadable. "You came here looking for a cure. There isn't one."

Her stomach clenched, but she refused to let the words settle in her bones. "There has to be."

"You don't understand what you're dealing with," he murmured.

Aelina's frustration flared hot. "Then make me understand."

Dorian's jaw twitched. He studied her for a long moment before he leaned forward, his voice dropping to something lower, something edged. "The sickness you've seen—the one that moves without pattern, that takes without warning—is not a sickness at all. It is a calling. A summons. Something is pulling them into the dark, and they are not resisting because they were never meant to."

Aelina's fingers curled into the fabric of her dress.

She had felt it—the way the afflicted faded without fight, the way their bodies seemed to empty before their hearts had even stopped beating. The way their eyes turned hollow, not from pain, but from something else.

Something worse.

Dorian watched her carefully, reading the thoughts racing through her mind. His voice was quieter when he spoke again. "I've seen it before."

Aelina's breath stilled.

She did not ask him where. She did not have to.

This was not just Iridale's suffering. It was his, too.

For a long moment, neither of them spoke.

Then, Aelina swallowed hard, forcing the lump from her throat. "Then tell me what to do."

Dorian exhaled, closing his eyes briefly before sitting straighter, rolling his shoulders back. "We start by finding the source."

Aelina frowned. "The sickness has no pattern."

"It does," Dorian said. "You just haven't seen it yet."

She wanted to argue. Wanted to tell him that she had spent weeks searching for connections, that she had looked at every victim, every location, every possible explanation, and had come up with nothing.

But something in his expression—something sure, something certain—made her pause.

"You know where it's coming from," she realized.

Dorian did not confirm it aloud. But he did not deny it, either.

Instead, he stood, his cloak shifting as he turned toward the map pinned against the far wall. Aelina had not noticed it before, but now, as she followed him across the room, she saw that it was old, the edges curled and browned with time, the ink faded in places where hands had touched it too many times.

He dragged a single finger across the parchment, tracing a jagged path north.

"Here," he murmured. "The sickness moves with the river. It touches villages that were once trade posts, places where the blood of Iridale's ancestors still lingers." His voice tightened slightly. "It is not spreading at random. It is following our lineage."

Aelina's heart pounded.

A curse did not spread like a plague. A curse did not fade. A curse chose.

Dorian stepped back from the map, exhaling slowly.

He did not have to say it for her to understand.

This was not a disease.

It was an inheritance.

Aelina stared at the map, her thoughts moving too fast, her pulse echoing against her ribs.

"How long," she whispered. "How long before it reaches Iridale?"

Dorian looked at her then, something unreadable flickering behind his golden eyes.

"It already has."

Her blood ran cold.

The wind outside pressed harder against the walls, rattling the windows, howling as though it carried the voices of those already lost.

Aelina's hands clenched at her sides, her nails pressing into her palms.

If Iridale had already been marked, then they were out of time.

She turned back to Dorian, meeting his gaze, steeling herself.

"Then we leave at first light."

Dorian studied her for a long moment, then—almost reluctantly—he nodded.

But Aelina did not miss the slight tension in his shoulders, the way his fingers flexed once, like something inside him already knew what awaited them at the end of this path.

The sickness was only the beginning.

Whatever lay at its center—whatever had begun to wake—was something much, much worse.

The wind howled through the broken windows of the ruined estate, dragging cold fingers across Aelina's skin, but she did not shiver. She had learned, long ago, that there were worse things than the bite of winter. Fear was colder. The feeling of helplessness, of knowing that time was slipping through your fingers like water, was colder. And now, standing beside Dorian, staring at a map stained by old blood and older curses, she knew what real cold felt like.

She had spent her life healing others, stitching together wounds, easing the suffering of those too weak to do it themselves. It had always been enough. Until now. Until her skills, her knowledge, her hands—steady and sure—were useless against something she did not understand.

Dorian had not moved since she spoke. His golden eyes flickered in the dim light of the dying fire, watching her in a way that made her uneasy—not because he frightened her, but because he saw too much.

He was weighing her, measuring the words she had said, the choices she had made to bring herself here.

And he was not convinced.

"You assume I'll go with you." His voice was low, edged with something unreadable.

Aelina turned to face him fully, crossing her arms. "You just admitted that you know what this is. That means you also know that ignoring it won't stop it. The sickness isn't just claiming villages anymore, Dorian. It's reaching your people. Your kingdom." She took a slow breath, steadying herself before adding, softer, "And you're the only one who can stop it."

Dorian let out a slow exhale, dragging a hand through his dark hair. He turned away from her, pacing toward the stone railing near the shattered window. The cold air from outside pressed into the room, making the flames in the hearth shudder.

"You think I haven't already tried?" His voice was quiet, but it carried something heavier than frustration. It carried defeat.

Aelina frowned, stepping closer. "What do you mean?"

Dorian's fingers curled against the stone, his gaze fixed on the ruins beyond. "This curse—this thing—has bound itself to my bloodline for generations. You think I haven't spent my entire life trying to break it? That I haven't hunted down every scholar, every sorcerer, every whisper of something that might end it?" His jaw clenched. "But it doesn't end. It only sleeps. It waits."

Aelina inhaled slowly, watching him. She had spent years treating wounds that could not heal, comforting people who did not want to be saved, but this was different. This was anger wrapped in exhaustion. This was the voice of a man who had fought against something for too long and had begun to wonder if fighting it at all was pointless.

"You still haven't answered me," she said, her voice softer now.

Dorian turned, his golden gaze meeting hers.

"Will you come with me?"

The moment stretched between them, the fire crackling in the silence. His lips parted slightly, and for a second—just a second—she saw something flicker across his face. Something hesitant.

Then he smirked.

It was not the kind of smirk that accompanied humor, nor the kind that carried warmth. It was sharp, edged with sarcasm and something else—something guarded.

"You're relentless," he murmured.

Aelina lifted a brow. "You're avoiding the question."

Dorian exhaled sharply, looking away again. He was silent for so long that she thought he might refuse her outright, might tell her that she had wasted her time, that she should leave at first light without him.

But when he spoke again, his voice was different. Softer.

"If we do this," he murmured, "you have to understand what it means."

Aelina straightened. "I understand more than you think."

Dorian shook his head. "No. You don't." His golden eyes burned in the dim light, steady and unrelenting. "This thing we're hunting—it's old, Aelina. Older than the sickness, older than the curse. It's been waiting a long time. And if we walk toward it—if we give it reason to notice us—it won't let us leave unchanged."

Aelina felt the weight of his words settle over her like a second cloak.

She thought of her village, of the hollowed-out bodies of those who had already been taken. She thought of the fear in the eyes of the ones who remained, waiting for the sickness to find them next.

And she thought of the way Dorian had stood in the doorway when she first arrived, his silhouette half in shadow, half in firelight, looking like something caught between two worlds.

Perhaps he had been fighting this battle alone for too long.

Perhaps it was time he stopped.

She took a step forward, closing the space between them. "Then we'll leave unchanged together."

Dorian's gaze flickered to hers, his brow furrowing slightly, as if she had said something he did not know how to respond to. For the first time since meeting him, he looked at her differently.

Not as an outsider.

Not as an inconvenience.

But as something else.

Something dangerous.

Something impossible.

His fingers drummed once against the stone before he finally nodded. "At first light, then."

Aelina exhaled, releasing a breath she hadn't realized she'd been holding.

She had won.

But as she watched the way Dorian lingered in the dark, the way his golden eyes reflected something haunted, she could not shake the feeling that she had also just agreed to something much bigger than herself.

Something that neither of them would walk away from unchanged.

The wind howled through the broken windows of the ruined estate, dragging cold fingers across Aelina's skin, but she did not shiver. She had learned, long ago, that there were worse things than the bite of winter. Fear was colder. The feeling of helplessness, of knowing that time was slipping through your fingers like water, was colder. And now, standing beside Dorian, staring at a map stained by old blood and older curses, she knew what real cold felt like.

She had spent her life healing others, stitching together wounds, easing the suffering of those too weak to do it themselves. It had always been enough. Until now. Until her skills, her knowledge, her hands—steady and sure—were useless against something she did not understand.

Dorian had not moved since she spoke. His golden eyes flickered in the dim light of the dying fire, watching her in a way that made her uneasy—not because he frightened her, but because he saw too much.

He was weighing her, measuring the words she had said, the choices she had made to bring herself here.

And he was not convinced.

"You assume I'll go with you." His voice was low, edged with something unreadable.

Aelina turned to face him fully, crossing her arms. "You just admitted that you know what this is. That means you also know that ignoring it won't stop it. The sickness isn't just claiming villages anymore, Dorian. It's reaching your people. Your kingdom." She took a slow breath, steadying herself before adding, softer, "And you're the only one who can stop it."

Dorian let out a slow exhale, dragging a hand through his dark hair. He turned away from her, pacing toward the stone railing near the shattered window. The cold air from outside pressed into the room, making the flames in the hearth shudder.

"You think I haven't already tried?" His voice was quiet, but it carried something heavier than frustration. It carried defeat.

Aelina frowned, stepping closer. "What do you mean?"

Dorian's fingers curled against the stone, his gaze fixed on the ruins beyond. "This curse—this thing—has bound itself to my bloodline for generations. You think I haven't spent my entire life trying to break it? That I haven't hunted down every scholar, every sorcerer, every whisper of something that might end it?" His jaw clenched. "But it doesn't end. It only sleeps. It waits."

Aelina inhaled slowly, watching him. She had spent years treating wounds that could not heal, comforting people who did not want to be saved, but this was different. This was anger wrapped in exhaustion. This was the voice of a man who had fought against something for too long and had begun to wonder if fighting it at all was pointless.

"You still haven't answered me," she said, her voice softer now.

Dorian turned, his golden gaze meeting hers.

"Will you come with me?"

The moment stretched between them, the fire crackling in the silence. His lips parted slightly, and for a second—just a second—she saw something flicker across his face. Something hesitant.

Then he smirked.

It was not the kind of smirk that accompanied humor, nor the kind that carried warmth. It was sharp, edged with sarcasm and something else—something guarded.

"You're relentless," he murmured.

Aelina lifted a brow. "You're avoiding the question."

Dorian exhaled sharply, looking away again. He was silent for so long that she thought he might refuse her outright, might tell her that she had wasted her time, that she should leave at first light without him.

But when he spoke again, his voice was different. Softer.

"If we do this," he murmured, "you have to understand what it means."

Aelina straightened. "I understand more than you think."

Dorian shook his head. "No. You don't." His golden eyes burned in the dim light, steady and unrelenting. "This thing we're hunting—it's old, Aelina. Older than the sickness, older than the curse. It's been waiting a long time. And if we walk toward it—if we give it reason to notice us—it won't let us leave unchanged."

Aelina felt the weight of his words settle over her like a second cloak.

She thought of her village, of the hollowed-out bodies of those who had already been taken. She thought of the fear in the eyes of the ones who remained, waiting for the sickness to find them next.

And she thought of the way Dorian had stood in the doorway when she first arrived, his silhouette half in shadow, half in firelight, looking like something caught between two worlds.

Perhaps he had been fighting this battle alone for too long.

Perhaps it was time he stopped.

She took a step forward, closing the space between them. "Then we'll leave unchanged together."

Dorian's gaze flickered to hers, his brow furrowing slightly, as if she had said something he did not know how to respond to. For the first time since meeting him, he looked at her differently.

Not as an outsider.

Not as an inconvenience.

But as something else.

Something dangerous.

Something impossible.

His fingers drummed once against the stone before he finally nodded. "At first light, then."

Aelina exhaled, releasing a breath she hadn't realized she'd been holding.

She had won.

But as she watched the way Dorian lingered in the dark, the way his golden eyes reflected something haunted, she could not shake the feeling that she had also just agreed to something much bigger than herself.

Something that neither of them would walk away from unchanged.

The fire had burned low in the hearth, its embers pulsing like dying stars, casting a dim glow against the stone walls. Shadows stretched long and deep, curling into the corners of the ruined hall, watching, as if they knew what had just been set into motion. The night outside had grown darker still, and with it came a silence so complete it pressed against Aelina's skin, making the small hairs along her arms rise.

Dorian had not spoken again since his quiet agreement. He stood near the far side of the hall, his back half-turned to her, his gaze distant as he traced the lines of the old map still pinned to the wall. There was something deeply unsettling about him in stillness. As if his body, his very presence, was meant for motion, for pacing, for hunting. Even the way his fingers rested lightly on the edge of the table, just barely grazing the wood, looked too controlled.

Aelina was good at reading people. It was part of being a healer—learning to see past what was spoken, past the walls people built around themselves, past the lies they told even to their own reflections.

And Dorian?

Dorian was holding something back.

The weight of it sat in his shoulders, in the tension at the back of his neck, in the way his breath came too slow, too measured. This was not just a man exiled from his kingdom, not just a prince with a curse too old to name. This was a man bracing himself for something inevitable.

Aelina exhaled softly, rolling her shoulders before standing.

"You don't have to pretend," she murmured.

Dorian stiffened, the only visible sign that he had even heard her. "Pretend what?"

Aelina stepped toward him, her boots making no sound against the worn stone. "That you haven't already decided where we need to go. That you don't already know exactly what's waiting for us on the other side of this."

Dorian finally turned to her, his expression carefully neutral. "You assume too much."

She lifted a brow. "Do I?"

A flicker of something—not amusement, not quite annoyance—passed over his face before he looked away again.

Aelina stopped just a few paces from him, crossing her arms. "I don't need you to tell me everything. I just need to know if I should be afraid."

His golden eyes found hers again, burning through the dim light, and for a moment, she swore the air between them thickened, charged with something neither of them had the patience to name.

"You should always be afraid," he murmured.

The words sent a shiver down her spine, but she did not look away.

Dorian sighed, dragging a hand through his dark hair, the strands falling loose from where they had been tied back. "We're heading north," he finally said, glancing once more at the map. "The river is the thread that connects every village that has fallen. It runs to the oldest ruins in the kingdom—the first temple to the Shadow God."

Aelina felt her stomach tighten.

She had read about those ruins. She had heard stories, the kind whispered between children around dying campfires, the kind meant to be warnings.

"That place is forbidden," she said quietly.

Dorian let out a dry, humorless laugh. "So am I."

Aelina frowned. "That's not what I—"

"You don't have to come." He turned fully toward her now, something careful, deliberate in his posture. "You don't owe these people anything. You could leave before dawn and pretend this was just another dead-end lead. Go back to your village and tend to what's left of it."

Aelina inhaled sharply, barely suppressing the frustration curling beneath her ribs. "If that were an option, do you think I'd be standing here right now?"

Dorian tilted his head slightly, studying her.

"You're infuriating," she muttered.

A smirk ghosted across his lips, the barest hint of something dangerously close to amusement. "So I've been told."

Aelina huffed, turning away before she did something stupid—like let herself feel anything other than utter irritation at his constant avoidance. "I need to prepare supplies if we're leaving at first light," she said, rubbing her temple. "Where do you keep—"

"Downstairs. Third door on the right."

She blinked. "You're actually going to let me near your things?"

Dorian shrugged. "If you're stupid enough to touch something cursed, that's on you."

Aelina groaned. "Wonderful. I can already tell this journey will be great."

Dorian's lips curled, something too sharp, too knowing behind his eyes. "Oh, little healer," he murmured, his voice dark with something she couldn't quite name. "You have no idea."

Aelina turned on her heel, shaking her head as she strode toward the corridor.

Dorian watched her go, his smirk fading just slightly.

The last echo of her footsteps vanished down the corridor, swallowed by the weight of the estate's ever-present silence. The fire in the hearth crackled once, a low, hollow sound, before settling into a slow burn. He exhaled, the breath leaving his lungs in something that was neither relief nor regret—just acceptance.

Aelina had no idea what she had just stepped into.

She was not the first to seek him out, not the first to demand answers, to ask for help that he could not give. But there was something different about her. It was in the way she looked at him—not with fear, not with reverence, but with an expectation that unsettled him more than he cared to admit.

And that was dangerous.

Dorian pushed away from the table, pacing toward the map still pinned against the wall. His fingers traced the path he had spoken of earlier, the river that cut through Iridale like an old scar, leading north toward the forgotten ruins where the first Shadow God had once been worshipped.

The first mistake of their ancestors had been made in that place.

The last mistake would be made there as well.

Dorian let out a slow breath, pressing his palm flat against the edge of the table. His body ached—not in the way of wounds, but in the way of something beneath the skin, something that lived in his bones and waited for nightfall to take its shape once more.

The curse had always been patient.

It could wait a little longer.

Aelina walked deeper into the ruin, guided by the faint glow of candlelight and the distant chill of something she could not name.

The hallway stretched long and empty, its walls lined with faded tapestries, their edges frayed from time and neglect. The dust that clung to them carried a scent beneath it—something old, something that did not belong to this world anymore.

Dorian had told her to find the storeroom. Third door on the right.

She counted each one carefully, her fingers trailing the rough stone, feeling the uneven cracks beneath her touch. When she reached the door, she hesitated, resting her hand against the iron handle. The metal was cold, too cold, as if untouched by the warmth of the estate.

Aelina exhaled and pushed inside.

The room was smaller than she expected. Wooden shelves lined the walls, some sagging under the weight of old supplies—dried herbs, glass vials, remnants of forgotten remedies. There were crates near the back, some marked with the royal insignia of Iridale, though the dust covering them told her that no one had touched them in years.

Aelina moved carefully, her fingers brushing the tops of bottles, checking for anything that might be useful. She found small pouches of powdered resin, dried bellroot, a flask of something she guessed was fire whiskey, and a half-broken mortar and pestle tucked behind a stack of unused candles.

It was a strange thing, standing in a place that had once belonged to royalty, knowing that the man who should have commanded this estate now lingered in the shadows of his own ruin.

She picked up one of the vials, turning it over in her palm.

"Looking for something specific?"

Aelina spun so fast that the vial slipped from her fingers, shattering against the stone floor.

Dorian leaned against the doorframe, watching her with far too much amusement for someone who had just nearly scared her to death. The candlelight flickered over his face, casting sharp shadows across his features, making him look more wolf than man.

"You could have made a sound," she muttered, pressing a hand against her chest.

He lifted a brow. "I did. You were just too focused on whatever potion you were about to steal from my shelves."

Aelina rolled her eyes and crouched to collect the broken glass. "I wasn't stealing. I was looking for supplies since, you know, we're traveling at dawn. I assumed you wouldn't mind."

Dorian stepped inside, slow, measured, his boots making no sound against the stone. He crouched beside her, picking up one of the larger shards between his fingers. He turned it once in the light, the reflection catching in his golden eyes, making them flicker like molten metal.

"You assume a lot about what I will and won't mind," he said, his voice lower now, almost... curious.

Aelina swallowed, her fingers tightening around the pieces of glass she had gathered. "You let me in. That has to count for something."

Dorian's lips curled, something between a smirk and something darker, something unreadable. "Does it?"

The air between them shifted.

Aelina was suddenly too aware of how close he was.

Too aware of the way his fingers had not yet let go of the glass, the way his gaze dipped—not to her hands, but to her mouth before flickering back up again, so fast she almost missed it.

Heat curled low in her stomach.

Dorian tilted his head slightly, as if he had noticed.

Bastard.

Aelina cleared her throat and stood, moving to deposit the glass shards on a nearby shelf. "I assume," she said, forcing her voice back to normal, "that if you were going to throw me out, you would have done it already."

Dorian watched her for a moment longer before standing as well, stretching lazily before leaning against the shelf beside her. "Maybe I just enjoy seeing what you'll do next."

Aelina scoffed. "You must be very bored."

"Endlessly."

Something too warm unfurled beneath her ribs, but she ignored it. Instead, she focused on the shelves, pulling out what she had gathered and organizing it into a small satchel.

She could feel Dorian's gaze on her, heavy and unrelenting.

"You don't trust me," she said after a moment.

Dorian hummed, a low, thoughtful sound. "That would require knowing whether or not you're trustworthy."

Aelina turned to him, lifting her chin slightly. "Would you like to find out?"

There was something sharp and heated in his eyes now, something dangerous, but not in a way that made her want to step back.

It made her want to step closer.

Dorian's smirk was slow, lazy. "Maybe I would."

Aelina huffed, shaking her head, breaking the moment before it became something else entirely.

"Then I suppose you'll have to wait and see."

Dorian let out a quiet chuckle, one that felt far too satisfied for her liking, before pushing off the shelf.

"At first light, then."

Aelina nodded, adjusting the strap of the satchel over her shoulder.

She did not look back as she walked past him, did not let herself see if he was still watching her, did not let herself acknowledge the fact that something had shifted in that moment between them.

Something that could not be undone.

The moment the door closed behind her, the warmth of the room seemed to leech away, leaving behind only cold stone and dying firelight. The silence stretched, pressing against his ribs like unseen hands. The weight of it was nothing new—he had learned long ago that silence was both a curse and a companion. But tonight, it felt different. Tonight, it lingered, the echoes of Aelina's presence still curling in the air, in the space she had filled only moments ago.

He ran a hand over his jaw, exhaling slowly.

This was a mistake.

She should not have come here.

And he should not have let her stay.

He had been alone for so long that he had forgotten what it felt like to have someone challenge him, to push back against the walls he had carefully built. She had looked at him as if he were a puzzle she intended to solve, as if she could somehow see past the sharp edges and the shadows curling at his feet.

It was dangerous.

Not for her.

For him.

Because the moment he let himself believe that he could be something other than this, that he could be more than a monster trapped in the ruins of his own making, was the moment he would begin to fall. And if there was one thing he had learned over the years, it was that falling never ended in anything but ruin.

Dorian clenched his jaw and turned away from the door.

The room felt too small now, the air too thick. He needed to breathe, needed to remind himself of what he was.

What he had always been.

The wind outside howled through the broken trees, rattling the shutters as the night deepened.

Aelina sat on the edge of the narrow bed in the guest chamber Dorian had reluctantly given her. The room was simple, bare, though the remnants of its former grandeur still clung to the edges—the carved wooden beams in the ceiling, the silver embroidery woven into the dust-laden curtains.

She let out a slow breath, rolling the tension from her shoulders, but it did little to ease the feeling that had settled deep in her bones. She had won tonight. Dorian had agreed to leave with her, to help her find the source of the sickness that had stolen so many lives.

But she could not shake the feeling that he was keeping something from her.

He had not hesitated when he traced their path on the map. Had not blinked when she told him about the sickness, about the way it was choosing its victims.

No.

Because he already knew.

Aelina frowned, running her fingers over the leather strap of her satchel. She had learned long ago that people did not hesitate over things that were new to them—they hesitated when they already knew the truth and were deciding how much of it to share.

Dorian knew exactly what was waiting for them.

The thought should have scared her.

And yet, when she closed her eyes, all she could see was the way his golden gaze had burned beneath the candlelight, the way he had watched her as if she were something unexpected.

Something dangerous.

She exhaled sharply and stood, stripping off the heavy cloak and unlacing the front of her tunic, letting the cool air of the room wash over her skin. Her body ached from travel, from exhaustion, from holding herself together when all she wanted to do was fall apart.

But she did not have the luxury of falling apart.

Not yet.

Not ever.

She slipped beneath the worn blankets, staring up at the ceiling. The wind outside continued its restless howling, rattling through the cracked stone, but it was not the only thing that kept her awake.

Because somewhere beyond this room, beyond these ruined walls, Dorian was awake, too.

And she knew, without question, that he was thinking of her just as much as she was thinking of him.

Dorian did not sleep.

He stood at the edge of the estate, his hands braced against the cold stone of the outer wall, staring into the night. The mist had crept in sometime after Aelina had gone to bed, rolling in thick tendrils across the overgrown courtyard, swallowing the trees and statues until they were nothing but shadows against shadows.

The air was wrong tonight.

It carried something beneath it, a whisper too soft to be wind, too steady to be imagined.

His fingers curled against the stone, his breath slow, measured. Waiting.

And then—

A shift.

Not a sound.

Not a movement.

But a change.

Like something beyond the mist had just turned its head in his direction.

Dorian clenched his jaw, ignoring the way his pulse hammered once, twice, against his ribs. The feeling did not go away. If anything, it deepened, sinking into his skin, pressing into his thoughts.

It was the same feeling he had gotten as a child, standing before the High Priest, listening to the old stories of what had been buried beneath Iridale's lands—stories that were never meant to be just stories.

Dorian inhaled slowly.

The mist curled through the courtyard, thick and restless, pressing against the outer walls like an uninvited guest, a force that had come not to pass through but to linger. The estate groaned under its weight, the stones old, weathered, tired—as tired as the bloodline that had once ruled from within them.

A voice, too soft to be real, whispered along the edge of his hearing. Not a word, not a name. Just a presence. A knowing.

His fingers curled against the stone railing.

It had been years since he had last felt it—this thing that moved just beyond the edges of sight, watching him with patience that no mortal thing should possess.

It had waited.

For him.

For this.

His jaw tightened, but he did not turn back to the mist, did not acknowledge its presence any more than he had to. If it wanted him, it would have to come for him directly.

And that was the one thing it would never do.

Dorian exhaled and stepped away from the wall, moving back through the ruined halls, his boots silent against the cold stone. The candlelight still flickered dimly, throwing long shadows against the worn tapestries, the remnants of a time when this place had been more than just a graveyard of his father's discarded heir.

His father.

Dorian felt the familiar flicker of something sharp crawl down his spine. A name he had not spoken aloud in years. The man who had cast him away, who had chosen his throne, his kingdom, his fear over his own blood.

Iridale was his.

And yet, it had never belonged to him.

Dorian reached the corridor where Aelina slept, slowing his steps, listening for any sign of wakefulness behind her door. Silence. Only the soft, steady sound of her breathing, light and even, as if she had already surrendered herself to sleep.

He frowned slightly.

He had expected her to resist. To linger on edge. To lay awake with thoughts of the journey ahead.

She trusted him.

She shouldn't.

Dorian stepped back into the shadows before he let himself linger too long, turning down another hallway, toward the room he had once used as his own. The fire had long since died in this one, leaving only the chill of winter seeping through the cracked walls.

He did not light a candle.

He did not undress.

Instead, he sat at the edge of the old, heavy chair near the window, resting his forearms on his knees, fingers laced together.

Aelina thought she had found the only path forward.

She thought he was her best chance.

But she did not yet realize that there was no path.

Not for him.

Not for her.

Because the thing waiting at the end of the road was something neither of them could run from.

And if he was right—if what stirred in the north was what he feared it to be—then he already knew the price of stopping it.

It would not be her who paid it.

It would be him.

The wind howled against the walls, and for the first time in a long time, Dorian let his eyes close.

Tomorrow, they would leave.

Tomorrow, the real battle would begin.

Chapter Two:

The Road to Ruin

The morning arrived in hushed tones, cloaked in mist and the biting chill of late autumn. The sky had not yet decided whether to yield to the dawn, leaving the estate draped in a soft, eerie half-light, as though the world itself hesitated to wake.

Aelina tightened the straps of her satchel, checking her supplies once more before slinging it over her shoulder. She was used to early departures, to the cold weight of exhaustion pressing into her limbs before her mind fully caught up with the day. But this morning was different.

This morning, she was leaving with a man who should not exist.

Dorian stood at the entrance of the ruined estate, adjusting the dark cloak over his shoulders, his posture lazy but too controlled, like a predator playing at indifference. His golden eyes flicked to her as she approached, scanning her quickly—assessing, always assessing—before turning back to the mist-shrouded path ahead.

"You're awake earlier than I expected," he murmured.

Aelina huffed, fastening her cloak. "You think I'd risk you leaving without me?"

Dorian smirked, slow and lazy. "And here I thought you trusted me."

Aelina rolled her eyes, stepping past him. "Let's just go before I change my mind."

Dorian chuckled under his breath but said nothing more as he followed her into the fog.

The path leading away from the estate was barely more than a forgotten road, half-swallowed by creeping ivy and the remnants of a kingdom that no longer remembered its own ghosts. The trees were dense here, their branches arching like skeletal hands, their roots thick and gnarled beneath the cracked stone path.

Aelina kept her pace steady, though she could feel the weight of Dorian's presence beside her, silent, steady, unsettling in ways she could not yet name.

"How far is the first village?" she asked after a few minutes of walking, breaking the quiet.

Dorian exhaled through his nose, glancing toward the sky, as if measuring the distance by instinct alone. "Half a day's journey, if we keep a good pace."

Aelina nodded. "And if we don't?"

Dorian smirked. "Then we hope whatever is watching us gets bored before nightfall."

She shot him a look. "Comforting."

"You asked."

Aelina sighed, shaking her head. "You're insufferable."

Dorian hummed in agreement. "And yet, here you are."

She didn't bother replying to that.

The road stretched onward, winding through the thickening trees, the mist curling around their ankles like restless spirits. The air here felt different, heavier, like something had settled into the land long ago and never truly left.

It was not magic in the way she had felt before—not the careful, measured power of a healer's hands, or the ancient sigils carved into temple walls. This was something older. Something that had existed long before men had dared to name it.

She felt it.

And from the way Dorian's shoulders tensed ever so slightly, she knew he felt it too.

"How long has it been like this?" she asked, keeping her voice low.

Dorian didn't look at her, his gaze fixed ahead. "Like what?"

Aelina gestured vaguely to the mist, the air, the way everything seemed to be listening.

Dorian was quiet for a moment before he finally spoke. "Since before I was born." His voice was unreadable, but there was something tired beneath it. "Iridale was always meant to fall. My father spent his life pretending otherwise."

Aelina studied him from the corner of her eye, the way his fingers flexed once before stilling again, the way his expression remained calm, despite the storm brewing beneath it.

"You don't talk about him much," she said carefully.

Dorian smirked, but there was no humor in it. "That's because there's not much worth saying."

Aelina didn't press further.

She knew what it was like to have wounds that never truly healed.

They walked in silence after that, the trees closing in tighter, the mist growing thicker, as if the very land itself knew what was coming.

And in the distance, just beyond the veil of fog—something moved.

Watching. Waiting.

And for the first time since they left, Aelina wondered if Dorian's warning about being afraid had not been a jest at all.

The mist thickened, curling through the trees like something alive, like something that knew it was being watched. The road ahead had vanished into the silver-white haze, obscured as though the world beyond it had ceased to exist. Aelina's breath slowed as she walked, her pulse steady but not calm.

She could feel it.

Something unseen. Something waiting.

Dorian walked beside her, his steps soundless against the uneven stone, his presence unnervingly still. He wasn't tense—not outwardly—but there was a subtle shift in him, a quiet edge in the way he held himself. His fingers hovered just slightly closer to the hilt of the dagger at his belt, his gaze flicking to the shadows between the trees as if he already knew what lay hidden there.

"You feel it, don't you?" Aelina murmured, keeping her voice low.

Dorian didn't answer immediately. His golden eyes remained forward, calculating, unreadable. When he finally spoke, it was soft, almost thoughtful. "I never stopped feeling it."

Aelina swallowed, resisting the urge to look over her shoulder. Because that was what it wanted.

She had seen it before, in dying men who swore they heard whispers in their final hours, in grieving women who claimed their husbands had stood at the foot of their beds after death. The unseen presence that lurked just beyond the veil of the living.

The mind had a way of filling in the gaps, of creating horrors where there were none.

Except she knew, in her gut, that this was not just her mind playing tricks.

It was real.

"You've traveled this road before," she said, her voice quieter now, as though speaking too loudly might make the thing lurking in the mist real.

Dorian nodded. "Many times."

"And yet, you still look like you're expecting something to lunge at us."

Dorian smirked, but it was a thin, sharp thing, void of real amusement. "That's because, eventually, something always does."

Aelina's throat tightened, but she kept walking. Kept her pace even, her breathing controlled. She had learned long ago that fear was a weapon, that showing it only sharpened the blade against your throat.

She had also learned that Dorian was not the type to make empty warnings.

The silence stretched, and for a moment, the only sound was the steady rhythm of their boots against stone. The mist pressed closer, thickening with every step, until the trees became hazy shapes, their outlines blurred as if the very world was unraveling around them.

Then—

Aelina felt it.

Not a sound. Not a movement.

A shift.

A pressure against the air, the kind that made the fine hairs on the back of her neck rise, the kind that made her fingers curl reflexively at her sides, the kind that whispered—

You are not alone.

She inhaled, slow and measured. "Dorian—"

"I know."

His voice was softer than before. Calm. Controlled.

But not reassuring.

Aelina's fingers twitched toward the dagger at her hip. She had trained to defend herself, had learned how to move in the presence of danger. But she had spent years fighting things that bled—diseases, infections, wounds that could be stitched closed.

This was something else.

Something that might not bleed at all.

Then—

A sound.

Distant at first, so faint she might have imagined it. But it grew, slow and deliberate, until it curled around them like a whispered breath against the skin.

A rustling.

Like leaves disturbed where there was no wind.

Aelina's grip tightened around the hilt of her blade, the cool weight grounding her.

Dorian had stopped walking.

That, more than anything, made her pulse quicken.

His golden eyes narrowed slightly, focused ahead, into the mist, where the road vanished into nothing. His posture had not changed, but there was something different about him now, something quietly coiled beneath the surface, waiting.

He was listening.

Waiting.

The silence thickened.

Then—

A second rustling.

Closer this time.

Too close.

Aelina turned her head slightly, her breath slow, controlled, her fingers curling around the handle of her dagger. "How many?" she murmured.

Dorian tilted his head, as if listening to something just beyond her ability to hear. "Three," he said. Then, after a pause, his voice dipped lower, unreadable—almost amused.

"No. Four."

Aelina exhaled through her nose. "Do they bleed?"

Dorian let out a quiet chuckle, the kind that should not have been reassuring but was anyway.

"Let's find out."

Then—

The mist moved.

A shape emerged, barely more than a shadow, barely more than a blur of shifting black against gray.

Aelina had one moment, one brief, fractured second, to make out the hollow place where a face should have been, the twisted curvature of limbs that did not belong to anything living—

Then it lunged.

And the fight began.

The creature moved too fast.

Aelina barely had time to react before it was upon them, a thing of shadows and something worse, its shape twisting, unfixed, like it had forgotten how to be human but still remembered how to hunt.

She sidestepped, her fingers tightening around the dagger at her hip, but before she could strike, Dorian moved first.

There was no hesitation in him.

No breath wasted.

No unnecessary motion.

One second, he was standing beside her, golden eyes calculating, and the next, he was gone—a blur of fluid, lethal grace, faster than any normal man should have been. His dagger flashed in the mist, cutting upward, a clean arc of steel, and the creature let out a sound that was not a scream but the memory of one, something high and distant, like the wind screaming through an empty place where a soul had once been.

Aelina staggered back, her heart hammering against her ribs as the shadow thing staggered too, dark ichor leaking from the gash in its side.

It should not have bled.

And yet, the thing looked down at its wound with something like confusion, as if it had forgotten it could be harmed at all.

Dorian didn't give it time to remember.

His second strike was just as swift—a silver arc in the dark, another clean, ruthless movement. The dagger buried deep into the creature's chest, sinking into the inky blackness where a heart should have been.

For a moment, the thing shuddered.

Then, without sound, without weight, it folded inward, its form collapsing into the mist, dissolving into something thinner than air, vanishing as if it had never been there at all.

The silence left in its wake was deafening.

Aelina exhaled too sharply, trying to steady her pulse. Her fingers still curled around the hilt of her dagger, but she had not used it. Had not even had the chance.

Because Dorian had moved before she could.

Because he had known exactly what to do.

Aelina turned to him, her throat tight with unspoken questions, with the weight of things she could not name. "What—"

She didn't get the words out.

The second one attacked.

It did not lunge for Dorian this time.

It went for her.

She barely managed to throw herself backward, the air shredding where she had been standing only moments before, as clawed fingers slashed through the space where her throat had been. The impact sent her skidding on the wet stone, boots scraping, hands catching against the dirt, but she didn't stop moving.

She rolled, coming up fast, her dagger raised, her body already turning—

Too slow.

The creature was on her.

A blur of darkness and bone, twisting limbs and something wrong. She could smell it now, the scent of decay and old ruin, something that had been dead for a long time but had not stopped moving.

Its hollow face twisted, its mouth opening in a shape that was not meant for speech, but Aelina did not wait to hear if it could speak at all.

She drove her dagger forward.

And for a second—just a second—she thought she had won.

The steel sank deep, right into the place where a human heart should have been.

But the creature did not shudder.

Did not bleed.

Did not fall.

Instead, it laughed.

A thin, brittle sound. A thing made of echoes.

And Aelina realized, too late—

This one was different.

Something sharp and invisible slammed into her chest, a force not of hands, not of claws, but of pure pressure, knocking the air from her lungs, sending her crashing backward. The world spun as she hit the ground hard, her breath leaving her in a sharp gasp, pain rattling through her ribs.

And then—

It was on top of her.

Its hands—if they could be called that—clamped around her throat, long fingers made of something not quite solid, not quite mist, but strong enough to hold her down. Its weight pressed against her, suffocating, and for the first time—

Aelina felt true panic.

She kicked, twisted, fought, but the thing did not move. Did not flinch. It only leaned in closer, its hollow face inches from hers, as if it were watching her die.

Distantly, she heard Dorian shouting her name.

And then—

A blur of movement.

A rush of gold and shadow.

The weight was gone.

Aelina gasped, air flooding back into her lungs as the pressure vanished, the grip around her throat ripped away. She rolled onto her side, coughing, sucking in breath after breath, but she barely had time to recover—

Because Dorian was not finished.

She pushed up on shaky arms, just in time to see him move.

Fast. Too fast.

His dagger was gone, discarded. He wasn't fighting with weapons anymore.

He was fighting with something else.

His hands gripped the thing's face, his fingers sinking into the shifting dark of its form, but instead of pushing it away—

He pulled.

And the thing—

It screamed.

It was not a sound meant for this world.

It was something old. Something hollow.

Dorian wrenched the thing's form apart, tearing it at the seams, its twisting limbs unraveling, its body convulsing, turning inward until it simply ceased to exist.

Aelina stared.

The silence that followed was deafening.

Dorian stood over the place where the creature had been, his shoulders rising and falling with slow, even breaths. His hands were shaking.

Not with fear.

With something else.

Something Aelina did not yet understand.

Slowly, he turned back to her.

Their eyes met.

Aelina should have said something. Should have asked what in the gods' names had just happened, should have asked what exactly he had done.

But she didn't.

Because in the dim light, beneath the mist and the weight of the moment, she finally realized something she should have known from the beginning.

Dorian was not just cursed.

He was not just a man abandoned by his kingdom.

He was something else entirely.

And whatever that something was—

It had just saved her life.

The world had not yet settled.

The mist still curled around them, thick as breath, whispering along the stone path, coiling in the spaces left behind by the creatures that were no longer there. The air had changed, though, sharp and electric, charged with something neither human nor entirely real, something that had come alive the moment Dorian had touched that thing.

That shadow.

Aelina did not move.

She remained on her knees, her pulse a thunderstorm in her ears, the phantom pressure of those hands—not hands, never hands, something else—still lingering against her throat. She inhaled slowly, steadying herself, but it was not fear that sat heavy in her chest now.

It was knowledge.

She had spent the past day walking beside Dorian, studying him, learning him, understanding that there was something beneath his surface that he did not want her to see.

But now she had seen it.

And there was no unseeing that.

Dorian had not fought like a man.

He had not killed like one, either.

His hands still trembled at his sides, his fingers curled as if they had forgotten how to unclench, as if he could still feel the thing he had pulled apart. The golden glow of his eyes had not fully dimmed, the firelight beneath them slow to fade.

Aelina swallowed, pushing herself to her feet.

"Dorian."

His name was a blade on her tongue.

He turned toward her slowly, like something waking from a dream. His breath was controlled, measured, but his shoulders were tense, his posture slightly wrong, as if the body he stood in was not entirely his own.

Aelina did not flinch.

She did not step back.

She only watched him.

Dorian's gaze met hers, and for a single, stretched-out moment, he did not speak.

The silence between them felt like a threshold.

Like a place they would never be able to return from.

And then—

He exhaled, slow and long, rolling his shoulders, his fingers flexing once before finally relaxing.

"It's over," he murmured. His voice was even. Controlled. But Aelina did not miss the way he turned his hands over once, staring at his own palms for half a second too long before letting them fall to his sides.

Aelina narrowed her eyes.

No.

Not over.

She took a slow step toward him, the scent of cold iron and something earthy, raw still thick in the air.

"What was that?" she asked, keeping her tone careful, controlled.

Dorian tilted his head slightly, a half-smirk creeping onto his lips. "I told you—things bleed if you make them bleed."

Aelina did not smile. "That wasn't a blade."

Dorian held her gaze. "No."

She inhaled deeply, trying to decide how far she could push him before he shut her out completely. "Then what was it?"

Dorian's smirk lingered, but it was thin, empty. "A story for another time."

Aelina felt her fingers tighten into fists. "Tell me now."

Dorian's eyes flickered. Just for a second. Just long enough for her to see that he did not want to tell her, but he also did not want to lie.

Then, he sighed, turning away from her, running a hand through his dark hair. "It's nothing you need to worry about."

Aelina's frustration burned hot.

"Nothing I need to worry about?" she echoed, stepping after him. "You just ripped something apart with your bare hands, and I'm supposed to pretend I didn't see it?"

Dorian stopped walking.

The weight of him filled the space between them, thick and unchangeable, a presence that could not be ignored.

His head turned slightly, just enough for his golden eyes to catch the dim light of the mist.

"You wanted my help," he murmured. "You have it."

Aelina's breath hitched slightly.

"That doesn't mean you get my secrets."

The words landed heavy, sinking into her chest, into the space between them that had begun to close but now felt endless once more.

Dorian turned away again, his long stride carrying him forward.

"We should keep moving," he said, voice lighter now, almost bored, amused, as if the past five minutes had not happened at all. "Unless you'd rather camp with the things that do not bleed."

Aelina did not move.

She stood there for a long moment, watching him, watching the place where the shadows had swallowed whatever had once been human, whatever had been called here to hunt them.

The sickness. The curse. The thing waiting at the end of the road.

It was all connected.

And Dorian was connected to it, too.

Aelina let out a slow breath.

Then, gripping the hilt of her dagger a little tighter, she followed him into the mist.

The mist hung heavy, pressing against Aelina's skin like damp cloth, thick and cloying, wrapping around her like unseen hands. The voice had faded, but its echo remained, carved into the marrow of her bones, whispering beneath her skin like a sickness she couldn't purge. She kept her breath even, kept her mind steady, but it wasn't enough. It had known her mother's voice. It had known exactly what to say, what words to shape into something sharp enough to carve into her ribs, to make her doubt.

She clenched her jaw and forced her mind to obey, to move past the thing that was no longer there. Dorian had already started walking again, his stride easy, too casual, like what had just happened was nothing more than an inconvenience, a distraction along the way. But Aelina saw the way his shoulders remained taut beneath his cloak, the way his fingers flexed and curled before relaxing, as if they had forgotten how to be still. He hadn't hesitated when he'd struck, hadn't paused or questioned whether the thing in the mist was real or an illusion.

She knew what that meant. He had done this before.

Aelina quickened her pace, falling into step beside him. The mist remained thick, but the presence that had lurked just beyond sight, that had whispered and reached for them, seemed to have pulled back, retreating like something that had been fed but was still hungry. Her mind still raced, questions tumbling over one another, fighting to be the first one spoken aloud. Instead, she exhaled through her nose, steadied herself, and asked, "How often does that happen?"

Dorian didn't stop walking. "More than you'd like to know."

Aelina swallowed against the unease curling in her stomach. She had expected danger on this journey, expected to face things that could kill them, but not like this. She had been prepared for swords and blood, for creatures that tore through flesh, for shadow mages who had long abandoned their humanity. But this? This was something else entirely. This was not a battle of weapons—it was a war for the mind.

She let out a slow breath, pressing a hand to the satchel at her hip, feeling the weight of the vials and herbs within. "And they always take the voices of the dead?" she asked, trying to keep her voice even.

Dorian's expression remained unreadable, golden eyes flickering beneath the pale light filtering through the mist. "Not always," he said, his voice softer now, measured, as if choosing his words carefully. "Sometimes, they just watch. Sometimes, they whisper. But if you listen long enough, they learn."

Aelina felt a chill crawl down her spine. "Learn what?"

Dorian's lips tilted, but there was no humor in it. "What you fear."

The words sat heavy between them, settling like a weight that neither of them could cast off. Aelina's fingers curled around the strap of her satchel, grounding herself in something real, something tangible. She had always known fear was a weapon, had always seen it used against men and kings alike. But she had never seen it take shape, never watched it wrap itself in something familiar and wear the voices of the dead like borrowed skin.

She studied Dorian from the corner of her eye, the way his face remained impassive, how he did not so much as glance over his shoulder, did not hesitate in his steps. He had not been surprised by what had happened. He had known what it was before it had even spoken.

That meant something.

She hesitated, then asked the question she already knew the answer to. "Has it ever spoken to you?"

Dorian's steps didn't falter, but she felt the shift in him, the slight stillness that lasted just a fraction of a second too long. When he finally answered, it was quiet, almost lost to the mist.

"Once."

Aelina waited for him to say more, but he didn't.

She wanted to push him, to demand the truth from him the way she had demanded it from so many others. But Dorian was not like the men she had known before. He gave away nothing unless he wanted to, and something told her that whatever had spoken his name in the dark, whatever had whispered to him in that same terrible voice, was something he had no intention of sharing.

So she let the silence stretch between them, let the mist swallow the space where the creature had stood, let the echoes of her mother's voice fade into something half-remembered and terrible.

But she did not forget.

And she knew—neither did he.

The path ahead was still hidden, still veiled in fog, but they did not turn back.

They never would.

The mist thinned as they pressed forward, but it never truly vanished. It clung to the trees in the distance, wrapping itself around the twisted branches like a veil, curling through the undergrowth as if reluctant to release them from its grasp. Aelina could still feel it in her lungs, thick and damp, carrying the scent of earth and something colder, something that did not belong to the world of the living. The air was heavier now, weighed down by the silence that had settled between her and Dorian, a silence that neither of them seemed eager to break. She told herself it was because they needed to focus, that speaking now would be a waste of breath, but the truth sat bitter on her tongue. She was still thinking about the voice.

She had heard echoes of the dead before, but never like that. There had always been distance, a separation between memory and reality, a space where grief could be acknowledged but not touched. But this—this had been different. That voice had not been a memory, had not been the soft recollection of something lost. It had been her mother. As if the mist had reached into the grave, had pulled her mother's voice from the earth and wrapped it around a body that had never belonged to her. The creature had known exactly how to cut into her, how to press its fingers into the weakest parts of her mind and whisper just the right words to break her open.

But she had not broken.

She had stood her ground. And though her heart had pounded, though her hands had trembled, she had not let it see her fall. That had to mean something.

Dorian had known. He had seen through it in an instant, had struck it down without hesitation, without doubt. The question burned at the edges of her mind, but she swallowed it down, knowing he wouldn't answer—not yet, not unless it suited him. He had lived with these things longer than she had, had walked through shadows that she had only just begun to glimpse. She had spent her life healing the sick, treating wounds that could be mended with poultices and herbs. But this was something she could not stitch closed, something she could not fight with vials of tinctures or whispered prayers over burning sage.

The world was darker than she had ever imagined, and Dorian had lived in that darkness for years.

The realization settled in her chest like a stone.

She glanced at him from the corner of her eye. He moved as he always did, with that impossible grace, every step effortless, every movement precise. He had barely made a sound since they started walking again, his expression carefully neutral, golden eyes fixed on the road ahead. His shoulders were loose, his posture easy, but there was something in the way he carried himself now that hadn't been there before. He was waiting.

She knew it in her gut. Dorian had never truly relaxed, never let himself sink fully into stillness. He was always listening, always watching, like something unseen was always watching him in return. He knew what lived in the mist, what lurked in the places between waking and sleep, and if he wasn't afraid, it was only because he had learned not to be.

She envied that.

Aelina let out a slow breath, willing her fingers to loosen from the hilt of her dagger. She had to focus. The road was still long, and whatever was waiting for them at the end of it would be worse than voices in the dark. Dorian had said they were following the river, that the sickness was moving with the water, creeping along the land like a slow, rotting plague. That meant the villages ahead would be worse than the ones already lost. And if she was right—if the magic in her blood still stirred when she reached for it—then they were heading straight into the heart of whatever was waking.

A flicker of movement caught her eye, and she turned her head sharply, but there was nothing. Just the skeletal trees stretching toward the sky, their bark stripped raw by time and wind, their limbs tangled together like gnarled fingers. The mist drifted lazily through them, twisting around the trunks before curling away again, but there was no sign of anything unnatural. Still, the feeling remained. That presence. That sense of being watched.

She swallowed, her pulse quickening. "We're not alone."

Dorian's expression didn't change. He didn't even turn his head. "We never are."

Aelina's throat tightened, but she didn't argue.

The path wound deeper into the woods, the air growing colder with every step. The trees loomed taller now, their branches weaving together overhead, blocking out the weak light of the sun. The forest felt old here, untouched, as though nothing living had dared set foot in it for years. The ground beneath her boots was soft, damp with the remnants of long-fallen leaves and earth that had never been disturbed. There were no signs of animals, no birdsong, no rustling in the underbrush. It was as if the forest itself was holding its breath.

Dorian slowed beside her, finally breaking his silence. "It's close."

She didn't ask what.

She could feel it.

Aelina's fingers hovered near her satchel, knowing she had nothing in it that could fight whatever was ahead of them. She had herbs for healing, vials of tinctures that could numb pain or ease a fever, but nothing that could fight this. Magic, perhaps, in the right hands. But she was not a mage. Her power had always been different—subtle, soft, something that mended rather than destroyed.

Dorian, though. He could destroy.

She had seen it.

And as much as she hated to admit it, she knew that when the time came, she would need him to.

Aelina inhaled deeply, steadying herself. "How much further?"

Dorian tilted his head slightly, listening. "Not far." His golden eyes flicked to her, unreadable. "But I don't think we'll be welcomed."

Aelina swallowed against the unease curling in her gut.

They kept walking.

The trees pressed in closer, their bark pale and brittle, as if the life had been drained from them long ago. The mist remained, curling between the roots like veins of something ancient, something waiting to be unearthed.

And then—

The village came into view.

Aelina stopped, her breath catching in her throat.

The houses were wrong.

She had seen abandoned places before—villages left to time, to war, to famine. But this was different. The buildings were standing, but they were not alive. The wood was too dark, as though soaked through with something unnatural. The windows were hollow, empty frames of glassless openings that looked like they had been carved out instead of broken. The doors hung open in some places, but there was no sign of struggle, no sign that people had fled.

They had simply vanished.

Aelina took a slow step forward. The air was heavier here, thick with something rotting but not dead. The scent of damp earth and something bitter filled her lungs, making her pulse quicken.

Dorian stood beside her, gaze locked on the buildings ahead. He didn't move, didn't breathe for a long moment. Then, in a voice lower than before, he murmured,

"They were here."

Aelina swallowed hard. "Who?"

Dorian turned his head slightly, and when he met her eyes, there was something dark in his expression.

"The ones who don't leave bodies."

Aelina's skin went cold.

The wind shifted, stirring the mist between the empty homes. And then, ever so faintly, from the darkness between the doorways—

Something moved.

The village stood in absolute silence, the kind that weighed heavy in the air, pressing down like an invisible hand. Aelina's breath was slow, steady, controlled, but the feeling in her chest—that cold, creeping unease—would not leave. The houses, though still standing, felt wrong, their structures warped, not in shape but in essence, as if something unseen had soaked into the wood, staining it with a presence that did not belong. She had seen abandoned places before, places where war or famine had driven people from their homes, where the remnants of their lives remained—broken furniture, scattered belongings, half-eaten meals left behind in the panic of escape. But here, there was none of that. There was no sign of flight, no overturned chairs, no footsteps in the dirt roads leading away. It was as if the people had simply stopped existing, had been taken, erased with nothing left behind to mourn them.

Dorian stood beside her, his golden eyes locked onto the open doorways, his expression unreadable but too still, too controlled. He had known what they would find before they had even arrived. Aelina clenched her fingers around the strap of her satchel, willing herself to focus, to push past the feeling slithering up her spine like ice. "How long has it been like this?" she asked, her voice barely above a whisper, as if speaking too loudly might wake something sleeping in the shadows of these empty homes. Dorian exhaled through his nose, slow, measured, before stepping forward. His boots made no sound against the dirt. "Not long." His voice was quiet, but not hesitant. He wasn't guessing. He knew. Aelina followed, her senses sharp, every instinct in her body screaming that something was watching, something unseen but undeniably there.

The village square was empty, but not in the way an abandoned place should be. There was no rot, no decay, no sign of nature reclaiming what had been left behind. The ground was undisturbed, no weeds creeping through the cracks of the stone paths, no birds overhead, not even the whisper of wind shifting through the buildings. Aelina's stomach tightened. It was unnatural, not just in what was missing, but in what remained. It was as if time had simply stopped here, leaving behind a place that should not exist anymore, but did. Dorian slowed in front of what had once been a tavern, its door swaying slightly in the breeze that she could not feel. His gaze flickered toward the threshold, assessing, calculating, before he finally spoke. "They were here." Aelina swallowed against the dryness in her throat. "Who?" Dorian turned his head slightly, just enough for his golden eyes to meet hers, and something in them was darker than before. "The ones who don't leave bodies."

Aelina barely had time to process the words before the sound came. It was faint, barely audible, but it reached her ears with the clarity of something meant to be heard. A rustling, soft, careful, as if whatever had made it had not wanted to be noticed, but had miscalculated. Her grip tightened on her dagger, her muscles going taut as her body prepared for something her mind had not yet caught up to. Dorian remained still, his posture unchanged, but she could feel the shift in him—the moment of waiting was over. He had been expecting this. He had known it would come. And he was ready. The silence returned, stretching too long, an empty pause that carried the weight of something unseen, something deliberate. Aelina's heartbeat hammered against her ribs, but she did not move, did not let the tension coil her body into hesitation. Whatever was out there, it was deciding. Waiting. And that meant it was not alone.

Dorian exhaled once, slow and deep, and the sound was enough to crack the fragile balance holding the moment together. The shadows moved. It happened fast—too fast. A shape burst from the open doorway of the tavern, something dark and shifting, something that did not belong to the realm of men. Aelina barely had time to register it before Dorian was already in motion. His dagger flashed, an extension of him, precise and merciless, a clean arc of silver through the air. The creature—or whatever thing had taken its place—lunged toward them, but Dorian was faster. He pivoted, sidestepping with a fluid grace that should not have been possible, his blade sinking into its form without resistance. And then, in an instant—it was gone. Not felled, not slain, but erased, like the mist had simply swallowed it whole, like it had never been there at all.

Aelina's pulse pounded in her ears, her grip on her dagger tightening until her knuckles ached. "What—" she started, but the words died on her tongue. Because the tavern was no longer empty. They were everywhere. Shadows moving between buildings, shifting in doorways, watching without eyes, waiting for something unseen to call them forward. The village was not abandoned. It had never been. The people had simply been replaced.

Dorian inhaled, slow and even, rolling his shoulders, preparing. "You should run," he murmured. Aelina turned toward him sharply, her heart slamming against her ribs. "Not a chance," she hissed. Dorian smirked, dark and knowing, but he did not argue. He hadn't expected her to leave. He had already accepted that they would fight together or die together.

The creatures did not move. Not yet. But the moment stretched too thin, like the pause before a storm, the air thick with the weight of something inevitable. The first attack had been a test, a question answered with steel. Now, the real fight would begin.

Aelina forced her breath to steady. The mist coiled around her ankles, whispering like breath against her skin. Dorian shifted beside her, his blade still slick with whatever passed for blood in these things, his stance relaxed but ready, a beast waiting for the hunt to begin.

Then—a sound. A voice, thin and distant, curling through the village like a child's laughter, like something that had once been human but had long since forgotten how to be. It echoed through the empty homes, through the hollow streets, a chorus of something wrong, something broken.

Then, the creatures moved.

And the world descended into chaos.

The world broke open.

The first creature moved in a blur of shadow and hunger, its form stretching and snapping back into something vaguely human, but wrong—twisted, as if it had been reshaped too many times and forgotten what it had once been. Its limbs bent at unnatural angles, fingers too long, its hollow face stretching in something that was not a scream but should have been.

Aelina didn't think. She reacted.

Her dagger was already in her hand, the leather grip biting into her palm as she sidestepped the first lunge, the thing's fingers slicing through the space she had just occupied. She swung upward, her blade catching something solid, and for a moment, she thought she had struck true. But the wound did not bleed, did not even seem to register. The creature simply twisted, its body folding in on itself, and then it was behind her.

Aelina's pulse spiked. Too fast. They were too fast.

Then—Dorian.

A flash of steel, a sharp, clean movement. He struck from the side, dagger sliding between where the creature's ribs should have been, twisting with a practiced, brutal efficiency. This time, it worked. The thing shuddered, its body convulsing, its shape unraveling before it collapsed into nothing.

Aelina barely had time to process before another shadow came at them.

They were surrounded.

The village, once eerily still, had come alive with movement. From the open doorways, from the alleyways between the houses, from the mist itself, they emerged. Dozens. Shapes without form, bodies that flickered in and out of existence, moving in ways that made Aelina's stomach turn. They did not walk. They did not run.

They simply appeared.

And then—they attacked.

Dorian moved before she could even draw breath. A blur of darkness and steel, his dagger slicing clean through the first creature before spinning, driving his elbow into the next one, his movements inhumanly smooth, more like a dance than a fight. He fought as if he had done this before—not once, not twice, but a thousand times.

Aelina had no time to watch him.

The next creature lunged at her, faster than she had expected, its clawed hands swiping for her throat. She ducked, her body moving on instinct, then drove her blade upward into its side. The impact sent a shock through her arm, and for a second, she thought it hadn't worked—

Then the thing jerked, its body spasming, and collapsed into the ground, fading into black mist.

She inhaled sharply. They could die.

She just had to figure out how to make them stay dead.

Dorian moved past her, quick and lethal, dispatching another creature with a clean, calculated motion, his blade flashing in the dim light. "You're thinking too much," he said, his voice maddeningly calm despite the chaos around them.

Aelina gritted her teeth. "I'm trying not to die, actually."

Dorian smirked, blocking a strike from another creature and shoving it back with nothing but raw strength. "Then move faster."

Aelina would have cursed at him if she hadn't been forced to dodge another attack.

Her body reacted before her mind could catch up, her instincts taking over, and this time, she did not hesitate. She struck without fear, without second-guessing. The blade found its mark, slicing cleanly across a shadowed throat, and the creature collapsed before vanishing.

She exhaled, then spun to face the next.

The fight became a blur—shadows twisting, steel flashing, mist curling at their feet as the creatures came, and came, and came. But no matter how many they cut down, more appeared.

Aelina's muscles burned, her breath ragged as she parried another strike, feeling the weight of exhaustion creeping into her limbs. She didn't know how long they had been fighting. Minutes? Hours? The creatures did not tire, did not slow. But she did.

And then—Dorian cursed.

Aelina barely had time to register it before a new sound filled the air.

A low, hollow chanting.

Not from the creatures.

From somewhere else.

The world lurched.

The mist thickened, rolling like a living thing, swallowing the village around them, blurring the buildings, the streets, the sky itself.

And then—they stopped attacking.

Aelina's breath came hard and fast, her body still locked in the momentum of the fight, but the creatures had stilled, frozen in place, their hollow faces turned toward the darkened sky.

Dorian's dagger was still raised, his breath even but his eyes sharp. He was watching them, waiting, because this was not a victory.

This was something worse.

Aelina's heartbeat slowed.

She could feel something now, something pressing against her chest, heavy and suffocating, something watching.

Then—

The mist parted.

And a new figure emerged.

Not like the others.

Not shifting or flickering or wrong.

Human.

Or close enough to it.

The figure was tall, draped in black, their cloak heavy with embroidery that shimmered faintly even in the dim light. Their face was hidden beneath a hood, but the power in the air shifted as they stepped forward, slow and deliberate, the chanting still whispering in the background.

Aelina's fingers tightened around her dagger.

This was not a creature.

This was a summoner.

Dorian's posture changed beside her. He did not lower his weapon. He did not move. But he knew who this was.

Aelina could feel it in the way his breath hitched—just barely.

The figure stopped, their head tilting slightly, as if studying them.

Then, a voice—low, smooth, terrible.

"Dorian."

The way they spoke his name was not a greeting.

It was a claim.

Aelina felt her stomach drop.

Dorian did not reply.

He did not move.

But his eyes burned.

And Aelina knew—this was not the first time they had met.

The figure stood in the mist, unmoving, but the power they carried pressed into the air like a slow-building storm, thick and electric, curling into the bones of the village as if it had always been there, waiting for them. Aelina could feel it settling over her skin, heavier than the fear coiling in her gut, heavier than the exhaustion creeping into her limbs. It was a presence that did not belong to the world of men, but had learned how to walk among them, how to shape itself into something that could be worn like a mask.

And right now, that presence had its gaze locked on Dorian.

He did not move. Not at first. His breath remained even, his grip on his dagger firm but not tense, and yet Aelina could feel the shift in him, the way his body had stilled just slightly too much, the way his golden eyes burned with something she had never seen before—something dangerously close to hatred. His entire being had become a single, controlled moment of silence, of waiting, of choosing how this would end. And then, finally, he spoke, his voice low and measured, the words precise, sharpened at the edges.

"I was wondering when you'd stop hiding."

The figure did not respond right away, but Aelina saw the smallest motion, the way their head tilted slightly beneath the hood, a slow acknowledgment, an amusement that sent something crawling up her spine. Then, their voice came again, smooth and deliberate, each word placed carefully, intentionally, as if meant to be savored.

"You've forgotten your place."

The air cracked around them, like the pressure had been torn open just enough to let something else seep through. Aelina stiffened, instinct screaming at her that they were standing at the edge of something much, much worse than they had prepared for. The creatures—the hollowed things that had attacked them moments ago—were still silent, still watching, as if waiting for permission. Not to attack, not to kill. To devour.

Dorian exhaled once, slow and deliberate, rolling his shoulders as if shaking off the weight pressing into the air. But Aelina saw the way his fingers twitched, saw the way he was already calculating, already deciding where to strike if this turned into something they couldn't walk away from. And that realization made her blood turn cold. Dorian did not plan for failure. He did not prepare for battles he thought he could win. He prepared for survival.

"Funny," he murmured, stepping forward just slightly, and the movement was so calculated, so predatory, Aelina almost forgot to breathe. "I don't remember having one."

The figure did not react right away, but Aelina felt the shift in the air, a slow, pulsing thing, like a heartbeat woven into the very fabric of the mist itself. It curled at the edges of her vision, creeping toward her ankles, sinking into the ground. Not just mist. Magic. Old magic. The kind that did not whisper. The kind that did not ask for permission.

Dorian felt it too.

Aelina saw it in the slight flicker of his eyes, in the tightening of his jaw, in the way he shifted his weight just enough—not to attack, but to pull her behind him if he had to.

And that terrified her.

Because if Dorian was preparing to shield her, it meant he did not know if they would win.

The figure let out a quiet hum, tilting their head in that same, slow amusement, and then they raised one hand. Not to attack. Not to strike.

But to call.

Aelina heard it before she saw it—the low, curling sound of something waking, something beneath them, something that had not been there before but had been waiting. The ground shuddered, just slightly, just enough to tell her it was real. And then, from the shadows of the empty doorways, from the cracks in the stone, from the hollow places where the villagers had once stood—something moved.

Dorian reacted first.

His dagger flew through the air, sharp and true, aimed directly for the figure's throat. But the moment before it could strike, before the blade could find purchase in whatever was beneath that hood, the mist devoured it.

Gone.

Swallowed whole.

Dorian's jaw ticked, but he did not hesitate.

He was already moving, already closing the distance between them, and Aelina barely had time to pull in a breath before he reached for the second dagger at his belt—

And then, the ground split open.

Aelina felt it beneath her boots, the sudden crack of the earth, a violent shudder that tore through the stones, sending a jagged line of darkness racing toward them. Instinct screamed at her to move, to run, but before she could react, something lashed out from below—not a shadow, not mist, but something solid, something alive.

It grabbed her ankle.

And yanked.

The breath was ripped from her lungs as she was dragged down, the world tilting, her dagger slipping from her grasp as she fell. The stone shattered beneath her, the world dropping away, and in the last, fleeting moment before she was swallowed whole, she heard Dorian's voice—not calm, not careful, but roaring her name.

Then—nothing.

Only darkness.

Only the cold.

Only the sensation of being pulled into something deeper than the earth, deeper than the world she knew.

And then—

A voice.

Not the figure's.

Not the thing that had spoken Dorian's name like a claim.

But something else.

Something that had been waiting.

"Finally."

Chapter Three:

Beneath the Veil

The world returned in pieces, in fragments of sensation before sight, warmth before sound, touch before memory. Aelina's mind stirred through the weight of unconsciousness, drifting first through the cold, the absence of breath, the slow, creeping realization that she was no longer falling. Her body was still, but not on stone, not in the depths of some endless abyss. There was heat against her skin, something solid beneath her, something that carried the slow, rhythmic movement of breathing.

She inhaled—not air, but scent.

Spice and smoke, something rich and wild, threaded with the faintest hint of metal, like steel warmed by the sun. It curled into her senses, familiar yet undeniably foreign, and the realization sent a slow shiver crawling up her spine. It was him.

Dorian.

Her lashes fluttered open, the dim glow of unseen firelight flickering across her vision, and she became fully aware of exactly where she was.

Pressed against him.

Not just beside him, not simply near enough to feel his presence, but wrapped in it. His arm was around her waist, firm and unmoving, a silent barrier between her and the unknown. Her head rested against his chest, her fingers curled loosely against his ribs, as if sometime between darkness and waking, her body had chosen him as its anchor. And he had not let go.

Aelina's breath caught, her pulse beating a traitorous rhythm against the stillness. It should have been awkward, should have made her tense, should have sent her scrambling away. But her body, traitorous and too aware, had already cataloged the details—the way his warmth had settled into her skin, the way his breathing remained steady, unbothered by her weight, as if he had always expected her to be there.

As if he had kept her there.

Her fingers twitched slightly, a movement so small she barely noticed it, but Dorian did.

Because his breathing changed.

Not much. Not enough to be obvious, not enough to be deliberate, but she felt it. A slow inhale, deeper than the rest, like he had just realized she was awake and was waiting.

She stayed still, listening, feeling the quiet tension now threaded beneath the surface of his stillness. He had not moved, had not made any effort to shift her away. But he was aware.

And suddenly, so was she.

The heat beneath her palm was not fabric, not leather, but skin.

Her mind registered the slow, steady rise and fall of his breath beneath her touch, the way the solid warmth of him pressed against her own body, the way her thigh had tangled slightly over his, their closeness something not accidental but not exactly purposeful either.

A mistake neither of them had corrected.

Slowly, carefully, Aelina tilted her chin, her gaze tracing the line of his throat, the sharp curve of his jaw, before landing on his face. His eyes were closed, his expression unreadable in the dim firelight, but she knew he was not asleep.

And then—he spoke.

"You're warm."

His voice was low, rough with something unreadable, and she hated the way it sent something curling low in her stomach, the way it unraveled something slow and dangerous beneath her ribs.

Aelina swallowed, resisting the urge to shift, because moving now would be an admission—of what, she wasn't sure. "You run hot," she murmured, her voice quieter than she intended.

One golden eye cracked open, half-lidded, knowing. "Mm. You're the one using me as a blanket."

Aelina's cheeks heated. Damn him.

She made to move, but his arm tightened, just slightly, just enough for her to feel it, to know that he had let her stay this way for a reason.

Not because he was holding her there.

But because he hadn't wanted her to leave.

The realization sent a shuddering pulse through her chest, something dangerous, something she could not name, and Dorian must have felt it, must have noticed the way she tensed, because his smirk—lazy, infuriatingly self-assured—curled against the edge of his lips.

"What?" he murmured, his voice dropping to something lower, softer, as if testing, as if daring her to acknowledge this moment at all.

Aelina clenched her jaw, ignoring the way his warmth had already settled into her skin, into the places between her ribs that should have been left untouched. "Nothing," she muttered, pushing herself up, forcing distance where there had been none.

Dorian let her go without a fight, but his gaze never left her, tracking her movements too carefully, too deliberately.

As if she were something fragile.

Or worse—something he was considering breaking.

She exhaled, dragging her fingers through her hair, trying to shake the lingering sensation of his touch, of his presence still pressed into her bones.

Only then did she take in their surroundings.

The chamber was dimly lit, the walls carved from black stone, flickering firelight casting restless shadows that danced along the surfaces like living things. The air was thick, charged with something old, something watching, though she saw no one else, no sign of the figure from before. The ground beneath her was smooth, polished, and too intact for a place that had collapsed beneath them. Wherever they were, they had been brought here.

Not by accident.

Dorian sat up beside her, running a hand through his hair, his expression shifting from amusement to something sharper, more alert. "We're not where we were."

Aelina shot him a dry look. "Brilliant observation."

He smirked again, but it didn't reach his eyes. "I try."

Her heart still thundered in her chest, not from fear, not from uncertainty, but from something worse, something treacherous, something that whispered of heat and stolen breaths and the way his arm had lingered around her waist longer than it should have.

Dorian exhaled, stretching, rolling the tension from his shoulders, before glancing at her with that too-knowing gaze, as if he could still feel her on him, just as she could still feel him on her.

"Best we figure out where we are," he murmured, voice still too low, too smooth, too full of the weight of something unspoken.

Aelina tore her gaze away, pushing herself fully to her feet, forcing herself to focus on the unknown threat, on their surroundings, on anything but the warmth still seared into her skin.

Because they had survived the fall.

But she wasn't sure if she would survive whatever this was.

The air here was different. Heavier. Alive.

Aelina could feel it pressing against her skin, slipping into her lungs, coiling through the hollow spaces of her ribs like unseen fingers. The chamber around them pulsed—not with sound, not with movement, but with something deeper, something ancient, as though the very stone had memory, as though the walls had learned how to breathe. It was not just a place. It was watching.

She exhaled slowly, forcing herself to steady the frantic rhythm of her heart. Her pulse still carried the echoes of what had happened, of the ground splintering beneath her, of the moment when the world had given way and swallowed her whole. The memory clung to her, a whisper of fear curling at the edges of her thoughts, but fear would not serve her now. Not here. She had survived. She was still breathing. But that did not mean she was safe.

Dorian stood beside her, his golden eyes scanning the chamber with a sharp, calculated focus, his entire body a study in quiet tension. He looked like something coiled and waiting, like a predator in the heartbeat before the strike. She had seen him fight before, seen the way he moved like the blade was merely an extension of himself, but this was different. This was not battle readiness. This was something deeper, something quieter, as if he recognized this place, as if he was listening to something she could not hear.

Aelina shifted, her boots scraping against the polished stone beneath them. The sound barely echoed. That, more than anything, unsettled her. A place this vast should have carried sound, should have allowed it to linger and stretch into the darkness beyond them. Instead, it simply swallowed it whole.

She turned, taking in their surroundings. The chamber stretched too far, wider than it should have been, the walls curving in unnatural ways, as though they had been shaped by something not human. The stone was dark, too smooth, polished to a gleaming obsidian that reflected the flickering light of unseen flames. Symbols—intricate, ancient sigils carved deep into the rock—spiraled in endless patterns along the walls, pulsing with a faint glow, as if whispering in a language just beyond her understanding. They looked old, far older than any ruin she had ever seen, but they were not abandoned. No dust clung to the surfaces, no cracks marred the edges. This place had been waiting.

She forced herself to take a slow breath, steadying the unease curling in her stomach. "Where are we?" she asked, her voice softer than she intended, as though speaking too loudly might draw something from the shadows.

Dorian didn't answer immediately. His gaze remained locked on the carvings, the sharp lines of his face cast in flickering light, his expression unreadable. When he finally spoke, his voice was low, distant, touched with something she could not name.

"Somewhere we weren't meant to find."

Aelina frowned, stepping closer to one of the walls, tracing her fingers lightly over the carved symbols. The moment her skin brushed the surface, a tremor ran through her, not painful, not forceful, but a sensation of something waking. It was subtle, like an exhale from the stone itself, a breath that had been held for too long. She jerked her hand back, the cold lingering in her fingertips, sending a shiver through her.

Dorian was watching her now.

Not with amusement. Not with that insufferable smirk. But with something else. Something she did not yet know how to name.

She swallowed and turned away from the sigils, forcing herself to focus. "You recognized that summoner." It wasn't a question.

Dorian's jaw tightened—just slightly, just enough. Not a flinch. But close.

"I recognized what they are."

Aelina arched a brow. "And what are they?"

Dorian's smirk returned, but it was thin, sharp as a blade, a shield thrown up in place of an answer. "A problem."

Aelina let out a slow breath, rolling her shoulders as she surveyed the space once more. If she pushed, he would deflect. He always did. But there was something different this time, something unspoken between them, a question neither of them dared voice aloud. Why had they been brought here? What was waiting for them in the dark?

She stepped forward, testing the air, feeling the faint shift of warmth and cold as she moved. The place was alive, in some strange way, in the way the air itself seemed to pulse. The sigils weren't just decoration. They were active.

And that meant something was feeding them.

Aelina turned back toward Dorian, ready to press him for more, but before she could open her mouth, the torches lining the walls flared, and the chamber shifted.

Not physically. The stone did not crack. The ceiling did not lower. But something changed.

The air became thicker, the weight of something unseen pressing down on her chest. A low hum thrummed through the stone, vibrating beneath her feet, through her bones. She gasped, stumbling back slightly as the carvings along the walls brightened, their glow shifting from dim silver to something deeper, something burning gold.

Then—a voice.

Low, resonant, layered over itself like a chorus of whispers.

"Welcome home, lost ones."

Aelina's breath hitched. Her stomach twisted.

Because the voice did not come from the walls.

It came from everywhere.

Dorian did not react—not outwardly, not visibly—but she felt the tension roll through him, felt the moment his body became a weapon waiting to strike.

The air shifted again, colder now, almost frigid. The voice returned, quieter this time, curling around them like a breath against the skin.

"You have wandered far."

Aelina's blood turned to ice. This was not some ancient ruin. Not some forgotten tomb.

This place knew them.

And it had been waiting.

She turned to Dorian, expecting anger, frustration, even fear.

Instead, she saw him smile.

Not the lazy smirk. Not the amused tilt of his lips.

Something darker.

Something that made her wonder if she had ever truly known what he was at all.

Aelina's breath shallowed, every instinct in her body screaming that they were standing on the edge of something they did not understand, something far older than them, far greater than anything they had ever encountered. The air thickened, charged with the weight of an unseen presence, the kind that did not simply watch but waited, the kind that did not need to be seen to be felt. The carvings along the walls pulsed in a slow, unnatural rhythm, as though they were not just markings, but veins, carrying something through the stone, something living, breathing, remembering.

And still, Dorian smiled.

Not in amusement, not in confidence, but in recognition, as though he had seen this before, as though the voice curling through the chamber, pressing against their skin like phantom hands, was expected. Aelina watched him carefully, her heartbeat thudding against her ribs, her fingers itching to reach for the dagger at her belt. But she knew, deep in her marrow, deep in the spaces between her thoughts, that no blade would serve her here. This was not something she could fight with steel and sharpened instincts. This was something worse.

Dorian took a slow step forward, his golden eyes tracing the flickering sigils on the walls, his breath steady, measured, like a man walking into an old memory. "You've been waiting a long time," he murmured, and his voice was not quite his own—lower, heavier, lined with something dangerous.

The voice did not answer right away. The silence stretched, thick and unyielding, before the walls exhaled. Not with wind, not with movement, but with presence, a shift in the very essence of the space around them. The flames in the sconces brightened, then dimmed, pulsing in the same strange rhythm as the sigils, as though the entire room was breathing along with them.

"Not for you," the voice finally whispered, and this time, Aelina felt it directly against her skin, curling around the shell of her ear like something that had leaned in too close. Her body locked up, her breath caught in her throat, and suddenly, the chamber did not feel vast at all. It felt tight, too small, as though the walls were no longer stone but something living, something watching her with intent.

Not for you.

The words clawed through her mind, lodging themselves deep, burrowing into places she did not want to examine. Aelina clenched her fists, her nails biting into her palms, grounding herself in the only thing she had left—her own control, her own refusal to be ruled by things she did not understand. She lifted her chin, pushing away the crawling sensation along her spine, the wrongness curling through the air.

"Then who?" she demanded, her voice steady, even though every part of her wanted to shrink away from whatever was listening.

The voice did not answer immediately, but the torches flickered, as though in amusement, as though something unseen found her curiosity entertaining. And then, slowly, like a whisper seeping through cracks in the walls, the reply came.

"The one you seek."

Aelina's stomach dropped.

For the first time since waking in this place, she felt something other than wariness, other than unease. She felt real fear.

Because she knew exactly what they meant.

She was here for answers. She was here to find the source of the sickness, the rot creeping across the land, poisoning villages, consuming entire bloodlines. She had thought it was the work of magic, the result of men who had dabbled too deep into things they should have left buried.

But now, as she stood in this living ruin, in a place that had known her name before she had spoken it aloud, she realized she had been wrong.

She was not here to find a plague.

She was here to find a man.

Dorian shifted beside her, his smile fading just slightly, just enough for her to see the sharp edges beneath it, the lines of tension in his shoulders, the subtle weight of recognition in his gaze. He knew what this meant. He had known the moment they landed here, the moment the voice spoke.

Aelina turned to him, and for the first time since she had met him, since she had placed her trust in him despite knowing she never should have, she felt something cold settle in her stomach.

"How long have you known?" she whispered, and she hated the way her voice thinned, hated the way it almost trembled.

Dorian did not blink. "Since before you ever asked the question."

Aelina's throat tightened, but she did not let herself recoil, did not let herself falter. She had always known Dorian carried secrets, had always seen the way he sidestepped her questions with a smirk, the way he buried his truths beneath half-spoken riddles. But this—this was different.

This was not just something he had kept from her.

This was something he had been guiding her toward all along.

The air shifted again, and the presence in the room leaned closer, pressing against her senses, whispering along the edges of her mind.

Aelina did not move.

She did not look away from him.

And then, the voice spoke once more.

"You cannot change what is already written."

The room darkened, the flames sinking into embers, and Aelina felt the weight of fate close around her like a cage.

She had always thought she was walking toward an answer.

She had never considered that she was walking toward a choice.

The room shuddered.

Not the walls. Not the floor. Something deeper. Something beneath the surface of the world itself, as though the very threads of fate had been pulled too tight, as though something old and unfinished had just taken notice. The sigils along the walls flared, burning gold for a single, breathtaking moment before darkening, their light retreating into the stone like a held breath. Aelina felt it in her chest—the weight of something shifting, something final, something that could not be undone.

And then—the whisper came again.

Not from the walls.

Not from the air.

From inside her own mind.

You were never meant to find him.

Aelina gasped, her hands flying to her head, fingers gripping at her temples as pain lanced through her skull, sharp and sudden, like something had reached inside and torn through the fabric of her thoughts.

The voice was not hers, not her own, but it fit too well, like a memory she had forgotten she ever had.

You were never meant to see.

Dorian moved then, too fast, too unnatural, a blur of dark fabric and sharp lines, his hands grabbing her shoulders, steadying her, grounding her. She barely registered the way his touch burned against her skin, too warm, too real, because the moment his fingers closed around her, the voice stopped. The pain was gone.

And for the first time, she realized what had just happened.

The room hadn't spoken to her.

Something else had.

Aelina's breath came in uneven pulls, her vision still spinning as she stared up at Dorian, her chest tight with something dangerously close to panic. He wasn't smirking now. He wasn't looking at her with that half-lidded amusement, that lazy, knowing expression. No, his golden eyes were sharp, narrowed, his mouth a thin, unreadable line.

"You heard it," he said, his voice low, but not quiet. Not gentle.

Aelina swallowed, still unsteady, still trying to find the edges of herself after something had just reached inside her mind and nearly pulled her apart. "That wasn't the room," she whispered, the words hoarse, raw. "That was something else."

Dorian exhaled slowly, and it was only then that she realized—he was furious.

Not at her.

At whatever had just touched her.

His grip on her arms tightened just slightly, like he was still deciding whether or not to let go. "I was hoping we had more time," he murmured, half to himself, half to her. Aelina blinked, pulse thrumming in her throat. "More time for what?"

Dorian's eyes met hers, and something inside them shifted—something dangerous, something protective, something she was not ready to name.

And then—

A sound.

Not the whispering voice. Not the pulsing magic.

A footstep.

Not theirs.

Aelina went still, her breath catching in her throat as her ears strained into the sudden silence. Dorian's entire body tensed, his golden eyes flicking toward the open archway at the far end of the chamber, where the darkness stretched deep and unbroken. The flames in the sconces dimmed further, their glow barely enough to push back the creeping shadows.

Then—another step.

And another.

Slow. Deliberate. Measured.

Aelina's fingers inched toward her dagger, her pulse a hammering rhythm of warning. Dorian was already ahead of her, his stance shifting, his weight balanced, every inch of him a weapon ready to strike. The moment stretched too thin, the air thick with the kind of tension that only existed before something shattered.

Then—

A voice.

Deep. Smooth. Too familiar.

Aelina's stomach dropped.

"I was wondering when you would get here."

She knew that voice.

She had heard it before.

But it was not possible.

Because the man stepping from the shadows—the man who had just spoken—

Was the same man she had buried three years ago.

Her brother.

Chapter Four:

The Dead Do Not Rise

The chamber seemed to contract around her, the air pressing against her ribs, thick with the weight of something impossible, something wrong. The torches along the walls flickered violently, their flames stretching too high, too wild, before dimming into trembling embers, as though even the fire itself had recoiled in recognition of what had just stepped from the shadows.

Aelina's breath hitched. Her pulse thundered. Her vision blurred for half a second, her mind refusing to make sense of what her eyes were seeing, of the impossible truth standing before her.

Her brother.

Elias.

Aelina's legs locked, her throat closing around the name before it could fully form. Her mind screamed it cannot be, but her body—her traitorous, desperate body—wanted to believe. Wanted to reach for him, to break through the wall of logic and let herself hope.

Because it was him. It was.

The face was the same, the sharp-cut jaw and the high cheekbones, the dark hair that always curled slightly at his temples when he let it grow too long. His frame was as she remembered—lean but strong, his shoulders broad, his presence steady, always steady, like a pillar she had once leaned against in the days before everything had fallen apart. He wore no armor, no robes of a noble healer, nothing of the life she had buried with him. Instead, his clothes were dark, heavy, his tunic embroidered with symbols she did not recognize, intricate sigils woven in silver thread that pulsed faintly beneath the dim light.

But it was his eyes that unraveled her.

Because they were wrong.

Not empty, not blank—but changed.

She had known his gaze better than her own reflection, had spent years looking into that deep, steady warmth, finding comfort in the way he had always looked at her as if he saw her, truly saw her, even when she tried to hide. But now—

Now, the warmth was gone.

The green of his irises had darkened, streaked through with something unnatural, something gleaming and silver, like moonlight reflected in a still lake. It wasn't lifeless. It was worse. It was aware.

Dorian had not moved.

Aelina could feel him at her side, the heat of him, his presence wrapped in controlled, deliberate stillness. He had been tense before, his body wound tight as a bowstring, but this—this was different.

Because Dorian did not look shocked.

He looked furious.

His golden eyes flickered, unreadable, locked onto Elias with an intensity that could have burned through stone. His breath was steady, too steady, his fingers relaxed at his sides—but Aelina wasn't fooled. He was calculating. Measuring.

He was preparing.

Elias took another step forward. Unhurried. Confident. His boots made no sound against the polished stone floor, and Aelina hated the way his presence filled the space, the way it swallowed the distance between them as if it had never existed at all.

His lips tilted at the corner—not a smirk, not amusement, but something softer. Something crueler.

"Aelina," he said, her name smooth as silk, wrapped in familiarity.

Aelina's breath staggered in her chest.

The sound of his voice unraveled something deep inside her, something she had kept buried beneath the weight of grief, beneath years of telling herself he was gone. That she would never hear that voice again.

And yet—here he was.

Here he stood, calling her name, speaking like he had never died at all.

Her fingers twitched, her pulse hammering against her ribs, desperate to reach for him, to touch him, to make sure he was real.

But Dorian—Dorian moved first.

Not forward. Between them.

It was not subtle.

It was not careless.

It was a deliberate barrier, his stance loose but unmistakably firm, as if he had decided something before she even had the chance to breathe.

Elias's gaze flicked to him.

Something changed. Something deepened.

And then—he smiled.

It was not relief.

It was not joy.

It was a secret. A promise.

"Ah," Elias murmured, tilting his head just slightly, watching Dorian with something just shy of amusement. "So. It's you."

Dorian's fingers curled into loose fists. His voice, when he spoke, was quiet, level, a slow-moving knife.

"You should be dead."

Aelina flinched.

The words cut through the air like steel, slicing through the veil of impossible, of hope, of anything she might have been willing to believe.

Because Dorian didn't say it as an insult.

He said it as a fact.

As something he knew.

Elias only smiled wider.

"And yet," he said, gesturing lightly to himself, his expression one of mock bemusement, "here I am."

Aelina staggered back a step, the weight of realization slamming into her like a fist to the chest. She turned to Dorian, her voice breaking before she could stop it.

"You knew."

It wasn't a question.

Dorian did not look at her.

He did not answer.

And that—that silence was worse than any confession.

Because she had suspected. She had seen the way he had guided her through this journey, the way he had never truly answered her questions, always redirecting, always pushing her forward without revealing exactly where they were going.

But she had not let herself believe—not fully.

Because if he had known, if he had always known—

Then he had never truly been on her side.

Elias exhaled, rolling his shoulders as if stretching after a long rest. "I was wondering how long it would take before you put the pieces together," he mused, watching her, measuring her reaction. "I'd hoped for a little more trust, but I suppose some wounds never heal, do they?"

Aelina's blood ran cold. Trust.

The word felt tainted, bitter.

She had trusted Dorian. She had chosen him, despite her better judgment, despite the warnings carved into his smirks and half-truths.

And now—

Now, she wasn't sure if she had ever truly known him at all.

Her heart pounded.

Her breath shook.

Elias stepped forward again, closing the space between them in one smooth, effortless motion, reaching out as if he had the right to touch her.

She did not flinch.

She did not move.

Because she wasn't sure if she would grab his hand—or drive a blade through his chest.

And for the first time in her life, Aelina was not certain which choice would be the right one.

The chamber seemed to contract around her, the air pressing against her ribs, thick with the weight of something impossible, something wrong. The torches along the walls flickered violently, their flames stretching too high, too wild, before dimming into trembling embers, as though even the fire itself had recoiled in recognition of what had just stepped from the shadows.

Aelina's breath hitched. Her pulse thundered. Her vision blurred for half a second, her mind refusing to make sense of what her eyes were seeing, of the impossible truth standing before her.

Her brother.

Elias.

Aelina's legs locked, her throat closing around the name before it could fully form. Her mind screamed it cannot be, but her body—her traitorous, desperate body—wanted to believe. Wanted to reach for him, to break through the wall of logic and let herself hope.

Because it was him. It was.

The face was the same, the sharp-cut jaw and the high cheekbones, the dark hair that always curled slightly at his temples when he let it grow too long. His frame was as she remembered—lean but strong, his shoulders broad, his presence steady, always steady, like a pillar she had once leaned against in the days before everything had fallen apart. He wore no armor, no robes of a noble healer, nothing of the life she had buried with him. Instead, his clothes were dark, heavy, his tunic embroidered with symbols she did not recognize, intricate sigils woven in silver thread that pulsed faintly beneath the dim light.

But it was his eyes that unraveled her.

Because they were wrong.

Not empty, not blank—but changed.

She had known his gaze better than her own reflection, had spent years looking into that deep, steady warmth, finding comfort in the way he had always looked at her as if he saw her, truly saw her, even when she tried to hide. But now—

Now, the warmth was gone.

The green of his irises had darkened, streaked through with something unnatural, something gleaming and silver, like moonlight reflected in a still lake. It wasn't lifeless. It was worse. It was aware.

Dorian had not moved.

Aelina could feel him at her side, the heat of him, his presence wrapped in controlled, deliberate stillness. He had been tense before, his body wound tight as a bowstring, but this—this was different.

Because Dorian did not look shocked.

He looked furious.

His golden eyes flickered, unreadable, locked onto Elias with an intensity that could have burned through stone. His breath was steady, too steady, his fingers relaxed at his sides—but Aelina wasn't fooled. He was calculating. Measuring.

He was preparing.

Elias took another step forward. Unhurried. Confident. His boots made no sound against the polished stone floor, and Aelina hated the way his presence filled the space, the way it swallowed the distance between them as if it had never existed at all.

His lips tilted at the corner—not a smirk, not amusement, but something softer. Something crueler.

"Aelina," he said, her name smooth as silk, wrapped in familiarity.

Aelina's breath staggered in her chest.

The sound of his voice unraveled something deep inside her, something she had kept buried beneath the weight of grief, beneath years of telling herself he was gone. That she would never hear that voice again.

And yet—here he was.

Here he stood, calling her name, speaking like he had never died at all.

Her fingers twitched, her pulse hammering against her ribs, desperate to reach for him, to touch him, to make sure he was real.

But Dorian—Dorian moved first.

Not forward. Between them.

It was not subtle.

It was not careless.

It was a deliberate barrier, his stance loose but unmistakably firm, as if he had decided something before she even had the chance to breathe.

Elias's gaze flicked to him.

Something changed. Something deepened.

And then—he smiled.

It was not relief.

It was not joy.

It was a secret. A promise.

"Ah," Elias murmured, tilting his head just slightly, watching Dorian with something just shy of amusement. "So. It's you."

Dorian's fingers curled into loose fists. His voice, when he spoke, was quiet, level, a slow-moving knife.

"You should be dead."

Aelina flinched.

The words cut through the air like steel, slicing through the veil of impossible, of hope, of anything she might have been willing to believe.

Because Dorian didn't say it as an insult.

He said it as a fact.

As something he knew.

Elias only smiled wider.

"And yet," he said, gesturing lightly to himself, his expression one of mock bemusement, "here I am."

Aelina staggered back a step, the weight of realization slamming into her like a fist to the chest. She turned to Dorian, her voice breaking before she could stop it.

"You knew."

It wasn't a question.

Dorian did not look at her.

He did not answer.

And that—that silence was worse than any confession.

Because she had suspected. She had seen the way he had guided her through this journey, the way he had never truly answered her questions, always redirecting, always pushing her forward without revealing exactly where they were going.

But she had not let herself believe—not fully.

Because if he had known, if he had always known—

Then he had never truly been on her side.

Elias exhaled, rolling his shoulders as if stretching after a long rest. "I was wondering how long it would take before you put the pieces together," he mused, watching her, measuring her reaction. "I'd hoped for a little more trust, but I suppose some wounds never heal, do they?"

Aelina's blood ran cold. Trust.

The word felt tainted, bitter.

She had trusted Dorian. She had chosen him, despite her better judgment, despite the warnings carved into his smirks and half-truths.

And now—

Now, she wasn't sure if she had ever truly known him at all.

Her heart pounded.

Her breath shook.

Elias stepped forward again, closing the space between them in one smooth, effortless motion, reaching out as if he had the right to touch her.

She did not flinch.

She did not move.

Because she wasn't sure if she would grab his hand—or drive a blade through his chest.

And for the first time in her life, Aelina was not certain which choice would be the right one.

Aelina's breath came slow and measured, but inside, her mind stormed with questions, each one more volatile than the last. The weight of betrayal sat sharp in her chest, the realization that Dorian had known about Elias, that he had guided her to this moment without a single warning, pressing against her ribs like a vice. The chamber still pulsed with energy, the torches burning in that strange, unnatural rhythm, but the flickering glow did little to chase away the shadows curling at the edges of her thoughts. Elias stood before her, his presence filling the space between them with something impossible, something undeniable. His voice had been the same. His face had been the same. But that light in his eyes, that silver-threaded gaze, was foreign. It was not the look of the brother she had once trusted above all others. It was something else entirely.

She forced herself to meet his gaze, ignoring the way her fingers still trembled, the way part of her ached to reach out, to prove to herself that he was real. "You died," she said, her voice sharper than she had expected, the words feeling strange on her tongue. Elias smiled, slow and knowing, as if she had said something amusing. "That's what you were told," he said, his tone even, devoid of anger or sorrow, as if the years that had passed between his last breath and this moment were nothing more than an inconvenience. The casual nature of his response sent a flicker of cold through her veins, a reminder that this was not a reunion. This was something else. A game, perhaps, or a test, and she did not yet know the rules.

Dorian remained still, his body a barrier between them, but his silence was no longer the relaxed confidence she had come to know. His shoulders were drawn tight, his hands loose at his sides, but she recognized the readiness in him, the controlled restraint of a man who was waiting for the right moment to strike. It unsettled her in ways she did not want to name. He was afraid—not in the way most men feared battle or death, but in a way that was deeper, more dangerous. Dorian was not afraid of losing. He was afraid of what would happen next. The thought sent a fresh wave of unease through her, because if there was anything she had learned about Dorian, it was that he did not scare easily.

Elias tilted his head, his sharp gaze shifting from Aelina to Dorian, studying him with something bordering on curiosity. "You've been watching over her, haven't you?" he mused, his voice smooth, laced with something just shy of amusement. "That must have been tiresome. She never did like being told what to do." Aelina bristled, the weight of his words grating against something raw inside her. "Don't talk like you know me," she snapped, stepping forward, ignoring the way Dorian tensed at her side. "You're not the same person I buried." The words felt heavy, leaden with the grief she had long since forced herself to ignore, and yet Elias simply smiled, the expression distant, unreadable. "No," he said, his voice soft but certain. "I suppose I'm not."

Aelina exhaled through her nose, forcing herself to think, to keep her emotions in check, even as they tangled into knots beneath her skin. "What happened to you?" she demanded, the question burning in her throat. Elias was silent for a moment, his gaze flickering with something unreadable, something careful. "I survived," he finally said, the weight of the words far greater than their simplicity. The answer was not enough, and they both knew it. But before she could press him further, before she could demand the truth he was keeping from her, he shifted his attention back to Dorian, his silver-threaded gaze narrowing slightly. "And you," he murmured, his tone lighter, but no less dangerous. "You've been leading her here all along, haven't you?"

Dorian's smirk was slow, deliberate, but Aelina could see the sharp edges beneath it, the restraint, the fury carefully tucked beneath the surface. "I told you once before," he said, his voice lazy, but his tone edged with something lethal. "I don't take orders from dead men." The chamber went quiet, the weight of the words settling over them like a storm about to break. Aelina's stomach twisted, her pulse pounding in her throat, because there was something in Dorian's voice, something layered beneath the sharpness of his words, that told her this was not their first encounter. She turned to him sharply, realization dawning like a blade to the chest. "You knew him," she said, not as an accusation, but as the only truth that made sense. "Not just that he was alive. You've met before."

Elias let out a slow breath, shaking his head slightly, his expression unreadable. "I thought she would have figured it out sooner," he mused, though there was no real mockery in his tone. "You've been slipping, Dorian." Dorian's jaw clenched, but his smirk did not falter. "Or maybe I just wanted to see how long it would take before she realized she was never the one asking the real questions," he said, turning his golden gaze to Aelina for the first time since Elias had appeared. "That was always your weakness, wasn't it?" His voice was quieter now, something dark coiled beneath the surface. "You only ever looked at the pieces in front of you. Never the ones moving in the shadows."

The words hit her harder than she wanted to admit. She had been so focused on finding answers, on unraveling the sickness, the rot spreading through the land, that she had never stopped to question the path she had taken to get here. She had followed Dorian because she thought she had chosen to. But what if she had never had a choice at all? What if she had been walking toward this moment since the very beginning, playing a role she had never known existed? The thought sent a wave of nausea curling in her stomach, because suddenly, it was not just Elias who felt unfamiliar. It was Dorian, too.

Elias sighed, rubbing a hand along his jaw, his movements slow, almost bored. "This has been entertaining," he mused, "but I didn't come here to play old games." His silver-flecked gaze settled on Aelina, sharp, assessing. "I came here because it's time." Time for what, he did not say. But Aelina knew, with a certainty that chilled her, that whatever answer was coming next, it would change everything. She took a slow breath, steadying herself, lifting her chin despite the weight pressing against her ribs. "Time for what?" she asked, her voice steady, even as her hands trembled at her sides.

Elias smiled. "To decide," he said simply.

And for the first time since stepping into the chamber, Aelina understood—this was not a battle to be won. This was a choice to be made. And no matter what path she took, she knew one thing with absolute certainty.

She would never walk away from it the same.

The chamber felt smaller now, though nothing had physically changed. The walls still stretched high, the carved sigils pulsing with that slow, deliberate rhythm, the torches still flickering in their unnatural pattern, but the air was different. It pressed in around Aelina, a weight she could not shake, as though the space itself had become aware of the choice hanging before her. Every breath felt heavier, drawn from an atmosphere that carried too much memory, too much intent.

Elias stood perfectly still, his silver-threaded gaze unwavering, his posture too controlled, too certain. He was not waiting for her answer—he already knew what it would be. That realization sent a fresh coil of unease through her, the sense that she had never truly been in control, that this moment had been laid before her long ago, waiting only for her to finally step into it. She tried to tell herself that wasn't true, that she was still the one deciding, but doubt crawled into the spaces between her thoughts, coiling like smoke, whispering like an old voice she had never wanted to hear again.

Dorian remained between them, unmoving, his presence a wall she had not realized she needed until now. There was something taut in him, something waiting to snap, like he had already played this game before and had no interest in entertaining it any longer. His golden eyes flickered, sharp with something she couldn't name, something that made her chest tighten. He had always carried secrets, had always walked with the weight of things left unsaid, but this was different. This was personal.

Elias exhaled slowly, as if he could sense the hesitation bleeding through her resolve, and when he finally spoke again, his voice was softer this time, quieter, but no less dangerous. "Aelina, I know this is difficult," he said, his tone gentle, laced with something that might have been genuine if it had come from the man she had once known. "But you have to understand—you were meant to be here. This moment was always going to come."

Aelina's stomach twisted, anger threading through the unease. She had spent her life trying to outrun the expectations placed upon her, trying to carve a path that was her own, and yet, at every turn, it felt like she was being pushed, guided, shaped into something she had never asked to be. First by the duty she had inherited, then by the sickness that had taken her family, and now by this—a prophecy she had never agreed to be part of, a fate she had never chosen.

She forced herself to take a slow breath, to ground herself against the rising tide of emotions threatening to pull her under. "What is it you think I have to decide?" she asked, keeping her voice level, though the words felt like broken glass in her throat.

Elias tilted his head slightly, his expression unreadable, though something flickered beneath the surface—not hesitation, but calculation. "You've been chasing the sickness, haven't you?" he mused, as though the answer didn't matter, as though he wasn't asking at all, but simply confirming what he already knew. "Following the traces, trying to piece together the cause, the reason, the cure."

Aelina stiffened, her breath shallowing. She had never told him that. She had never spoken those words to anyone but Dorian, and even then, she had kept the truth close, unwilling to expose the depths of her fears, of her need to understand. But Elias spoke as if he had been there all along, watching her unravel the pieces.

Dorian's smirk was slow, deliberate, and edged with something dangerous. "You always did love talking in circles," he muttered, his tone almost bored, though the sharpness in his posture had not faded. "Maybe get to the part where you actually say what you want."

Elias let out a quiet hum, his gaze flicking back to Dorian for a brief moment, and for the first time, his expression darkened. There was a history there, something bitter, something unspoken, and the weight of it settled between them, thick enough that Aelina could feel it pressing into her skin. She didn't know what had happened between them, didn't know how they knew each other, but whatever it was, it was deep, woven into the fabric of whatever had led them all here.

Still, Elias did not rise to the bait. He simply looked back at her, his silver-threaded gaze steady. "You're looking for the wrong thing, Aelina," he said, his voice quieter now, more intimate, as if the words were only meant for her. "The sickness isn't what you think it is."

Aelina's breath caught, her fingers curling into fists at her sides. "And what exactly do you think it is?"

Elias held her gaze for a long moment, studying her, as if deciding how much she was ready to hear. Then, with a slow, deliberate exhale, he said the words that shattered everything.

"It's me."

The chamber lurched.

Aelina's body went still, her mind rejecting the words before they could fully register. No. No, that wasn't possible. The sickness was a force, a spreading decay, a blight that had touched entire villages, entire bloodlines. It was ancient magic, twisted and unchecked. It was something unnatural.

But Elias was standing before her.

Whole. Unbroken. Alive.

Her thoughts reeled, grasping for something—**anything—**that made sense, but all she could see was the bodies she had tried to save, the people who had withered beneath the weight of the sickness, the villages that had collapsed under its grip. And Elias—**her brother, the man she had mourned—**was telling her it had come from him.

The torches flickered violently, the sigils on the walls pulsing faster now, as if the very air was responding to the weight of his words. Dorian let out a slow breath beside her, shaking his head slightly, and when he finally spoke, his voice was low, edged with something dark and unreadable.

"Well," he murmured, tipping his head slightly. "That's a bit dramatic."

Elias chuckled softly, a sound that should not have belonged in a conversation like this. "And yet," he mused, his lips curling just slightly, "here we are."

Aelina's pulse pounded in her ears, her mind still struggling to bridge the impossible gap between what she had known and what had just been laid before her. She had spent years searching for the source of the sickness, desperate to understand what had taken so much from her.

And now, standing before her, his silver-threaded eyes burning in the dim light, was the answer.

Her brother.

The thing she had been hunting all along.

The world around her felt suspended, as if time had slowed, holding its breath in anticipation of what she would do next. The air was thick, not just with the weight of Elias's words but with something older, heavier, more insidious. The sigils on the walls pulsed in slow, deliberate succession, no longer flickering at random but beating in time with the silence that stretched between them. The chamber was listening. The very stone seemed to be drinking in the moment, as if it had waited for this revelation as much as she had.

Aelina's heart pounded against her ribs, but she forced her breath to remain steady, fighting the whirlwind in her mind. She had seen what the sickness had done—the bodies reduced to husks, the veins blackened like withered roots, the slow, inevitable unraveling of life itself. She had spent years searching for its source, chasing traces of magic that had no name, following paths that always led to empty answers. And now, standing before her, impossibly alive, was the man who had once been her brother—telling her he had been at the heart of it all.

Her voice, when she finally spoke, was raw, edged with something that was not anger but something dangerously close to it. "What do you mean, it's you?" The question left her lips sharper than she had intended, each syllable carrying the full weight of disbelief, of the battle between her logic and the quiet, aching part of her that wanted to deny what stood before her. "People are dying, Elias. Villages are falling apart. You're telling me that's because of you?"

Elias did not look away. He met her gaze with the same calm certainty that had always defined him, the quiet self-assurance that had made him the kind of man others trusted without question. But now, that certainty was laced with something else—something unreadable, something that did not belong to the brother she had buried. "Not by choice," he murmured, his voice almost soft, like he was offering her something fragile, something she could still break if she wanted to. "But yes, Aelina. It comes from me."

Dorian shifted beside her, his stance still relaxed, but she could feel the coiled energy beneath it, the way his body remained ready, waiting, as if he expected something to strike from the darkness. His golden gaze flicked between them, sharp and assessing, before he let out a slow breath, shaking his head slightly. "I have to say," he drawled, the edges of his smirk sharpened by something colder, "I expected a lot of things when we got here. But this? This is almost impressive."

Elias chuckled under his breath, tilting his head as if considering the words. "You always did appreciate a good twist, didn't you?" His expression did not change, but Aelina caught something beneath the surface of his amusement, something pointed, something deliberate. This was a conversation they had not had for the first time.

The realization sent a fresh chill through her, though she refused to let it show. She turned to

Dorian then, her fingers curling into fists at her sides. "How long have you known?" The words were quieter now, but no less sharp. No less dangerous.

Dorian sighed, running a hand through his dark hair before giving her one of those infuriating looks, the ones that sat between exasperation and reluctant honesty. "Not as long as you think," he admitted, and though his tone was lighter, his gaze remained heavy. "But long enough to know that this meeting was inevitable."

Aelina exhaled through her nose, struggling to contain the emotions threatening to unravel inside her. Of course, Dorian had known. Of course, he had guided her here with purpose, not just on the path to understanding the sickness but straight into the center of something far more dangerous.

She turned back to Elias, taking a step forward before she could stop herself. "Then explain," she demanded, her voice carrying the kind of edge that left no room for deception. "If this was always going to happen, if you're the reason for the sickness, then tell me—what are you?"

Elias considered her for a long moment, and for the first time, she thought she saw something flicker behind his composure—not hesitation, not fear, but something deeper. Something like grief. "I'm not what you remember," he finally said, and his voice had changed, lower, heavier, weighted by something he did not want to say. "And I'm not what you think I am either."

The torches flickered, the flames twisting unnaturally, curling toward him like they were drawn to his presence. The sigils along the walls pulsed faster, no longer rhythmic but erratic, and the air grew thick, charged with unseen energy. Aelina felt it press against her skin, wrapping around her like an invisible hand, pulling at the strands of her magic, seeking something.

Elias exhaled slowly, and when he spoke again, his voice carried a weight that made her chest tighten. "I didn't survive that night, Aelina." His silver-threaded gaze darkened, something shifting behind his irises, something inhuman rising just beneath the surface. "I was remade."

Aelina's pulse slammed against her ribs.

She heard the words, understood them, but her mind could not accept them, not fully. Remade. Not resurrected. Not saved. The difference was a chasm that stretched impossibly wide, a void that could not be crossed without stepping into something irrevocable.

Dorian's breath was slow beside her, controlled, but she could feel the tension threading through him, the way his muscles tightened as though preparing for what came next. He had heard it too. He had understood the implication. And unlike Aelina, he had expected it.

The chamber shuddered again, the air shifting as something unseen rippled through the space, something ancient and waiting. Elias did not flinch. He simply held her gaze, patient, as if giving her time to come to terms with what she already knew to be true.

Aelina swallowed against the tightness in her throat. "Then what are you now?"

Elias's smile was slow, edged with something unreadable, something almost sad.

"Something that cannot be undone."

The chamber pulsed.

Aelina's stomach twisted, her heart pounding as the weight of those words settled deep into her bones. She had come searching for answers, for the truth behind the sickness, but she had not been prepared for this.

She had not been prepared to find that the thing she had been chasing had a face. Had a voice.

Had been the person she had once loved most in this world.

And whatever had remade him, whatever had brought him back—

It was still here.

Aelina's breath was steady, but only because she forced it to be. Inside, her mind was a storm, churning with the weight of what she had just heard, what she had just seen. Elias stood before her, real and whole, yet carrying something terribly, impossibly wrong. The torches continued their erratic flickering, casting long shadows that twisted unnaturally along the carved stone, making the chamber feel smaller, more suffocating. The air around her buzzed with unseen energy, as though something old and unrelenting was watching, waiting for her reaction. She had spent so long searching for answers, following the sickness, chasing ghosts, only to find that the ghost had come to her.

Elias was not dead. But he was not alive in the way she had once known.

Her fingers twitched at her sides, an instinctive urge to reach for something solid—a weapon, a vial, a truth she could actually hold. But there was nothing here that would ground her, nothing here that would give her what she needed. The brother she had mourned had become something else. The sickness she had been hunting had led her back to him.

Elias took a slow step forward, his expression unreadable, though the silver in his gaze flickered with something she could not quite name. "I know what you're thinking," he murmured, his voice threaded with that same impossible calm. "That this doesn't make sense. That I can't be standing here, speaking to you. That this is some kind of trick." He tilted his head slightly, studying her as if waiting for her to deny it. "But you feel it, don't you?" His voice dropped lower, softer. "You know I'm real."

Aelina swallowed, her throat dry, her pulse hammering against her ribs. She did not want to admit it, but he was right. Whatever strange magic had brought him back, whatever force had wrapped around his bones and pulled him from the grave, it was not an illusion. She had seen tricks before, had fought creatures that could mimic the faces of the dead, but this was not that. This was Elias.

And yet—it wasn't.

Dorian had remained silent, still standing between them, but Aelina could feel the sharp weight of his presence, could feel the storm coiling beneath the surface of his controlled exterior. He had known this was coming—not the full truth, perhaps, but enough. His golden eyes flickered, his body still loose but poised, like a blade held in an assassin's grip, waiting for the right moment to strike or withdraw. When he finally spoke, his voice was smooth, quiet, but lethal.

"You're right about one thing," he murmured, tilting his head slightly, his smirk laced with something sharper than amusement. "This doesn't make sense." His gaze darkened, his voice lowering. "So why don't you start explaining?"

Elias chuckled, a sound that was too easy, too familiar, and that was what made Aelina's stomach churn. He had always been able to do that—disarm people with his words, with the effortless way he made them believe he was always in control. But there was something in his expression now, something too knowing, too patient, that made her blood run cold.

"You think I haven't tried?" Elias asked, spreading his hands in a slow, deliberate motion, as if he were making an offer rather than answering a demand. "You think I haven't spent every moment of my second life trying to understand what I've become?"

His silver-threaded eyes darkened slightly, the flickering torchlight catching the strange luminescence beneath his irises. "I didn't ask for this, Aelina." His voice was softer now, but it did not lack weight. "I woke up in the ruins of my own grave, alone, with no memory of how I got there. No pulse. No warmth. Just an emptiness where something used to be."

Aelina's breath hitched slightly, her throat tightening. She had imagined his death a thousand times, had wondered how much pain he had endured, if he had known in his final moments that he would never see the sunrise again. And now he was telling her that those final moments had not been the end at all. That something had reached into the grave and pulled him back.

The sigils along the walls pulsed harder, a tremor running through the stone beneath them, as if the chamber itself was reacting to his words. The air grew colder, not from the touch of wind but from something unnatural, something unseen.

Dorian exhaled through his nose, shaking his head slightly, his smirk fading into something more like irritation. "So that's it?" he mused, golden eyes locked onto Elias with a gaze so sharp it could have cut through steel. "You woke up cursed and just decided to let the world rot around you?"

Elias's expression didn't change, but Aelina saw the flicker of something behind his gaze, something coiled, waiting. "Do you think I wanted this?" he asked, his voice quieter, but charged. "Do you think I haven't tried to stop it?" His jaw tightened, the calm mask slipping just slightly. "This sickness isn't something I control, Dorian. It's something I am."

Aelina inhaled sharply, the words striking something deep inside her, something she did not know how to name. She had always believed the sickness was something created, something wielded by a dark force, by men who had lost their humanity in the pursuit of power. But this—this changed everything.

Her voice was hoarse when she finally spoke, barely above a whisper. "Then what happens if you die again?"

The question hung between them, heavy, and Elias stilled. His silver-threaded eyes locked onto hers, something shifting behind his expression, something she could not name. And then, finally, he smiled.

"You don't want to know."

A shiver raced down her spine, her body reacting before her mind could fully comprehend what that meant. It was not a threat. It was a warning.

Dorian let out a slow breath, shaking his head slightly. "Well, that's not ominous at all," he muttered, rubbing a hand along his jaw before flicking his gaze back toward Elias. "So, let me get this straight. You wake up, magic stitched into your bones, and instead of figuring out how to undo it, you just... let it spread?"

Elias didn't flinch. "I tried to contain it. I failed."

Aelina's hands curled into fists. "Then why did you let me chase it?" she demanded, the frustration rising in her voice. "Why lead me here if you knew it would end like this?"

Elias studied her for a long moment before he answered. "Because I needed you to see it for yourself."

The air tensed, the torches dimming further, and Aelina felt it again—the presence, the weight of something else in the chamber with them. Not Elias. Not Dorian. Something greater.

And in that instant, she knew.

They were not alone.

Elias took a slow step back, his silver-threaded gaze flicking toward the darkness beyond the chamber's edge. His voice, when he spoke again, was almost too quiet to hear.

"It's already here."

And the shadows moved.

Aelina's breath tightened in her chest as the shadows twisted, stretched, shifting in ways that defied logic, defied form. They did not move like mist curling from the flame of a dying torch, nor like the creeping dark at the edges of twilight. They moved with purpose. With hunger. Shapes slithered at the chamber's edges, rising and falling in unnatural waves, and the moment Elias spoke, they stilled—watching. Waiting.

The air grew thick, heavy with something unspoken, unseen, but no less real. The torches dimmed to nothing but embers, their weak glow casting trembling light along the polished obsidian floor, stretching shadows into grotesque, impossible lengths. It was not an absence of light—it was something else entirely. The feeling of a presence curling through the cracks of reality, seeping through the places where the world had thinned.

Dorian exhaled sharply, shifting his weight slightly, but he did not reach for his blade. That, more than anything, sent a fresh wave of dread through Aelina's spine. Dorian always reached for his blade. He had fought his way through ambushes, through assassins, through men and creatures alike who thought they could outmatch him, and yet here, now, standing on the precipice of something neither of them understood—he waited.

Elias's silver-threaded gaze flickered toward the growing darkness, his features unreadable, but Aelina could feel the tension creeping into him, the way his breath slowed, the way his shoulders locked in something close to readiness, close to resignation. His next words were quiet, but they carried through the space like a stone dropped into still water.

"You don't want to see it."

The moment the words left his mouth, the chamber trembled.

Not a quake, not a shift in the earth, but a pulse, a single, slow heartbeat in the air itself. Aelina staggered slightly, a wave of nausea rolling through her stomach as the weight of something unseen pressed against her chest, pressing into her ribs like a breath exhaled from the void. The shadows stretched farther, curling toward them, not reaching—pulling.

Dorian muttered something under his breath, his golden eyes flashing with something dangerously close to recognition, to understanding. His head tilted slightly, and when he spoke, his voice was too careful, too slow. "What did you bring us into, Elias?"

Elias didn't answer immediately. He stood motionless, his hands loose at his sides, his gaze locked on the shifting dark. His voice, when it came, was distant, like he was speaking from somewhere far away. "This isn't about me," he murmured, but there was something off about the way he said it—something that sounded like a lie.

The shadows trembled again, and then—they split open.

Aelina's heart slammed against her ribs as the darkness peeled apart like a living wound, the black mist curling away to reveal a shape rising from the abyss. It was not a man. It was not a beast. It was something in between, something older than the words she had for it, something that should have never been able to step foot in this world.

She could not see its face. Could not tell where it began or ended. Its form flickered, shifting between the solidity of flesh and the weightless nothing of a nightmare slipping through waking thought. Its presence pressed against her mind, whispering in tongues she did not know, languages she had never heard but somehow understood.

You sought the truth.

The voice did not come from the creature's mouth. It did not seem to have one. It came from everywhere. From inside her own skull. From the spaces between the moments she had lived and the ones she had forgotten.

Dorian's breath was slow beside her, but she could feel the way his muscles had locked into something close to stillness, as though moving, speaking, acknowledging it too much would be enough to make it real.

But it was real.

It was already here.

Elias exhaled once, a breath so quiet it was barely there, and then he did something she did not expect.

He knelt.

Aelina's breath hitched, her pulse spiking, every part of her body screaming that this was wrong, that Elias should not be bowing to anything. But he did not hesitate, did not falter. He lowered himself to the ground like a man honoring a god, his silver-threaded eyes lifting to the thing in the dark without fear, without defiance—with acceptance.

And then—he spoke.

"You said it would be her."

The air split.

The moment the words left his mouth, the thing in the shadows shifted, its presence folding in on itself, and Aelina felt something cold slide into her veins. Not physically. Not with hands or blades. With will.

With intention.

A spark ignited in her chest, a flicker of something ancient and unbidden, something that did not belong to her but had always been waiting for her to claim it. The torches in the chamber guttered completely, plunging them into a darkness that was not absence, but presence, a living void curling around them.

Aelina gasped, her vision swimming, her lungs tightening as something unseen reached for her. Her body locked, her blood roared in her ears, and through the ringing, through the cold, through the dark pressing into her ribs like unseen fingers—

She heard Elias's voice.

"You were always part of this."

The world fractured.

And then—nothing.

Only silence. Only cold.

Only the feeling that, whatever had just happened—

She would never be the same again.

Chapter Five:

The Mark of the Void

Aelina awoke to the sensation of falling.

Not the violent, heart-stopping plummet of gravity pulling flesh toward the earth, but something worse—a slow, endless descent through nothingness, as if the world had unraveled around her and left her to drift in the remnants of what remained. Her body felt weightless, suspended in a place that was neither dark nor light, where shadows did not stretch and time did not breathe. It was not cold, not warm—only vast, endless, empty.

She tried to move, but there was no ground beneath her, no air to push against, no sound to anchor her. Only the steady thrum of something unseen, something vast pressing against the edges of her mind, curling into the hollow spaces of her bones. She wasn't alone. She wasn't sure she ever had been.

Then—a voice.

It came from everywhere and nowhere, layered over itself, shifting between octaves as if it could not decide what it should be. It did not whisper. It did not echo. It simply was.

"Now you understand."

Aelina's chest constricted, her breath catching on something unseen, unfelt, unknown. The voice did not belong to Elias. It did not belong to the creature in the dark. It belonged to this place, to the nothingness around her.

Memories came back in pieces—Elias kneeling, the shifting thing in the darkness, the way her blood had turned cold as something reached for her, claimed her, marked her. But what had happened after that? Where was she?

The pressure in the air deepened, wrapping around her like the weight of a storm pressing against fragile glass. Then, all at once, she stopped falling.

She felt ground beneath her feet, solid but not stone, not earth. The nothingness receded, or maybe it had never been there at all. Aelina inhaled sharply, staggering forward as sensation rushed back into her body, her limbs heavy, her heartbeat erratic. The air was thick, heavy with the scent of ancient parchment, of metal, of something burned and long since extinguished.

She lifted her head—and the world came rushing back.

She stood in a vast, open chamber, far larger than the one she had been in before. The walls stretched impossibly high, disappearing into a blackened expanse that was neither sky nor ceiling. Sigils burned along the floor, intricate symbols shifting in and out of recognition, pulsing in a rhythm that was not entirely separate from her own heartbeat. The air itself shimmered with an unseen force, humming in the back of her skull like a memory she could not place.

And she was not alone.

Dorian stood several feet away, his golden eyes sharpened with something dangerously close to fury. He was tense, his body coiled like a predator about to strike, but he was not looking at her. His gaze was fixed on something beyond her, something she could not yet see. His breathing was controlled, measured—but Aelina could feel it in the air, the way his magic bristled just beneath his skin, how it curled at his fingertips, waiting for him to decide if he needed to use it.

Slowly, she turned.

Elias stood at the edge of the sigil-marked floor, his posture too relaxed, too knowing, as if he had expected this. As if he had been waiting. The silver-threaded glow in his eyes had deepened, the unnatural light pulsing faintly in the dimness of the chamber. He watched her not with cruelty, not with triumph, but with certainty.

"You were always meant to come here," he said, and his voice held weight now, carried by something more than breath, more than will.

Aelina's hands clenched at her sides, the weight of his words sinking in, the anger beginning to push through the haze of confusion. "Where is here?" she demanded, her voice steadier than she felt.

Elias's lips tugged into a slow, knowing smile. "Where you've always been headed."

The torches that lined the walls flickered—not fire, not light, but something deeper, something shifting, something alive. The sigils beneath their feet pulsed once, and then the shadows in the farthest reaches of the chamber moved.

Aelina froze.

She had seen shadows move before, had seen magic twist the laws of reality in ways that could not be explained. But this—this was different.

The darkness did not creep forward like mist. It expanded.

And as it did, something stepped from it.

A figure, taller than any human, shrouded in robes that moved as if made from the void itself. Its presence was impossible to comprehend, shifting in shape and mass, like her mind could not fully decide what it was seeing. Its face was hidden, but the weight of its gaze was undeniable.

Dorian's breath left him in a slow, careful exhale, his fingers twitching toward the hilt of his dagger, but he did not move. Aelina could feel the tension in him now, the barely contained instinct to fight, to run, to do anything but stand still in the presence of something that should not exist.

Elias did not look away.

"You're ready now," he murmured.

Aelina's stomach turned, her fingers curling into fists, every instinct in her body screaming that this was a moment she could not undo. She had thought the sickness was the end of the mystery, thought finding Elias would give her the truth she had been chasing.

But this—this was only the beginning.

The figure took another step forward, and the chamber pulsed again, a low, resonant sound rippling through the air. Aelina's breath hitched, her body locking in place as the weight of it pressed against her ribs, settling into her bones like something that had been waiting to take hold of her.

And then, it spoke.

"The mark is upon you, child. And the choice will come soon."

The chamber shuddered, the sigils flashing with one final, blinding pulse of light—

And the world, as she knew it, shifted forever.

The chamber breathed around her, the air shuddering with unseen movement, as though the very stone had exhaled in the wake of the words spoken. The weight of them pressed into her ribs, a slow, crawling thing that wrapped around her spine like unseen vines, rooting her in place. Aelina's heartbeat was too loud, too erratic, thudding in her chest like a war drum she could not silence.

The figure before her did not move, and yet its presence expanded, filling the space with something ancient, something unknowable. It was not merely standing in front of her; it was in the air, in the walls, in the very marrow of her bones. Its robes, dark as the space between stars, did not ripple with the wind, did not shift with movement, but seemed instead to drink in the light around them, swallowing the glow of the sigils, leaving only an eerie, pulsing radiance that flickered like dying embers beneath her feet.

Aelina wanted to speak—demand answers, deny the claim, anything—but her tongue felt heavy, thick, as though it no longer belonged to her. The pressure of something unseen and watching coiled around her throat, not enough to strangle, but enough to remind her that this was not a place of mortal authority. Whatever had spoken—**whatever had marked her—**was not bound by the rules of men.

Dorian's voice cut through the thick silence, low and edged with something that might have been anger, might have been fear. "What exactly do you mean by 'mark'?" He did not move, but his posture shifted—a fraction, a breath, his weight tilting just slightly onto the balls of his feet, ready to react. It was the kind of stillness Aelina recognized, the kind that came right before violence.

The figure tilted its hooded head, too fluid, too unnatural, as though its body did not follow the same rules as theirs. When it spoke again, it was not one voice, but many, layered atop one another, reverberating in a way that did not belong in the physical world.

"The brand has been placed, and the burden has begun. It cannot be undone. It cannot be forsaken."

Aelina's stomach twisted, her pulse a roaring current beneath her skin. "I didn't agree to anything." The words came out harsher than she intended, but the fire in them was real, burning through the confusion, the fear, the weight of standing before something that should not exist.

Elias exhaled through his nose, tilting his head slightly, but he did not look surprised. If anything, there was something close to amusement in his expression, his silver-threaded gaze glinting beneath the torchlight. "You never had to," he murmured. "It was always waiting for you."

Her breath caught, sharp and quick.

No.

No, she would have known. She would have felt something, would have sensed that her fate had been twisting itself around her throat like a noose long before she had stepped foot in this chamber. She had fought for control her entire life, fought against the idea that she was nothing more than a pawn in someone else's story, but now—now, she was beginning to wonder if she had ever been the one steering the path at all.

Dorian's fingers twitched at his sides, his expression dark, unreadable. "That's not how this works," he muttered, golden eyes flicking between Elias and the robed figure, his stance still loose, but his magic bristled just beneath his skin. Aelina could see it, the way the air around his hands wavered, the way the unnatural shadows retreated from him. "You don't just claim someone without their consent. Fate doesn't get to decide who she becomes."

The hooded figure shifted. The air trembled.

"Fate does not decide."

The voices were layered again, thick with something impenetrable, unyielding. The figure raised a hand—or what should have been a hand, for the moment its sleeve lifted, the darkness underneath shifted, revealing not flesh, not bone, but something void-like, something endless. It reached outward, extending fingers that were not fingers at all, just the impression of shape, the mimicry of something that had once been human but had long since forgotten how to be.

Aelina's body seized with cold.

"The mark is chosen."

The moment the words left the figure's unseen lips, pain lanced through her.

A fire—not real fire, not heat, but something deeper, something laced beneath the surface of her skin, curling through her veins. It was not like the pain of a wound, not sharp or sudden. It was pulling, as though something had reached into her chest and was dragging her forward, trying to pull something from her that had been buried for too long.

Her knees nearly buckled, her breath coming out in a sharp, ragged gasp. Dorian moved instantly, his hand catching her arm before she could fall, his touch steady, grounding. The moment his fingers closed around her wrist, the pain—for a flickering second—eased.

Elias stepped closer, watching her carefully, but he did not move to help.

Of course he didn't.

Of course, he had known.

Her breathing steadied, her teeth clenched so tightly her jaw ached, and slowly, she forced herself to look down.

And there it was.

The mark.

Burned into the inside of her left wrist, just above her pulse, a symbol she had never seen before but somehow recognized. It was not ink, not paint, not something carved into flesh—it was deeper, something beneath her skin, as though it had always been there and had simply been waiting to reveal itself.

A single, curving design, intricate and sharp-edged, woven into itself like a knot with no beginning and no end. And at its center—a single point of silver, pulsing with a faint, impossible light.

Dorian swore under his breath. "That's not just a mark," he muttered. "That's a seal."

Aelina's stomach dropped.

She knew what that meant.

A mark could be burned away, erased, severed with magic.

But a seal was permanent. A seal meant binding, inescapable, irrefutable.

A seal meant she belonged to something now.

She sucked in a slow, shaking breath, her fingers flexing, trying to ignore the way her wrist still thrummed with a dull, aching pulse. "What does it do?" she forced out, looking up at the hooded figure, her vision sharp with fury, with demand.

It did not answer.

Instead, it turned.

The shadows shifted again, folding inward, and the figure began to step back, retreating as if it had finished its task, as if it had already won.

"You will know when it is time."

The darkness closed in behind it, the sigils on the floor flickering one last time before dimming to silence.

And just like that—it was gone.

Aelina stared at the empty space where it had stood, her body still tense, her mind still spinning, the weight of the seal still pulsing against her wrist like a second heartbeat.

Elias exhaled softly, shaking his head, his expression unreadable. "Well," he mused, a faint smirk tugging at the corner of his lips. "That went better than expected."

Dorian turned to him, his golden eyes dark and unreadable.

And then—he punched him.

Elias barely had time to react before Dorian's fist connected with his jaw, the sharp crack of bone against bone echoing through the chamber like a gunshot. The force of the hit sent Elias staggering back a step, his head snapping to the side, but he didn't fall. Instead, he rolled with the impact, his body moving with unnatural grace, absorbing the blow as though he had expected it.

Aelina stood frozen, her wrist still pulsing, her breath still uneven, but the sudden violence snapped something back into place inside her. The room was no longer filled with shadows shifting at the edges of reality, no longer held in the grip of that inhuman presence. Now it was just them—three people, bound together by something none of them had asked for.

Elias exhaled sharply, lifting a hand to his jaw, his fingers grazing the bruised skin with a slow, almost amused curiosity. He rolled his shoulders, tilting his head slightly before finally looking at Dorian, silver-threaded eyes flashing with something dangerous. "Well," he muttered, voice edged with something close to amusement. "That was uncalled for."

Dorian didn't smile. Didn't smirk. Didn't even move. His posture remained loose, controlled, but Aelina could see the tightness in his shoulders, the sharp way his breath came too slow, too measured, like he was keeping something caged just beneath the surface. "Was it?" His voice was low, even, but there was nothing light about it. "Because I think it was overdue."

Elias chuckled softly, shaking his head, but there was no true humor in it. "You always did like making a mess of things, didn't you?" He flexed his jaw once, testing the damage, before finally meeting Aelina's gaze. His amusement faded slightly, replaced with something heavier, something unreadable. "And you—" His silver-threaded gaze flickered toward her wrist, lingering on the pulsing mark that had burned itself into her skin. "How do you feel?"

Aelina's fingers twitched, her nails pressing lightly into her palm as she forced herself to keep her breathing steady. How did she feel? The answer coiled inside her, twisting and writhing, but she could not put it into words. Not yet. Not with all of this still sitting too raw in her chest. She swallowed once, then lifted her chin, leveling her gaze at him with a steadiness she didn't quite feel. "I feel like you should start explaining. Now."

Elias hummed under his breath, rubbing his jaw absently, but she could tell he was weighing something. Deciding how much to say, how much to withhold. He had always been good at that—revealing just enough to keep her from pushing too hard. But this time, she wouldn't let him get away with it.

Dorian crossed his arms, his golden eyes flashing with irritation. "For once in your life, Elias, just stop dancing around the truth and say it. You let her walk into this, knowing exactly what it was. That thing branded her like it had a claim on her, and you're standing here pretending like it's nothing. So talk."

Elias exhaled slowly, tilting his head back as if contemplating the ceiling—or whatever stretched beyond it. When he finally spoke, his voice was calm, careful. "It was never my place to tell her," he said simply, lowering his gaze to Aelina once more. "This was always going to happen, whether she knew or not."

Aelina took a slow step forward, closing the distance between them, the pulse in her wrist thrumming louder, sharper. "And what exactly is 'this'?" she demanded. "What did that thing do to me?"

Elias studied her for a long moment, then sighed. "It marked you as a conduit," he said finally.

The word felt heavy, unfamiliar, yet dangerously close to something she had always feared. Her throat tightened, but she didn't let the panic rise. Not yet. "A conduit for what?"

Elias hesitated—just for a breath, just long enough for her to see it. That flicker of doubt, of uncertainty.

And that was the moment she knew.

Whatever had happened here—**whatever had been set into motion—**Elias did not know how to stop it.

Aelina's pulse roared in her ears. "Tell me," she pressed, her voice lower now, edged with something sharp.

Elias exhaled, rubbing a hand over his face before finally answering. "For whatever force put that mark on you," he murmured, and this time, his voice lacked the usual amusement, the infuriating distance he always carried. This was real. This was a confession. "It means you are bound to it now. To its will, its knowledge, its power." His gaze flickered, the silver threading in his irises gleaming beneath the torchlight. "You aren't just part of this anymore, Aelina. You are its vessel."

The world lurched.

Aelina took a step back, her breath shaking, though she refused to let it show. "No," she whispered, the word almost involuntary. "That's not possible."

Elias's lips pressed into a thin line. "It already happened."

Dorian let out a slow, dangerous breath, his golden eyes sharp, cold. "That's not something you just accept."

Elias's gaze flicked to him, and something shifted in his expression—not pity, not anger, but a strange kind of understanding. "You think I don't know that?" His voice was quieter now, more dangerous. "You think I wanted this for her?"

Dorian's jaw tightened, but he didn't respond.

Aelina could barely hear them. The words conduit. Vessel. Bound. kept circling in her mind, crashing into each other, shattering against the walls of her thoughts. She had spent her life trying to control her fate, trying to carve her own path despite what others wanted for her. And now—now she had been marked. Claimed. Tied to something she did not understand, something that had already begun to sink into the marrow of her bones.

A slow pulse of heat throbbed beneath her wrist, a whisper of something moving just beneath the surface of her skin. The mark was not silent. It was awake. It was waiting.

She swallowed hard, forcing the fear away, locking it down deep where it could not touch her. If she let herself feel it now, it would consume her.

Elias sighed again, softer this time. "You need to understand," he murmured, and there was something almost pleading in his voice. "This isn't something you can run from."

Aelina lifted her gaze to his, and for the first time, she let him see the fire behind it. "I wasn't planning on running."

Something in Elias's expression shifted—just slightly.

Dorian smirked faintly, though there was no humor in it. "That's good," he murmured, rolling his shoulders, tension still coiled beneath his movements. "Because something tells me we won't have the luxury of running anyway."

The torches flickered violently, a sudden gust of cold rushing through the chamber.

Aelina's pulse pounded.

The mark beneath her wrist flared.

And from somewhere beyond the chamber walls—something stirred.

The air in the chamber thickened, pressing against Aelina's skin like the weight of an unseen tide. The sigils etched into the floor gave a single, final pulse, their glow sinking into the stone as if retreating into the veins of the world itself. Whatever had marked her, whatever had claimed her, was not gone—it was merely waiting.

Aelina's wrist still burned, the seal pulsing like a second heartbeat, its rhythm not her own. The sensation coiled beneath her skin, neither pain nor comfort, just an undeniable presence, something she could not shake, something watching her from the inside out. She gritted her teeth, flexing her fingers as if she could force it away, but the moment she did, a whisper of heat curled through her veins, humming with recognition.

Dorian had not moved. He stood just to her side, close enough that she could feel the faint shift of his breathing, the quiet tension threaded through him. His golden eyes had not left Elias, but Aelina could sense the way his attention flickered to her—measuring, waiting, expecting. He had seen enough magic in his life to know when something wasn't finished.

Elias exhaled, his silver-threaded gaze drifting toward her wrist, noting the mark, acknowledging the shift that had settled over her. "It's begun," he murmured, almost to himself, though his voice carried through the chamber like a prophecy spoken aloud. His expression was unreadable, carefully composed, but there was something in the way his fingers curled at his sides, something that hinted at restraint.

Aelina swallowed hard, forcing her voice steady. "What happens now?" The words should have been a demand, a sharp-edged challenge, but they came out quieter, heavier. She hated the way they felt on her tongue, hated the uncertainty wrapped around them.

Elias's gaze lifted back to hers, and for the first time since he had stepped from the shadows, he looked almost—weary. "That depends on you," he said, tilting his head slightly. "But I can tell you this—you don't have much time."

Aelina's pulse spiked, and she hated the reaction, hated that her body reacted before her mind could catch up. "Time for what?" she asked, though she wasn't sure she wanted to hear the answer.

Elias sighed, and something shifted in his posture, something that made the breath still in her throat. "The mark is a link," he said, his voice careful, measured. "Not just to the entity that placed it, but to something older. Something that's been waiting for the right vessel." He hesitated, as if weighing his next words, then let them fall like stones into deep, unseen water. "And now that vessel is you."

The chamber seemed smaller then, the walls pressing inward, the space around her suddenly suffocating. Aelina shook her head, a bitter laugh scraping its way up her throat, but there was no humor in it. "You're telling me I'm supposed to be some kind of... what? A conduit for a power I didn't ask for?"

Elias's silver-threaded gaze remained steady. "I'm telling you that you already are."

The silence that followed was too sharp, too final.

Dorian exhaled, his fingers twitching slightly at his sides. "That's not how this works," he muttered, his tone edged with irritation, though there was something beneath it—concern, tightly reined in, barely visible. "Magic isn't sentient. It doesn't wait for people, it doesn't choose."

Elias gave him a slow, knowing smile. "Are you sure?"

The question lingered in the air, sinking into the cracks between them, curling into the spaces where doubt had already begun to take root. Aelina hated the way it made her stomach twist, the way it settled inside her chest like something undeniable.

She turned her wrist over, staring at the mark again, the intricate, curling design that pulsed with its own quiet rhythm. It didn't burn anymore, but she could feel it, like a whisper under her skin, a presence she could not ignore. "And if I don't accept it?" she asked, lifting her gaze back to Elias, watching his expression shift slightly at the question.

He was quiet for a moment, and when he finally spoke, there was no amusement left in his voice. "Then it will take you anyway."

Aelina's breath caught.

Dorian stiffened beside her, and for the first time since the mark had burned its way into her skin, she saw real anger flicker in his golden eyes. "That's not an option," he said, his voice low, controlled, but there was violence threaded beneath it, a promise he was ready to keep.

Elias's smirk returned, faint and knowing, but there was something tired beneath it. "You think I don't know that?" His voice softened, his gaze flickering between the two of them. "You think I haven't tried to change it?" His hand lifted slightly, fingers brushing over the high collar of his tunic, and for the first time, Aelina realized—he had a mark, too.

The same intricate weave of symbols, the same pulsing glow beneath the skin.

Elias had been marked before her.

Her stomach turned to ice. "How long?" she whispered.

Elias exhaled, rolling his shoulders slightly, as if shaking off an unseen weight. "Long enough to know what happens next."

The torches lining the chamber flickered, the light dimming slightly, and Aelina swore she could feel the air shift. The mark on her wrist gave a slow, deliberate pulse, as though it had been waiting for the moment she realized the truth.

She wasn't the first.

She wouldn't be the last.

And whatever had marked her—**whatever had marked Elias—**wasn't finished yet.

Dorian turned to her, his golden eyes steady, assessing. "You're not doing this alone," he said, and it wasn't a question, wasn't even reassurance. It was a fact. A promise.

Aelina clenched her jaw, forcing herself to breathe, forcing herself to lock down the storm inside her. She didn't have the luxury of fear. Not now. Not when the battle had already begun, and she had no choice but to fight it.

She lifted her gaze to Elias. "Then tell me," she murmured. "What happens next?"

Elias's silver-threaded gaze darkened.

"The real question, sister," he murmured, "is what happens when you can no longer stop it."

The air in the chamber shifted, heavy with something unseen, something vast pressing into the edges of reality. Aelina felt it now, the pulse beneath her skin, the weight of something she did not understand coiling deep inside her bones, waiting. It was not just the mark on her wrist—it was what lay beyond it, what had seeped into her when the sigils had burned, when the shadows had whispered her name. She had been hunting the sickness, chasing the answers, but the truth had always been chasing her.

Dorian exhaled sharply, his golden gaze flicking between her and Elias, his stance loose but coiled with readiness. "So let me get this straight," he muttered, rolling a shoulder as though shaking off an unseen weight. "You're saying she's a conduit, and that whatever put that thing on her is just... waiting?" His fingers tapped against the hilt of his dagger, a slow, rhythmic sound, and Aelina knew him well enough to recognize it for what it was—frustration carefully measured, anger held just beneath the surface.

Elias met his gaze with an unreadable expression, something between patience and inevitability. "Not waiting," he corrected softly. "Becoming."

Aelina's stomach tightened, the air in her lungs turning to stone. Becoming. The word coiled in her mind, pressing against the fragile threads of understanding she had left. She had thought she was meant to stop the sickness, to find its source and cut it from the world before it could consume anything else. But what if she was not meant to destroy it? What if she was meant to carry it?

She swallowed hard, her fingers curling slightly, feeling the burn beneath her wrist like an ember waiting to catch flame. "Then how do I stop it?" Her voice was steady, but inside, her mind reeled. She needed answers, she needed a path, something to hold onto before the ground disappeared entirely beneath her feet.

Elias's silver-threaded gaze lingered on her, measuring, waiting. When he finally spoke, his voice was quiet, almost resigned. "You don't."

Silence.

The word sank into the chamber, into the stone, into her. Dorian let out a slow, sharp breath, his hand tightening around his dagger, and for the first time, Aelina saw something rare flicker across his expression—uncertainty.

"You're lying," Dorian said, but the words did not carry their usual bite. They were too soft, too deliberate, like a man trying to convince himself of something he already knew was false.

Elias tilted his head slightly, his smirk faint, but there was something in his gaze, something like regret. "No, I'm not."

Aelina forced herself to move, to shake off the weight pressing against her ribs. "Then what happens when I lose control?" The words felt foreign in her mouth, like she was speaking of someone else, like she was asking about a fate that did not belong to her. But the mark on her wrist pulsed, a steady, knowing beat, and she knew—this was not someone else's fate. This was hers.

Elias hesitated, but just for a breath. "Then the world learns what it means to fear you."

The torches shuddered, their light twisting, stretching the shadows against the walls. Aelina felt her pulse slow, felt the way her breath seemed to deepen, to sync with something else, something not entirely hers. The sigils beneath them dimmed, then flared, and for a single, terrible second, she felt something else—something just beyond her reach, something that had been watching her long before she had ever stepped into this chamber.

She was not alone.

Not anymore.

Dorian took a step closer, his voice quieter now, but no less sharp. "That's not an option." It was not a plea. It was a promise.

Elias's expression did not change, but the way his gaze softened—**just slightly, just enough—**made Aelina's chest tighten. "Then you're already running out of time."

The air pulsed.

Aelina's breath caught, the mark flaring hot against her skin, burning without fire, pressing without weight, whispering without sound. Something inside her stirred, woke.

And from somewhere beyond the walls—something answered.

The torches died.

The darkness swallowed them whole.

Chapter Six:

The Hollow Awakening

The moment the torches died, the darkness wasn't empty.

It was not the absence of light but the presence of something else entirely. It moved, thick and tangible, curling around Aelina's skin like a second breath, whispering in tones she could not hear but could feel. The chamber, once vast and sprawling, now felt endless, without boundary, as if the very concept of walls and floors had been swallowed whole. Even the weight of the air had changed, pressing against her ribs, sinking into her bones like fingers reaching into her very being.

Her pulse thundered in her ears, the mark on her wrist pulsing in time with it—a steady, growing rhythm. It wasn't pain. It wasn't fire. It was something deeper, something threading itself through her veins, binding, claiming, becoming.

Aelina sucked in a sharp breath, trying to focus, trying to find something solid in the void that had consumed them. The shadows around her were not still—they moved, shifted, breathed as if alive. She turned, her heart hammering against her ribs, but there was no light, no form, only the sense that she was being watched from all sides.

Then—a voice.

"Do you feel it now?"

Elias.

His voice was calm, too calm, but she could hear the weight beneath it, the edge of something deep and knowing. She turned sharply toward where she thought he had been standing, but she could not see him. The shadows had taken everything, swallowed everything, and yet—he was still there.

Her breath was slow, controlled. "What is this?" The words came out steady, but her fingers twitched at her sides, itching for something—anything—she could use to ground herself.

Elias's voice was closer now, though she hadn't heard him move. "This is what it means to be chosen."

Aelina clenched her jaw, her stomach twisting. "I didn't ask for this," she bit out.

Elias chuckled, and this time, there was something almost sad beneath it. "Neither did I."

A flicker of movement—not Elias, not Dorian.

Something else.

Aelina whirled, instinct tightening in her limbs, but there was nothing to see, nothing to fight, nothing to stop. Just the endless dark, just the whisper of something old, something hungry stirring at the edges of her thoughts.

Then, suddenly—warmth.

A hand closed around her wrist, solid, steady, dragging her back into something real.

Dorian.

His grip was unshakable, fingers firm but not crushing, grounding her in a way that sent a shudder through her chest. The heat of his touch bled through the cold sinking into her skin, and for the first time since the torches had died, she felt real again. Not a vessel. Not a conduit. Just herself.

His voice came next, low and sharp, cutting through the weight pressing against them. "Elias, I swear to the gods, if you don't start explaining, I will drag you into the light myself and beat the answers out of you."

Aelina almost laughed. Almost.

Elias sighed, the sound distant, and suddenly—the torches flared back to life.

The chamber reappeared in a burst of flickering golden light, shadows recoiling, twisting back into the corners as if retreating into the cracks of the world. The air was still thick, but the crushing presence was gone, or at least... watching from a distance.

Elias stood where he had been before, unmoved, unaffected, watching her.

But Dorian's hand had not left her wrist.

Aelina felt the moment he realized it, the slight shift of his fingers, the tension running through his frame. And yet—he did not let go.

Not yet.

Elias exhaled, rolling his shoulders as if shaking off the weight of something unseen. "There," he said, his voice lighter, though his gaze never left Aelina. "Now you know."

Aelina yanked her wrist free from Dorian's grasp, not because she wanted him to let go, but because she needed to move, needed distance, clarity, air. "Know what?" she demanded, stepping forward, her breath still uneven, her skin still humming with something she did not understand.

Elias tilted his head slightly, the silver in his irises catching the flickering torchlight. "That it's waking up."

The words sent a chill down her spine.

Dorian scoffed, crossing his arms, his golden eyes dark with frustration. "You're being cryptic again. Try actual answers for once."

Elias's smirk flickered, brief and knowing. "You keep thinking there's one answer to give." His gaze flicked to Aelina's wrist, where the mark still glowed faintly beneath her skin. "But she's not ready for the truth."

Aelina bristled, something inside her snapping. "Then make me ready."

The words hung between them, heavy, final.

Elias studied her for a long moment, and for once, there was no amusement in his expression. No patience. No cryptic riddles.

Just truth.

"You don't control it yet," he said simply. "But soon, it will control you."

Silence.

Aelina's heartbeat thundered, but she kept her face steady, kept her shoulders square. "Then what do I do?"

Elias exhaled, and this time, there was real weight in it. "You learn."

The flames in the torches flickered again, as if something unseen had exhaled with him.

Aelina lifted her chin. "Then teach me."

Elias smirked, slow and knowing, but behind it—something colder, something uncertain. "I hope you mean that, sister," he murmured, his silver-threaded gaze sharp with something that almost looked like pity. "Because once you start, there's no stopping."

Aelina inhaled, steadying herself.

She already knew that.

She had known it the moment the mark burned itself into her skin.

Dorian said nothing, but when she turned slightly, she caught the way his gaze lingered on her wrist, the sharp tension in his jaw. He wasn't afraid of her.

But he was afraid of what came next.

The torches flickered.

And in the space between heartbeats, she thought she heard something else.

A whisper. A name.

Not spoken in the chamber.

Spoken inside her own mind.

And it was not her own voice.

Aelina's breath shook.

She was running out of time.

Aelina's fingers twitched at her sides, the lingering warmth of Dorian's touch already fading, replaced by the slow, curling throb of the mark on her wrist. It wasn't pain, not exactly—it was something worse. It was a constant, pulsing reminder that something inside her wasn't entirely hers anymore.

She sucked in a slow breath, trying to push back the crawling sensation beneath her skin, trying to ignore the way Elias watched her with that infuriating knowing smirk, as if he had already foreseen every thought running through her mind. He always had that look—like he was three steps ahead, already watching her arrive at a conclusion he had reached long before her. She hated it.

Dorian was still beside her, arms crossed, golden eyes sharp as he studied Elias like a man considering whether or not to throw another punch. He wasn't smiling now. The easy arrogance he usually carried was gone, replaced by something heavier, something that sat deep in his chest, thick and unreadable. His jaw was tight, his stance loose but poised, and Aelina knew—he was waiting for Elias to give him a reason to react.

Elias, as always, remained unbothered.

Aelina took a step closer, her heartbeat settling into something measured, steady. "If you're going to teach me," she said, her voice quiet but unwavering, "then do it now. No more waiting. No more games."

Elias tilted his head, the smirk on his lips twitching, almost as if he were amused by her defiance. "You always were impatient," he mused. "You used to hate when I was right. That hasn't changed, I see."

Aelina's fingers curled into fists. "I don't have time for this, Elias."

For a moment—**just a moment—**his expression shifted. The amusement faltered, something deeper flashing across his silver-threaded gaze, something old, distant.

"Neither do I," he admitted.

That took her off guard.

Dorian's brow furrowed slightly, his arms tightening across his chest. "What does that mean?"

Elias exhaled, running a hand through his hair, his smirk fading completely now. "You don't think the thing that put that mark on her is just going to wait around, do you?" He looked back at Aelina, and this time, there was something almost resigned in his voice. "That thing—the one that branded you, the one that branded me? It doesn't like to be ignored. And it never stops watching."

Aelina's throat tightened. She had felt it, hadn't she? Even before the torches had gone out. That subtle, unshakable presence. The feeling that she was being watched, even when no one was there.

"You're saying it's aware of me," she murmured, the words heavier than she intended.

Elias met her gaze. "I'm saying it's waiting for you to fall."

Silence stretched between them.

Dorian let out a slow, deliberate breath. "Fantastic," he muttered, rubbing a hand along his jaw, fingers brushing over the fading bruises left from their last fight. "Because that's exactly what we needed. Another omniscient nightmare lurking in the background."

Aelina could feel his frustration, feel the way his instincts were screaming at him to fix this, to fight it, to put a blade between whatever unseen force was circling them and her. Dorian was a man of action, a man who could cut his way through most problems, but this? This was something he couldn't fight.

Elias, on the other hand, had already made peace with it.

That alone made Aelina's chest tighten.

She shook her head, forcing herself to focus, to push away the rising unease slithering through her ribs. "Then we don't give it the chance," she said, meeting Elias's gaze. "You said I need to learn how to control this? Fine. Teach me."

Elias was silent for a moment, then—**slowly, deliberately—**he extended a hand toward her.

Aelina hesitated.

She had fought to find him, had spent years believing him dead, had stood over his grave and mourned. But now, standing before him, so very alive yet so very different, she wondered if she was about to make a mistake. If trusting him, if taking that hand, meant stepping into something she could not walk away from.

But hadn't she already?

Hadn't that choice been made the moment the mark burned itself into her flesh?

Her fingers twitched, her pulse steady but not calm, and then—she reached out.

The moment their hands touched, the world shifted.

It wasn't just magic, wasn't just some unseen force pulling at her. It was a storm, a weightless plunge into something vast and endless, her senses flooding with a thousand memories that weren't hers.

A flicker of fire against the night.

The sound of something screaming.

Blood pooling in the cracks of stone.

A whisper, curling through the air, speaking in a language she did not know, but somehow, she understood.

And then—pain.

Aelina gasped, ripping her hand away, stumbling back as the chamber snapped back into place around her. Her breath came hard and uneven, her body trembling from the force of whatever she had just seen, just felt.

Elias exhaled, shaking out his fingers, as if the exchange had drained something from him, too. "Well," he murmured, rolling his shoulders. "That's one way to start."

Dorian was beside her in an instant, his presence a grounding force, his hand hovering just close enough to catch her if she collapsed. "What the hell was that?" His voice was sharper now, threaded with something dangerously close to anger. Not at her. At Elias.

Elias flexed his fingers, smirking faintly. "That was a taste of what she's bound to."

Aelina swallowed hard, her chest still tight, the weight of what she had seen, what she had felt, settling into her bones like something she would never be able to shake. "That wasn't just magic," she whispered. "That was something else."

Elias's silver-threaded gaze met hers, and this time, there was no amusement left.

"That was the beginning," he said quietly.

Aelina's breath stilled.

Dorian swore softly under his breath, rubbing a hand through his hair, frustration rolling off him in waves. "I'm starting to think punching you a second time would be justified."

Elias laughed, the sound dry and knowing, but Aelina wasn't listening.

She was still hearing the whisper.

Still feeling the fire.

Still seeing the blood in the cracks of stone.

And in the back of her mind, just beneath the edges of thought—something waited.

Watching.

Listening.

And it was only just beginning.

Aelina forced herself to steady her breathing, but the remnants of whatever had just happened still clung to her, coiled beneath her skin like an ember waiting to ignite. The flickers of memory—or were they visions?—had been too vivid, too real, and she could still feel the burn of unseen fire licking at the edges of her mind. Her wrist throbbed in tandem with the mark, and the whisper that had curled through her thoughts like smoke had not fully left her. It lingered in the back of her mind, waiting, watching.

Elias observed her carefully, his silver-threaded gaze unreadable, his posture too relaxed for someone who had just dragged her into something she did not understand. The ease with which he carried himself, the way he remained unmoved by what had just happened, made her stomach twist. He had expected this. Maybe he had even wanted it.

Dorian exhaled sharply, stepping in front of her, his stance shifting into something protective, intentional. His golden eyes burned, his frustration no longer masked behind sarcasm or amusement. "You knew that would happen," he accused, his voice low, but edged with something sharp, something close to barely restrained fury. "You knew what touching her would do, and you let it happen anyway."

Elias tilted his head slightly, as if considering that statement. Then, with a slow, deliberate smirk, he said, "Yes."

Aelina's breath hitched, but not with surprise. With realization. Of course he had known. Of course he had let it happen. The truth was a thread she had not fully pulled on yet, but it was there, unraveling in front of her. He wasn't just trying to teach her. He was testing her.

Dorian's shoulders tightened, his fingers flexing at his sides as if he were barely holding himself back. "You are really making it hard for me not to punch you again," he muttered, his voice strained with the effort it took to stay still.

Elias sighed, shaking his head slightly, as if Dorian's anger was a predictable inconvenience. "You don't get it," he said, crossing his arms. "She doesn't have time to ease into this. The moment that mark appeared, she became a target. We don't get the luxury of playing this slow." His gaze flicked back to Aelina, and there was something different there now—something heavier, something that almost looked like regret. "And if she can't handle this, she won't survive what's coming next."

Aelina swallowed hard, resisting the instinct to look at her wrist again. She didn't need to. She could feel it. The presence of something ancient, patient, waiting. The visions, the pulse beneath her skin, the way the air in the chamber still carried the lingering taste of something unseen—he was right. As much as she hated to admit it, Elias was right.

She lifted her chin, forcing herself to push past the unease crawling through her ribs. "Then what's next?" she asked, her voice steadier than she felt. "What do I have to do?"

Elias studied her for a long moment before speaking, and when he did, there was no amusement left in his tone. "You have to learn how to use it before it uses you," he said. "And that means we leave. Now."

Dorian frowned, crossing his arms tighter over his chest. "Leave? To where, exactly?"

Elias exhaled, running a hand through his dark hair before fixing Aelina with that knowing stare. "You've been chasing answers for years, trying to track the sickness back to its source," he said. "I'm telling you now—you were looking in the wrong places." He stepped closer, the weight of his presence shifting, becoming more imposing, more real. "I know where it began. And I know what's waiting at the end of this path."

Aelina's pulse pounded, the truth pressing into her, sharp-edged and undeniable.

This wasn't just about finding a cure anymore.

This was about finding the source.

And stopping it.

Dorian sighed through his nose, shaking his head slightly as if he already knew where this was going, as if he had already resigned himself to whatever madness was about to unfold. "Of course you do," he muttered, throwing a glance at Aelina. "And let me guess—we don't have a choice."

Aelina knew the answer before Elias even spoke.

She wasn't running from this.

She wasn't turning back.

She wasn't the same person she had been before walking into this chamber.

And maybe she never would be again.

Elias gave a small, knowing smile. "No," he said. "You don't."

The torches along the walls flickered violently, the flames twisting in the unseen wind. The chamber, once heavy with lingering energy, now felt on the verge of something breaking, something shifting.

Aelina exhaled, bracing herself for whatever came next.

Because there was no turning back now.

Chapter Seven:

The Path of Ash and Blood

The cold air of the underground corridors clung to Aelina's skin like a second layer, thick with the weight of old magic and the whispers of the past. The torches along the stone walls flickered in a strange, unpredictable rhythm, as if the flames themselves were uneasy, sensing what was coming. Each step she took sent echoes shivering down the narrow hall, bouncing against the worn, ancient stone that had long since forgotten the touch of sunlight.

Dorian walked beside her, his presence solid, grounding, though his golden eyes flicked toward her more than once, as if measuring something he couldn't quite put into words. She had felt it since leaving the chamber—the tension humming between them, an unspoken worry he didn't want to voice, or maybe just didn't know how to. She wasn't sure which would have been worse.

Elias led the way ahead of them, his stride unhurried but deliberate, his posture too relaxed for someone who had just dropped the weight of prophecy on her shoulders. He had always been like that—effortless, unreadable, carrying the knowledge of too many things and revealing too few. Now, though, she could see the faintest tightness in his movements, the way his fingers curled and uncurled at his sides. Even he wasn't unaffected.

The silence stretched, thick and unbearable.

It was Dorian who finally broke it, his voice low but edged with something sharp. "You still haven't said where we're going."

Elias didn't look back, but the corner of his mouth twitched, half amusement, half something else. "I did," he said. "You just weren't listening."

Dorian scoffed, dragging a hand through his dark hair, frustration simmering just beneath his skin. "Gods, I hate you."

Elias chuckled under his breath, though there was no real humor in it. "You're not the first."

Aelina exhaled through her nose, pushing past the bickering, trying to focus on the pieces of truth Elias had given her so far—the mark, the sickness, the force that had been waiting for her long before she had ever known it existed. "The source," she said, her voice steady despite the storm still roiling beneath her ribs. "That's where we're going, isn't it?"

Elias inclined his head slightly. "Clever girl."

Dorian muttered something under his breath that sounded a lot like a curse.

Aelina ignored them both, pressing forward. "You said I was looking in the wrong places," she continued. "Then tell me—where is the right one?"

This time, Elias slowed his pace slightly, glancing over his shoulder at her, his silver-threaded eyes gleaming in the dim torchlight. Something unreadable moved behind them, something vast and knowing. "Not far," he murmured. "But far enough that you should prepare yourself."

Aelina's jaw tightened. Prepare herself. As if she hadn't spent years preparing, as if she hadn't already felt the weight of this before she even understood what it was. She had spent too long searching, too long fighting against shadows without names. Now she had one—and she was ready to face it.

The corridor opened abruptly, spilling them into a vast, underground cavern. Aelina inhaled sharply, the air suddenly different here, heavier, tinged with something metallic. The walls stretched high into darkness, their surfaces slick with veins of glowing silver, pulsing softly like the breath of something half-asleep. At the cavern's center, an archway of blackened stone loomed, its surface carved with symbols she did not recognize—symbols that seemed to shift when she wasn't looking directly at them.

And beyond the archway—nothing.

Not darkness. Not stone.

Just emptiness.

Dorian halted beside her, his expression darkening. "Elias," he said, voice slow, wary. "What the hell is that?"

Elias took a step forward, standing just before the threshold of the archway, tilting his head slightly as if listening to something the rest of them could not hear. "A doorway," he said.

Aelina's stomach twisted. "To where?"

Elias looked at her then, his gaze sharp, knowing, and utterly serious.

"To the beginning."

Aelina's breath hitched.

Dorian let out a slow, steadying breath, dragging a hand down his face. "Of course it is."

Elias smirked. "It's adorable how you always act surprised."

Dorian shot him a glare that could have burned through steel. "I don't act surprised. I act pissed."

Aelina ignored them both, stepping forward until she stood just before the archway, close enough to feel the strange, thrumming pulse emanating from the stone. She lifted a hand, hovering her fingers just above the surface, and immediately—heat coiled up her arm, sinking into her bones, tracing along the pathways of the mark.

She yanked her hand back, her breath catching.

It had recognized her.

Elias nodded as if he had expected that. "Only those who bear the mark can pass through."

Dorian stiffened slightly beside her. "You could have mentioned that before."

Elias waved a hand dismissively. "You worry too much."

Aelina clenched her jaw, stepping closer again, ignoring the way her pulse pounded against her ribs. "What happens when I go through?"

Elias was quiet for a beat, then said, simply, irrevocably: "You see the truth."

The cavern went silent.

The torches that lined the stone walls flickered, the light stretching unnaturally, casting long, twisting shadows that did not belong to them. The archway pulsed again, the symbols flashing brighter, stronger, as if sensing that it was time.

Aelina exhaled, slow and measured, then turned to Dorian.

His golden eyes were already on her, and she hated the way she could see the conflict written across his face. He didn't like this—any of it. He didn't trust Elias, he didn't trust whatever lay beyond that archway, and most of all—he didn't trust that she was safe.

She gave him a small, steady nod.

Dorian muttered another curse, rubbing a hand along his jaw before exhaling sharply. "Fine," he said. "Let's get this over with."

Elias grinned. "That's the spirit."

Aelina turned back to the archway.

She didn't let herself hesitate.

She took a step forward—

And the world split open.

The moment Aelina stepped through the archway, the world fractured. It wasn't like stepping into another room, another space—it was like stepping out of existence altogether. The stone beneath her feet was suddenly gone, the cavern, the torches, even the sound of her own breathing vanished in an instant. For a moment, there was nothing. Not darkness. Not light. Just an overwhelming sense of absence, of weightlessness, of something vast and infinite pressing in from all sides.

Then, like a sharp inhale after drowning, the world snapped back into place.

She was standing again, but the ground beneath her was not stone, not earth. It was smooth, glass-like, reflecting the vast, open sky above her—except it was not a sky. The heavens stretched endlessly, swirling with colors she could not name, deep blues and silvers, streaks of white light twisting through a sea of stars. But the stars were not fixed, not distant—they moved, pulsed, shifted like embers caught in a silent wind. The air was thick with something unseen, something ancient, pressing into her lungs with each breath she took.

Aelina turned, her pulse hammering against her ribs, and found Dorian at her side, his expression locked somewhere between awe and unease. His golden eyes flicked across the landscape, taking in the sky that wasn't a sky, the endless reflection beneath their feet, as if the world had been turned into some vast, endless mirror. "This is..." he trailed off, shaking his head slightly. "Gods, I don't even know what this is."

Elias appeared beside them, stepping through the nothingness as if he had merely walked through a door. His silver-threaded gaze flicked upward, following the strange, shifting stars, before settling on Aelina. "Welcome to the In-Between," he said, voice quiet but weighted. "This is where the world begins and ends. Where the past and future exist at once."

Aelina's breath hitched slightly. The In-Between. She had read about it, stories and myths of a place that existed outside of time, where the dead whispered, where magic was not bound by mortal rules. But no one had ever seen it and returned to tell the tale.

She swallowed hard, her fingers twitching slightly as she took a slow, steadying breath. "Why are we here?"

Elias's smirk was faint, but there was no humor in it this time. "Because this is where the sickness was born."

The words settled into her bones, cold and heavy, curling into the spaces where doubt and fear had been waiting. She had spent years chasing shadows, following the rot as it spread, searching for something she could trace back to a single moment, a single place. Now she was here, standing at the edge of what should not exist, and the truth was suddenly too large, too vast to comprehend.

Dorian exhaled sharply, rubbing a hand over his face. "Of course it was," he muttered, but there was no sarcasm in his voice this time, only exhaustion. His golden eyes flicked to Elias, narrowed with suspicion. "So, what? We just walk in here and the answers will present themselves?"

Elias tilted his head slightly, the silver threading in his irises pulsing faintly, reflecting the shifting stars above. "Not exactly," he murmured. "This place isn't like the mortal world. It responds to the ones who step inside it." His gaze flicked toward Aelina again, and something distant, unreadable passed through his expression. "It's waiting for her."

Aelina's fingers curled into fists at her sides, the mark on her wrist thrumming in response, as if something had reached out to touch it. The moment she had stepped through the archway, it had awakened again, stirring beneath her skin, recognizing something in the air that she could not see.

The In-Between was alive.

Dorian's expression darkened, his jaw tightening. "I don't like this," he muttered. "I don't trust it."

Elias smirked, but there was no real amusement behind it. "That's because you weren't meant to."

Before Dorian could snap back, the ground beneath them shifted.

It was not an earthquake, not the tremor of something breaking—it was fluid, seamless, as if the very reality of this place had decided to move. Aelina's breath caught as the reflection beneath their feet rippled outward, the sky above twisting, the stars rearranging themselves in patterns she could not decipher.

Then, from the vast nothing ahead of them—a figure stepped forward.

Aelina froze.

It was not shadow, not mist. It was solid, real, yet it did not belong here. It was clad in armor that pulsed like molten metal, shifting between silver and black, woven with intricate sigils she recognized but could not name. The helm obscured its face, but she felt its gaze settle on her, heavy and knowing.

Dorian reacted first, his body shifting instinctively between Aelina and the figure, one hand hovering near his blade, but he did not draw it yet. He had fought too many things that were not meant to be fought to know that this might be one of them.

Elias was the only one who remained still.

Aelina exhaled slowly, steadying herself, then stepped forward. "Who are you?" she demanded, her voice steady despite the thrumming tension beneath her skin.

The figure tilted its head slightly, as if considering the question. When it finally spoke, its voice was layered, distant, familiar in a way that made her bones ache.

"You already know me."

The words sent a cold shudder down her spine.

Elias exhaled softly. "Well," he murmured, crossing his arms. "That didn't take long."

Aelina barely heard him.

Because suddenly, the truth slammed into her.

She did know this figure.

She had seen it before, in pieces, in memories that were not hers. In the flickering images Elias had forced into her mind. In the fire. In the blood. In the cracks of a dying world.

This was not a stranger.

This was a memory of what she was meant to become.

And it had been waiting for her all along.

Aelina's breath came slow and measured, though every instinct inside her screamed to retreat, to deny what stood before her. The figure did not move, did not breathe, but it watched—not with eyes, but with an awareness that pressed against her skin, curling through her ribs like unseen fingers. The shifting metal of its armor pulsed with a slow, deliberate rhythm, as if it had a heartbeat, as if it were something more than mere steel and sorcery. The sigils etched into its form glowed faintly, their patterns woven in a language she could not read but somehow understood. Every part of her recognized this presence, not just from the visions Elias had forced upon her, but from something older, something buried in the marrow of her being.

Dorian's muscles had coiled with tension, his body angled protectively in front of her, though she could feel the conflict in him, the indecision pulling at his instincts. He wasn't afraid, but he wasn't reckless either—he knew the danger of fighting something you didn't understand. His golden eyes flickered with a sharp, assessing focus, taking in every inch of the figure, measuring its movements, or lack thereof. But despite the unease radiating from him, his presence remained steady, unwavering, a grounding weight in a place that felt like it was constantly shifting beneath her feet. It was an anchor she hadn't realized she needed until now.

Elias, on the other hand, stood with infuriating calm, his silver-threaded gaze locked on the figure as if this moment had already played out in his mind long before they had stepped through the archway. His posture was loose, relaxed, but Aelina knew better than to mistake it for indifference. He was watching carefully, waiting, his expression unreadable. It was the way he had always been—as if he existed half in the present and half in whatever future he had already decided would come to pass. She hated that about him, hated that he always seemed to be holding some secret that she was just one step too slow to uncover.

The figure took a single step forward, its movements too smooth, too precise, as though gravity did not fully apply to it. The air around it seemed to shift with its presence, thickening, pulsing in tandem with the light that traced through its armor. The voice came again, layered, distant, and yet too close, curling through her thoughts as if it had always been there, waiting for her to finally hear it. "You know me, Aelina. You have always known me." The sound of her name from its lips—if it even had lips—sent a cold shudder through her spine, but she refused to recoil, refused to show any sign of weakness.

She exhaled slowly, forcing herself to steady the tremor in her chest. "I don't know you," she said, though the words tasted like a lie even as they left her mouth. The mark on her wrist flared, burned, as though answering for her, as though it knew something she did not. She fought the instinct to clutch at it, to press her fingers against her skin in a futile attempt to silence the pulse of something ancient stirring beneath her flesh. But the figure simply tilted its head, the movement eerily deliberate, as though it were considering whether to correct her or let her deception unravel on its own.

Elias finally spoke, his voice quiet but edged with something she could not quite place. "That's not entirely true," he murmured, and though his words were directed at her, his gaze remained locked on the figure. "This place exists outside of time, outside of fate as we understand it. What you see is not the past, not the future—it's what has always been." His lips curled slightly, but there was no amusement in the expression, only something knowing, something almost sad. "You are not meeting something new, Aelina. You are meeting something that has been waiting for you since the moment you were born."

Dorian let out a slow, sharp breath, dragging a hand through his hair as though trying to physically pull himself from the insanity unfolding before him. "Fantastic," he muttered under his breath, the irritation in his tone failing to fully mask the concern beneath it. "So now we're just casually speaking to eldritch nightmares that claim to know you?" His golden eyes flicked to her then, sharp and searching, and for a brief moment, there was something else there—worry, frustration, something that looked dangerously close to fear. Not for himself. For her.

Aelina clenched her jaw, keeping her gaze locked on the figure before her. "If you know me," she said, voice steadier now, more controlled, "then tell me what you want." The words carried an unspoken challenge, an unwillingness to be pulled into whatever game was being played here. She had spent her life chasing shadows, trying to unravel the sickness that had plagued the world, and now, for the first time, one of those shadows had a face. She would not run from it.

The figure was silent for a long moment, the glow of its armor pulsing in a slow, steady rhythm. Then, finally, it took another step forward, and the world shuddered with the weight of its presence. "You were chosen," it said, the words sinking into her like stones into deep water. "You were always meant to bear the mark. But you do not yet understand its purpose."

Aelina inhaled sharply, the truth settling heavy in her chest. The mark. The sickness. The power Elias had warned her of. It had never been random, never been a curse without direction. It had always been waiting for her. And now, she was finally standing in the place where it all began.

Elias exhaled softly, shaking his head as if this was the moment he had been waiting for all along. "Then tell her," he said, his silver-threaded eyes flashing. "Tell her what it means before it's too late."

The figure did not hesitate, did not waver. Instead, it lifted a hand, palm facing upward, and the air between them rippled, warped, twisted like heat distorting the horizon. Aelina felt it before she saw it—a pull, a shift, the sensation of something unraveling and reforming all at once. And then, the space above the figure's palm tore open.

Aelina stared into the abyss.

Not darkness. Not light.

A memory that had not yet happened.

Her breath caught as the image took shape—a battlefield of ruin, the sky split open with storms of fire and shadow. The land itself was broken, carved through with jagged fractures where the earth had split apart, and at its center stood a figure, motionless amid the chaos. The same armor, the same sigils pulsing with power, but it was not the creature before her.

It was her.

Aelina felt the air leave her lungs, her body locking in place, unable to look away. The version of herself in the vision was unrecognizable, draped in shadows that pulsed with a force that did not belong to the mortal world. The mark on her wrist—**the same one that had bound itself to her—**now spread up her arm, through her chest, reaching like veins of silvered darkness beneath her skin.

And in her hand, held like a weapon she had wielded a thousand times before—was fire.

Not ordinary fire. Something ancient, something living, something made of the same power that now pulsed beneath her flesh.

The image flickered once. Then it was gone.

Aelina staggered back, the cold air of the In-Between rushing into her lungs, her body trembling with something she could not name. The figure lowered its hand, watching her in silence.

"This is your fate," it said, and the words were not a warning.

They were a promise.

Aelina's breath came shallow and quick, her heart hammering against her ribs as if it, too, was trying to escape the weight of what she had just seen. The image burned behind her eyes, seared into her mind like an ember pressed too deep—a battlefield swallowed by ruin, a sky bleeding fire, a version of herself she could not recognize. The power she had glimpsed in that vision was not something wielded. It was something born, something claimed, something that had already begun to take root inside her.

The figure before her remained still, watching, as though waiting for the realization to fully sink into her bones. There was no satisfaction in its posture, no cruelty in its voice—only certainty. It had shown her what she would become, what the mark had already decided for her. It had not asked for her permission. It had never needed it.

Dorian shifted beside her, his golden eyes still locked onto the place where the vision had flickered out of existence, his fingers twitching slightly at his sides. He had seen it too—had seen the fire in her hands, the devastation at her feet, the way the power had crawled through her veins like something waiting to be unleashed. When he finally spoke, his voice was low, carefully restrained. "No."

The word came sharp, edged with defiance, but Aelina could hear what lay beneath it—the fear. Not of the vision, not of the thing standing before them. Fear for her.

Elias, standing a few feet away, exhaled softly, tilting his head just enough that the flickering silver in his gaze caught the unnatural starlight above them. "It doesn't care whether you refuse," he murmured, his voice quieter now, almost... sympathetic. "You saw it, Aelina. The path has already begun."

She swallowed hard, her fingers curling at her sides, a sharp ache settling into her chest. She had spent her life trying to find the source of the sickness, trying to carve a way forward in the face of something unstoppable. But this wasn't a path she had chosen—this was something far worse. This was a destiny she had walked into unknowingly, a fate that had already been written long before she ever touched its pages.

Her wrist throbbed again, the mark pulsing in quiet acknowledgment, and she fought the urge to rub at it, to claw at the sigil burned into her flesh as if she could tear it away. But the figure before her had already told her the truth—this was not something that could be removed. It was not something that could be undone. It had waited for her. And now, it would not let go.

Dorian took a slow step forward, his shoulders tense, his voice controlled but unwavering. "Then we change it," he said, his gaze locked onto Elias now, his frustration shifting into something colder. "I don't care what she saw. I don't care what you think is inevitable. Nothing is written in stone."

Elias's smirk was faint, but there was something tired in it. "Then you don't understand what this place is." He turned to Aelina again, his expression softening for the briefest of moments. "The In-Between only shows what is already true."

The ground beneath them shuddered again, and Aelina stiffened, her pulse spiking as a low, distant sound began to rise. Not a voice, not a whisper—something deeper, something guttural, something ancient. It was coming from beyond the reflection beneath their feet, beyond the swirling abyss where reality and time had begun to fray.

The figure before them did not move, but when it spoke again, the words settled like iron into Aelina's chest.

"You are running out of time."

The words sent a chill down her spine, cold and final, and before she could react, the world shifted. The endless sky above them fractured, the stars twisting, warping, turning to embers as something cracked through the fabric of the In-Between. The pulse in her wrist flared again, hard enough to steal the breath from her lungs, and she knew—whatever had been waiting beyond the archway had found them.

Elias moved first, already turning, already stepping toward the rip in reality, but Aelina's feet felt rooted to the ground, her chest tightening as something unseen pulled at her. The vision had shaken her, had shattered something inside her she wasn't sure could be put back together.

Dorian grabbed her arm, his fingers warm, steady, and the moment his touch met her skin, the pull loosened just slightly. He didn't say anything—he didn't need to. The tension in his grip, the way his breath **slowed just enough to control his own fear—**it was enough.

The cavern was breaking apart around them, the archway flickering as the doorway began to seal itself. Elias glanced over his shoulder, eyes flashing. "Aelina, now."

She hesitated—just for a breath.

Then, she ran.

The last thing she heard before stepping through was the figure's voice, whispering through her thoughts like a shadow curling into the marrow of her bones.

"You will return."

And then the world collapsed.

Chapter Eight:

The Sins of the Past

Aelina fell.

Not through space, not through time, but through something deeper, heavier, more consuming. It wasn't the weightless, endless drift of stepping into the In-Between—it was a plunge, a violent rip through reality itself. She didn't know if she was screaming. The air had been stolen from her lungs, her senses stripped away, her body weightless and untethered. For a moment, there was nothing. No ground. No sky. No self.

Then—impact.

The world slammed back into her, reality rushing in like a crashing wave. She hit something solid and unyielding, the breath knocked from her chest, pain splintering through her ribs as her body skidded across cold stone. The sharp scent of dust and damp earth flooded her lungs, and the moment she tried to breathe, she choked—coughing against the thick, ancient air that burned her throat.

Her vision blurred, the dim torchlight above her a flickering haze of gold and shadow. Aelina forced herself to move, to push against the pain screaming through her limbs, but everything felt wrong—too heavy, too raw, too real. The mark on her wrist was searing now, its presence no longer just a dull hum beneath her skin but a raw, open wound that pulsed with each erratic beat of her heart.

Footsteps. Fast. Near.

Dorian's voice broke through the haze, sharp with panic he never allowed himself to show. "Aelina." Then stronger, angrier—desperate. "Aelina, look at me."

She tried. Gods, she tried.

Her vision swam as she lifted her head, and the moment she did, a shadow moved in front of her—tall, sharp, dangerous. Dorian. His golden eyes burned, his hand already reaching for her, but she could see the tension in him, the rigid set of his shoulders, the way his breath came sharp and shallow. He had landed better than she had, but not by much. There was blood on his temple, already trailing down his jaw. She wanted to reach for him, to say something, but before she could—

A second figure appeared behind him.

Elias.

Unharmed, of course. He stood with effortless ease, his silver-threaded gaze scanning their surroundings as if this was all some mild inconvenience. He did not stagger, did not gasp for breath—he simply existed in the aftermath, untouched by the chaos.

Aelina hated him for it.

"Where are we?" she managed, her voice hoarse, the taste of blood sharp on her tongue.

Elias tilted his head slightly, as if considering how much he wanted to tell her. Then he exhaled through his nose, shaking his head. "Not where," he murmured. "When."

Aelina's blood ran cold.

Dorian stiffened beside her, his golden gaze snapping toward Elias with something between frustration and fear. "Don't start that cryptic bullshit," he warned, his voice sharp enough to cut. "Just tell us where the hell we are."

Elias smirked, but there was something else behind it—something cautious. "We didn't just leave the In-Between," he said. "We left time."

Aelina's heart lurched, her fingers twitching against the cold stone beneath her. The air here was different—heavier, older. The moment he said it, she felt it—the way the space around her seemed to breathe differently, the way the light in the torches flickered with an unfamiliar rhythm. It was subtle, but it was enough.

Dorian let out a slow, controlled breath, the kind that barely masked the growing storm behind his eyes. "Fix it."

Elias actually laughed.

Aelina's patience snapped. "Fix it," she repeated, this time with a sharp edge that even she hadn't expected. "Elias, I swear to the gods, if you don't start giving me real answers, I will make sure you regret it."

Elias raised a brow, clearly entertained by her anger, but his smirk faded just slightly. "You wanted answers, little sister," he murmured. "This is where they begin."

Aelina forced herself to her feet, ignoring the sharp protest in her ribs, ignoring the way her body still felt like it didn't fully belong to her. She could still feel the weight of what she had seen in the In-Between, the fire in her hands, the power waiting beneath her skin like something patient and cruel. But she would not let it own her—not now. Not ever.

She lifted her chin. "Then start talking."

Elias sighed, as if they were exhausting him, which only made her want to punch him in the throat. But his gaze sharpened as he turned away, stepping toward the far side of the cavern they had landed in. Aelina followed his gaze, and her breath caught.

The walls were covered in markings, carved deep into the stone—symbols older than any language she had ever seen, the same twisting sigils that had flickered across the figure's armor in the In-Between. They pulsed faintly, their edges glowing as if still alive, as if they had been waiting for something to awaken them.

Or someone.

Aelina exhaled slowly, realization settling into her chest like a weight she wasn't ready to bear. "This place," she murmured, stepping closer. "This is—"

"The first mark," Elias confirmed.

Dorian swore under his breath.

Aelina barely heard him. The weight of the truth was too heavy now, too thick to ignore. This was the first. The beginning. The place where whatever power had tainted the world had begun to sink its claws into time itself.

Elias turned to face her fully, his expression finally serious, finally devoid of amusement. "Now do you understand?" His voice was quieter, but it held something raw, something real. "This was never about stopping what's coming, Aelina." His silver-threaded gaze met hers, the finality in them like a lock snapping into place. "It's about choosing who survives it."

Her stomach turned.

The torches flickered.

The mark on her wrist burned.

And somewhere, deep within the stone walls, something shifted.

Watching.

Waiting.

And now, it knew she was here.

Aelina exhaled slowly, forcing herself to keep her breathing even despite the cold weight settling into her chest. She had always suspected the truth behind the sickness ran deeper than what she could see, but now—**standing here, in the place where it had all begun—**the reality of it pressed down on her like unseen hands. This wasn't just about fighting a disease, about stopping an unseen force from consuming the world. This was about a choice that had already been made, long before she was ever born.

Dorian was tense beside her, his fingers flexing at his sides as he studied the carvings along the walls. His golden gaze flicked over the symbols, searching, measuring, trying to make sense of something that should not exist. He was a man built for battle, for tangible enemies and visible threats, but there was nothing to fight here—just history, waiting to be rewritten in blood. His frustration rolled off him in waves, but his silence was heavier than any outburst.

Elias took a slow step forward, his boots barely making a sound against the stone. His silver-threaded eyes traced the sigils, his expression unreadable, distant. "I told you," he murmured, voice quiet but steady, "this was always going to happen." He reached out, running his fingers along one of the ancient carvings, and the moment his skin met the stone, the entire cavern shuddered.

Aelina tensed, stepping back instinctively, her pulse spiking as the markings along the walls flared with sudden light. The glow was not warm, not natural—it was cold, shifting, sentient, pulsing with the same rhythm that had burned into her wrist. The ground beneath them rumbled, deep and slow, as if something beneath the surface had awakened.

Dorian reacted instantly, his blade drawn in one fluid motion, the silver edge catching the unnatural light. "Elias," he growled, his voice low and edged with warning, "what the hell did you just do?"

Elias didn't move, didn't react to the threat of steel at his back. He didn't need to. He simply turned his head slightly, the faintest smile pulling at the corner of his lips. "I opened the door."

The air shifted.

Aelina barely had time to react before the space ahead of them rippled, the light from the sigils coalescing into something solid. The walls trembled, the stone groaning as it gave way, breaking apart like the pieces of a puzzle realigning themselves. And then—a passage appeared.

It had not been there before.

It had not existed before.

Dorian let out a slow, measured breath. "Right. Of course you did." He dragged a hand through his dark hair, his grip still tight on his blade as he shot Elias a glare sharp enough to cut. "And I suppose you're about to tell us we have to go through it?"

Elias turned fully now, his expression unreadable, but for once, there was no amusement in his gaze. Only certainty. "You already know the answer."

Aelina ignored their exchange, stepping forward until she stood at the mouth of the passage. The air was different here—heavier, humming with something unseen. The darkness beyond the threshold was not natural, not empty. It felt like something was waiting on the other side, something that had been sealed away for too long. The mark on her wrist pulsed once, a sharp, deliberate warning, and she felt it then—recognition.

This place knew her.

It had been waiting.

She swallowed, her throat tight, her mind already running through the possibilities of what lay beyond. They had come here looking for answers, chasing the past in hopes of stopping the future. But something about this felt different. This wasn't just about knowledge. This was about revelation.

Dorian stepped beside her, his presence solid, grounding. He was tense, but his golden gaze flicked toward her with something close to certainty. He wasn't trying to stop her. He had seen the same things she had, felt the same warnings ripple through the air, but he wasn't turning back.

Elias smirked slightly, watching them both with quiet satisfaction. "No turning back now."

Aelina exhaled sharply, steadying herself.

Then, without another word, she stepped forward and crossed the threshold.

The moment Aelina crossed the threshold, the air shifted violently—as if the space itself rejected her presence, as if something unseen recognized her entry and reacted. The passage swallowed her in an instant, and for a brief, terrifying moment, there was nothing. No ground beneath her feet, no air to breathe—just a crushing stillness, a silence so absolute it pressed against her like unseen hands gripping her ribs.

Then—light.

Not natural light. Not fire, not torches, not the distant glow of the stars. This light was alive, moving, curling around her as if trying to read her, to measure her worth. The air felt thick, charged with something ancient and waiting. She clenched her jaw, willing herself not to react, not to let it see her hesitation.

Then, just as suddenly as it had swallowed her, the stillness released her, and she stumbled forward onto solid ground.

Dorian was behind her in an instant, his hand gripping her elbow before she could fall. His warmth was immediate, solid, grounding, but his posture was still tense, coiled. He had felt it too—the shift, the watching presence, the way this place breathed around them as if it were alive.

Elias stepped in last, leisurely as ever, though Aelina didn't miss the way his gaze scanned the walls, the floor, the very air. Even he wasn't unaffected.

They were no longer in a cavern.

The space around them stretched into an impossibly high chamber, the ceiling disappearing into darkness, the walls carved with thousands of shifting sigils, their edges glowing faintly, pulsing as if whispering to one another. The floor beneath them was smooth black stone, too perfect, too untouched, as though no one had stepped foot here in centuries.

Aelina swallowed hard, her pulse slow, steady—but her nerves screamed. This place was wrong. Not in a way that suggested danger, not yet—but in a way that unraveled something deep in her chest.

It knew her.

It had been waiting.

Dorian's grip on his blade tightened, his golden eyes flicking across the sigils on the walls, as if expecting them to shift into something monstrous at any moment. "I don't like this," he muttered. "Feels like a damned tomb."

Elias hummed under his breath, stepping further into the chamber. "A tomb?" He ran his fingers along one of the glowing sigils, his silver-threaded eyes gleaming with something unreadable. "No, Dorian. This is a memory."

Aelina stiffened.

"A memory of what?" she asked, her voice quieter than she wanted it to be.

Elias turned, his expression strangely distant. "Of what came before."

The words settled into her bones, heavy and inevitable, and before she could fully grasp them, the chamber answered.

The walls flared with sudden light, the sigils burning brighter, shifting, rearranging themselves into something new—something recognizable. Aelina's breath caught as the symbols melded together, forming a single, massive sigil at the center of the chamber.

And then the stone beneath their feet rippled.

Aelina staggered, but this time, she didn't fall. She watched as the ripples spread outward, moving like waves across the floor, the reflection of something ancient breaking through the surface.

And then—the figures appeared.

Not flesh and blood, but shadows of the past, their forms woven from the light itself, flickering and half-real. Aelina's stomach twisted as she saw them—hundreds of them, standing in rows, their forms clad in armor carved with the same sigils lining the walls. Their faces were empty voids, hollow where their features should have been, and yet, she could feel them watching.

Dorian's breath left him in a slow, controlled exhale. "Tell me that's not what I think it is," he muttered, his voice barely above a whisper.

Elias's silver-threaded gaze locked onto the figures, and for the first time since entering this place, his usual smirk was gone. His jaw tightened, his fingers flexing at his sides.

"It's them," he said. "The Firstborn."

Aelina's chest tightened.

She knew that name. Everyone knew that name.

The Firstborn—the ones who had wielded magic before it had been fractured, before the sickness had begun to spread, before the world had been torn apart by its own power. They were the ones who had stood at the dawn of magic, the ones who had built the foundations of everything that was now crumbling into ruin.

And now, they stood before her.

Not living. Not dead.

Just waiting.

The chamber's light shifted again, and as it did, one of the figures stepped forward.

Unlike the others, this one was sharper, clearer, more defined. The sigils carved into its armor burned with a deep, silver fire, and when it raised its head, Aelina knew.

It was the same figure from the In-Between.

The same shadow of herself that had been waiting.

The figure raised a hand, palm open, as if offering something.

And then—it spoke.

"You were never meant to be free of us."

The words slammed into Aelina like a punch to the ribs, stealing the breath from her lungs.

The walls trembled, the figures behind the Firstborn shifting, as if waking from a long, endless sleep.

Dorian moved before she did, stepping between her and the apparition, his blade raised in warning, his body a shield she hadn't asked for but couldn't deny she needed. "I don't care who they were," he growled, his golden eyes burning with fury. "They're dead now."

Elias exhaled, but there was something almost pained in his expression. "That's the thing," he murmured.

"They never died."

The chamber shuddered.

The Firstborn took another step forward.

The mark on Aelina's wrist burned white-hot.

And then—the past bled into the present.

The moment the past and present collided, the chamber erupted with sound.

Aelina felt the shift inside her bones, a deep, shuddering weight that dragged her under before she had the chance to fight it. The figures of the Firstborn didn't merely remain still—they expanded, filled the air, pressing against the edges of reality as if they had always been waiting to slip through the cracks of time. The walls trembled under their presence, the ancient sigils glowing white-hot, their energy rippling outward in thick, twisting waves.

The one who had stepped forward—the reflection of herself, the thing that had haunted her since the In-Between—did not lower its hand. Its silver-fire gaze locked onto her, seeing through her, into her, as if searching for the pieces of itself that still remained buried inside her flesh.

"You carry what is ours."

Aelina's pulse spiked, her breath shallow, her instincts screaming at her to move, to run, to fight. But she did not. She stood her ground, fingers twitching at her sides, the burn of the mark on her wrist now a roaring fire beneath her skin.

Dorian, however, was done waiting.

His blade flashed as he stepped forward, the steel catching the eerie silver glow of the chamber, his body shifting into a stance that was equal parts calculated and reckless. "If you don't start making sense," he bit out, voice sharp as a knife, "I'll carve the answers out of you myself."

The Firstborn did not react—not in the way they should have. No shifting of posture, no drawing of weapons. Instead, the figure in front of them tilted its head, almost as if amused by Dorian's threat.

"You think steel can harm what is already inside her?"

Aelina's breath hitched.

Dorian went still.

Elias exhaled slowly, shaking his head. "Well," he muttered under his breath, "this is going exactly as terribly as I thought it would."

Aelina snapped toward him, her frustration boiling over into something dangerous. "You knew," she hissed, her voice too sharp, too raw. "You knew we'd find them, that they'd be waiting. You knew they weren't dead."

Elias sighed, rubbing a hand through his hair. "Knowing and believing are two different things," he murmured, though there was no smirk this time, no amusement in his silver-threaded gaze. "I suspected. I hoped I was wrong." His eyes flicked toward the Firstborn, his lips pressing into a thin line. "I wasn't."

Aelina's hands clenched into fists, but before she could press him further, the Firstborn moved.

Not toward them.

Toward her.

She barely had time to react before the world lurched, the air collapsing inward, pulling her under. Her vision blurred, twisted, fractured like shattered glass, and then—

She wasn't in the chamber anymore.

She was somewhere else.

Somewhere before.

A Memory Not Her Own

The battlefield stretched wide before her, jagged cliffs rising in the distance, the sky above an endless storm of silver fire. The ground beneath her feet was not stone, not earth, but something slick and dark, something pulsing with magic that refused to fade. And before her, thousands stood—not men, not mortals, but warriors cloaked in the same shifting armor as the Firstborn. Their sigils burned against the storm-lit air, their hands gripping blades that pulsed with unholy light.

She was among them.

No—she was leading them.

Aelina tried to move, tried to speak, but her body did not obey. She was trapped inside the vision, forced to witness through another's eyes, another's hands, another's fate.

A voice—her voice, but not hers—rang through the storm.

"They will not stop. We end it here."

The army before her bowed their heads, their weapons raised, and in the distance, through the haze of smoke and silver fire, another force loomed. Another army.

But this one—this one was human.

Aelina's breath caught in her throat as she watched the two sides begin to move toward one another, slow, deliberate. The war was about to begin, but something was wrong. The warriors around her—they were not defending.

They were purging.

Her stomach twisted. No. This wasn't the battle she had always read about, the one the scholars spoke of in whispers. This wasn't the war against the sickness.

This was the moment it had begun.

The Firstborn had not been the saviors of magic.

They had been its executioners.

Aelina tore herself free.

She gasped, her vision snapping back to the present, the chamber returning around her in a rush of cold air and flickering light. Her body trembled violently, her heartbeat too loud, too uneven, her skin damp with sweat.

Dorian was already at her side, his hands gripping her arms before she could collapse, his golden eyes wild with worry. "Aelina," he said, his voice low, steady, anchoring. "What just happened?"

She could barely breathe.

The Firstborn still stood before her, unmoving, waiting.

Elias was watching, watching too closely, his silver-threaded gaze unreadable.

Aelina swallowed hard, her throat tight, her ribs burning with each breath.

She knew the truth now.

The sickness, the war, the corruption that had seeped into the world and consumed everything—

The Firstborn had started it.

And the power inside her?

It was theirs.

The mark on her wrist pulsed one final time, as if acknowledging what she had finally come to understand.

She wasn't just their descendant.

She was their continuation.

And the past wasn't finished with her yet.

Aelina's breath came in sharp, uneven pulls, her chest rising and falling like she had just surfaced from drowning. But she wasn't drowning. Not in water. Not in air. She was drowning in history, in truths that had been hidden beneath centuries of lies, in the weight of something too large to fight and too cruel to ignore.

Dorian's grip on her arms was the only thing keeping her upright. His warmth, steady and grounding, was the only proof that she was still here, still real, still separate from the nightmare she had just witnessed. But his golden eyes were dark with something dangerous, something frustrated and raw, and she knew what it was. Fear. Not for himself. For her.

"Aelina," he said again, slower this time, voice treading carefully between demand and concern. "Tell me what just happened."

She tried to find her voice, tried to form words that would make sense, but the weight of what she had seen still crushed her. Her fingers twitched at her sides, nails pressing into the palms of her hands as if she could claw herself back to the present, back to a world that wasn't bleeding between past and future.

"They weren't fighting to save magic," she whispered, the words barely audible, barely hers. "They weren't protecting the world from the sickness." She swallowed hard, the taste of something bitter and old curling at the back of her throat. "They created it."

The silence that followed was absolute.

Dorian didn't move. Didn't breathe. His fingers tightened just slightly on her arms, as if making sure she wasn't about to collapse, as if holding onto her was the only thing keeping him from losing his balance.

Elias, however, didn't flinch.

Aelina's head snapped toward him, her breath sharp with accusation. "You knew."

It wasn't a question.

Elias tilted his head slightly, his silver-threaded eyes unreadable, distant in a way that made her want to break something. He had stood there, watching, letting her piece it together, letting the past carve itself into her ribs like a blade.

"I suspected," he said, his voice calm, too calm. "But I couldn't tell you until you saw it yourself. You wouldn't have believed me."

Her stomach twisted with anger and something worse—betrayal.

"You let me walk into that memory blind," she hissed, her voice trembling, but not with fear. With rage. "You knew what I was going to see, and you—"

Elias finally moved, stepping toward her, and though his posture was loose, his eyes were not. "And now you know the truth," he said, his voice quieter, edged with something unreadable. "Now you understand why I couldn't tell you. Because it's not just a story, Aelina. It's you."

The words landed hard, heavy, irreversible.

Her wrist burned again, hot and unrelenting, and she pressed a hand against it instinctively, as if she could quiet it, as if she could press herself back into a body that did not bear the weight of an entire forgotten war.

Dorian finally moved, stepping between them, his stance shifting into something protective, territorial. "That's enough," he said, his voice a low, warning growl. "She doesn't need riddles right now, Elias. She needs the truth."

Elias let out a slow breath, his gaze flicking to Dorian as if measuring how much to say, how much to withhold.

"She already has it," he murmured. "She just doesn't want to accept it."

Aelina's fists clenched.

She wanted to hit him. Hard.

But she didn't.

Because despite the anger in her chest, the betrayal twisting in her ribs, she knew—he was right.

Dorian turned slightly, his gaze flickering toward her, the sharpness in his eyes softening just slightly. "Aelina," he said, and it wasn't an order, wasn't even a question. It was a tether, something meant to pull her back from whatever spiral Elias had just thrown her into. "Tell me what you need."

The simplicity of it almost undid her.

She could still feel the memory pressing into her, sinking into the marrow of her bones. But Dorian was here. Solid, real, unshaken. He wasn't pushing her to accept something she wasn't ready for. He was giving her control—something Elias had taken the moment he let the past swallow her.

She exhaled slowly, steadying herself.

"I need to get out of this place," she murmured. "I need air."

Dorian nodded once, decisive. "Then we leave."

Elias sighed, rubbing a hand over his jaw. "And go where, exactly?"

"Anywhere," Dorian snapped, his patience breaking, the simmering frustration in him finally boiling over. "Unless you have another cryptic doorway to history you want to shove her through, I suggest we get her as far away from this chamber as possible before she—"

He stopped.

But Aelina knew what he was about to say.

Before she becomes what they were.

Before she loses herself to whatever is already inside her.

She swallowed hard, ignoring the way her mark pulsed again, whispering something she couldn't quite hear.

Elias studied her for a long moment, then exhaled. "Fine," he said, stepping past them toward the exit, his smirk returning just enough to make her want to punch him again. "But don't think running is going to change what's happening to you, Aelina. The past isn't finished with you yet."

Aelina didn't answer.

She just turned, following Dorian as he led her away from the chamber, away from the flickering sigils, away from the ghosts of a war she hadn't known she was a part of.

But she felt it, deep inside her, beneath her skin, curled around her bones like something waiting.

Elias was right.

The past wasn't finished with her.

And neither was the power inside her.

As Aelina walked away from the chamber, from the whispering sigils and the ghosts of a war she had not chosen, the weight of it did not leave her. The echoes of what she had seen—**what she had been forced to witness, to understand—**pressed into the spaces between her ribs, tightening with every step she took.

Dorian remained close at her side, his presence steady, a constant in a world that had begun to slip through her fingers. He didn't speak, but she could feel his tension, could sense the war churning beneath his skin—a fight not against an enemy, but against something far worse. Against the knowledge that no matter how hard he tried, he couldn't protect her from this.

Elias moved ahead of them, his posture relaxed, but his steps too measured, too careful. He was waiting—for her to break, for her to demand more answers, for her to admit the truth that was already curling its way into the core of her being. She would not give him the satisfaction.

The air in the tunnel was thick, damp with the weight of centuries of secrets, and yet Aelina still felt the presence of the chamber behind her. It had let her leave, but it had not let her go. The mark on her wrist pulsed again—not in pain, not in warning.

In recognition.

As if it knew—as if it had always known.

The past was not something she could walk away from.

It was coming for her.

And when it did, she would have no choice but to face it.

Chapter Nine:

The Hollow Crown

The night sky stretched wide above them, the wind cool against Aelina's skin as she stepped out into the open for the first time since entering the ruins. She inhaled deeply, the scent of rain-soaked earth and distant firewood curling through the air, a sharp contrast to the stale, magic-thick atmosphere of the underground. But even here, beneath the stars, she did not feel lighter.

She felt watched.

Dorian exhaled next to her, his hand still hovering just close enough to steady her if she needed it. "Better?" he asked, his golden eyes sharp, still searching her face for signs of what she wasn't saying.

She nodded, but the motion felt hollow. "For now."

Elias emerged behind them, stretching his arms above his head, as if they had just finished a casual stroll instead of uncovering the foundations of a forgotten war. "Well, that was productive," he said, glancing at Aelina with too much amusement, too much certainty. "What's next, oh bearer of the mark?"

Aelina turned toward him, her stomach tight, her pulse too slow, too heavy. She didn't have an answer.

But something in the night did.

A low, distant sound echoed across the valley—a horn, deep and reverberating, its call stretching through the darkness like a warning carried on the wind.

Dorian's body went rigid instantly. Elias's smirk flickered.

Aelina's heart slammed against her ribs.

Because she knew that sound.

It was the sound of war.

And it was coming for them.

The moment the horn's call faded into the night, the world shifted. The stillness that followed wasn't empty—it was expectant. Aelina could feel it pressing into her skin, a warning in the very air itself, in the earth beneath her feet.

Dorian was already moving, his golden gaze scanning the darkened landscape, his hand steady on the hilt of his blade. He didn't need to say anything. Aelina knew. This wasn't something distant, something they could ignore.

This was for them.

Elias sighed dramatically, rubbing the back of his neck. "Well," he mused, "that didn't take long."

Aelina ignored him. She took a step forward, listening, feeling. The pulse of her mark was slow, deliberate, but not in warning. No, this was different. It wasn't fear she felt creeping into her chest.

It was recognition.

"They're already here," she murmured.

Dorian's grip on his blade tightened. "How many?"

She closed her eyes for a brief moment, her breath steadying, trying to sense the presence beyond the shadows. It was still new—this ability, this connection to something greater than herself. It was like listening to a song she had only just learned the words to, like tracing the edges of something she didn't fully understand.

But she knew one thing.

"More than us," she admitted, opening her eyes, locking onto Dorian's. "And they know exactly where we are."

He exhaled sharply, muttering a curse under his breath. "Of course they do."

Elias smirked, crossing his arms lazily. "That does tend to happen when you wake the ghosts of the past." He tilted his head slightly, his silver-threaded gaze flicking toward the tree line beyond the valley. Watching. Waiting. "The question is—do we greet them? Or do we run?"

Aelina's jaw tightened. They couldn't afford to run. Not now. Not when the past had already caught up to them.

She turned to Dorian, who was already watching her, waiting for her decision.

"We stand," she said, her voice steady, final.

Dorian nodded once. "Then we find the high ground."

Elias let out an exaggerated sigh but followed as Dorian led the way up the slope, the three of them moving swiftly toward the nearest ridge, away from the open valley where they were exposed. The wind had shifted, carrying the scent of something foreign, something unnatural—a mix of steel and charred magic, of something long since corrupted.

Aelina didn't need to see them to know what was coming.

Shadowborn.

Dorian must have recognized the scent too, because his posture tensed further. "This isn't just a scouting party."

"No," Elias murmured, his smirk gone now, replaced by something colder, sharper. "This is a hunt."

The words settled heavily between them, but Aelina refused to let them take root in her chest.

She had spent too long chasing the truth.

Now, the truth was coming for her.

The wind shifted, curling around them like unseen fingers, carrying the unmistakable scent of charred magic and rotting air. Aelina fought the instinct to shudder, to rub at the mark on her wrist as the cold pulse of it deepened, sharpened, called. The Shadowborn were not here yet, but they were close. She could feel them, could sense the weight of something wrong pressing at the edges of the night.

Dorian moved ahead, his steps deliberate, his golden eyes sharp as he scanned the ridgeline for an advantage. He was already working out the battle in his head, measuring distances, calculating angles, reading the land like a second language. His fingers flexed around the hilt of his sword, but he hadn't drawn it yet. Not yet. He was waiting—waiting to see if this would be a fight or a slaughter.

Elias remained at Aelina's side, unnervingly calm. His silver-threaded gaze flicked across the valley below, lips curving slightly, as if he were listening to something no one else could hear. When he spoke, his voice was quiet, but not without amusement. "They're watching us."

Aelina's stomach twisted. "How many?"

Elias tilted his head, as if tasting the air, as if he could pluck the knowledge from the night itself. "Enough that running would be useless," he said, his smirk deepening. "Enough that if we stay, we either win or die."

Dorian let out a sharp exhale, dragging a hand through his hair. "You really have a way of inspiring confidence, don't you?"

Elias chuckled. "You're still standing here, aren't you?"

Dorian didn't bother with a response. Instead, he turned back to Aelina, his expression shifting from irritation to concern. "Are you feeling anything?" he asked, his voice low, measured. He wasn't asking about fear. He was asking about the mark.

Aelina hesitated, then nodded.

It was faint at first—a whisper curling along the edges of her thoughts, a pull just beneath her skin, the quiet hum of something expectant, waiting. But now it was more than that. It was reaching.

She didn't know if it was calling to the Shadowborn, or if they were calling to her.

Elias hummed under his breath, watching her carefully. "It's waking up."

Aelina's breath hitched. "What does that mean?"

Elias lifted a brow. "You tell me."

Before she could snap at him, before she could force herself to pull away from the sensation creeping into her chest, the valley below shifted.

A shadow moved.

Not one. Many.

Dorian went rigid beside her. "There."

Aelina's gaze locked onto the treeline at the edge of the valley, where the forest seemed to breathe. The darkness between the trees was thick, twisting, stretching into something not entirely natural. Then, slowly, the figures began to step forward—tall, too thin, moving with a grace that was both wrong and hypnotic.

Shadowborn.

Aelina's pulse slammed against her ribs. She had fought them before—small groups, stragglers, the remnants of something older and unkillable. But this was different.

This was an army.

Dorian muttered another curse, drawing his sword with a slow, steady motion. The metal gleamed in the moonlight, its edge sharp, unforgiving. He squared his stance, but Aelina didn't miss the shift in his posture—the recognition that this was going to be bad.

Elias, as always, looked unbothered. "Well," he mused, watching the approaching figures with a lazy sort of interest. "At least they're punctual."

Aelina ignored him. Her pulse pounded, the mark on her wrist burning now, the same way it had in the

In-Between, the same way it had when she had seen the past bleeding into the present.

The Shadowborn were not just hunting her.

They were expecting her.

She exhaled slowly, willing her body to steady itself, willing her mind to clear. Fear would not help her here. Only action would.

She turned to Dorian, his golden eyes already waiting for her command.

"We don't let them get any closer," she said, her voice steady, final.

Dorian nodded. No hesitation. "Then we hold here."

The wind shifted again, and the Shadowborn moved faster.

The fight had already begun.

The moment Elias vanished beneath the swarm of Shadowborn, something inside Aelina broke.

It wasn't rage—not the sharp, calculated kind that fueled warriors in battle. It wasn't fear, either. It was something deeper, something older, something that had been waiting beneath her skin for far too long.

The mark on her wrist flared violently, heat searing up her arm, curling into her ribs like a living flame. The pain was immense, burning through her blood, through her bones, through every part of her that had once belonged solely to herself. She barely registered Dorian shouting her name—barely felt his hands grabbing at her, trying to stop her from moving forward.

But it was too late.

The magic answered her.

It did not come gently.

It erupted.

The ground beneath them shattered outward, a violent wave of energy ripping through the battlefield, knocking Dorian backward, sending him skidding across the dirt. The Shadowborn sensed it immediately—felt the shift, the raw and uncontrollable force gathering around her, responding to her grief, her fury, her need.

And they hesitated.

That was their mistake.

Aelina's hands lifted on instinct, and power tore from her like a storm unleashed.

It wasn't fire, not truly—it was something wilder, something purer, something that did not belong to this world. White-hot light cascaded outward, sweeping through the battlefield like a tidal wave, crashing into the Shadowborn with a force that shattered the very air.

The creatures screamed.

Aelina felt their pain as if it were her own—felt them unravel, felt their existence burn away beneath the sheer magnitude of what she had become. The closest one disintegrated on impact, its form twisting and curling in on itself until it was nothing but smoke in the wind. The others—**those who had been strong enough to resist steel and fire—**were not strong enough for this.

She did not stop.

She could not stop.

The mark on her wrist blazed brighter, the symbols along her skin shifting, expanding, growing—not a wound, not a brand, but a seal breaking.

And the magic inside her?

It wanted out.

The remaining Shadowborn began to retreat.

Aelina barely recognized the sound that tore from her throat—a battle cry, a command, a demand for their destruction. She was not done.

She was just beginning.

The light swelled, rising from her hands, from her very breath, twisting into something raw and ancient and unrelenting. The sky itself seemed to shudder beneath its presence. The earth beneath her feet cracked.

She could destroy them all.

She would.

But then—a voice.

Not Elias.

Not Dorian.

A whisper.

"Enough."

The magic slammed back into her like a collapsing wave, the force of it ripping through her body, pulling her back into herself, into her own skin, into the limits she had almost broken. She staggered, gasping, her vision blurring at the edges, her knees buckling beneath the weight of power she no longer controlled.

And then—arms caught her.

Solid. Familiar.

Dorian.

His voice was sharp, panicked, full of something too raw to name. "Aelina, stop! You have to stop!"

She barely had time to process his words before the battlefield went silent.

The Shadowborn—the ones who had not yet been burned away—were gone.

Not dead. Gone.

Retreated.

Fled.

Because of her.

Aelina's breath hitched, her body trembling as she stared at the empty battlefield, at the scorched ground, at the lingering trails of silver-white fire curling through the air.

She had done this.

She had become something else.

But then—Elias.

Her stomach dropped, her body moving before she could think, before she could even breathe. She shoved out of Dorian's grip, her legs barely holding her, her hands still shaking from the magic that had nearly consumed her.

Elias was on the ground.

Blood.

Too much of it.

For the first time since she had met him, Elias looked fragile.

His dark hair was matted with blood, his skin too pale beneath the silver glow of his eyes, which flickered like dying embers. The Shadowborn had torn through him, their claws carving deep wounds along his arms, his chest. The jagged gashes still pulsed with remnants of their magic, black veins spreading outward from the wounds, as if the corruption had tried to sink into him, to drag him into the darkness with them.

Aelina dropped to her knees beside him.

She wasn't even aware of what she was saying—just his name, over and over again, sharp and desperate, her hands shaking as she reached for him.

His eyes barely opened.

But his lips twitched—that damn smirk, even now, even dying.

"Hell of a fight," he rasped. His voice was rough, strained, the usual arrogance threaded through with something weaker.

Aelina's throat tightened.

"Shut up," she snapped. But her voice cracked.

His eyes flickered, something knowing in them.

But then—his breath hitched. His body tensed.

Aelina barely had time to react before he seized, his entire frame arching off the ground, his face twisting in agony.

The Shadowborn's corruption was spreading.

Aelina's pulse slammed against her ribs.

No.

No.

Not like this.

Not Elias.

Her hands hovered over him, her magic still burning beneath her skin, still raw, still untamed.

She had destroyed creatures born of darkness, had wielded magic that even the Shadowborn feared.

But could she save him?

Dorian knelt beside her, his breathing sharp, ragged, his golden eyes locked onto Elias's wounds. He wasn't asking for permission. He was waiting for her choice.

Because this wasn't a matter of whether she wanted to try.

This was a matter of whether she was willing to risk what she had become.

Aelina swallowed hard, her heartbeat thundering, her fingers trembling as she placed them over Elias's wounds, over the spreading darkness that threatened to take him.

The mark on her wrist pulsed again.

And then—she let go.

The magic rushed from her, silver-white fire spilling from her hands, sinking into him, fighting against the corruption like light waging war against the void.

Elias let out a shuddering breath, his body jerking beneath her touch.

Dorian's voice was sharp. "Aelina—"

But she wasn't listening.

She wasn't thinking.

She was saving him.

Or she was damning herself.

Either way—it was too late to stop.

The moment Aelina let the magic take her, the world fractured.

The fire that spilled from her hands was not ordinary, not clean, not something that belonged to the realm of mortals. It was raw power—ancient, untamed, something that did not heal so much as consume, something that did not mend so much as claim.

Elias jerked beneath her, his back arching violently, his breath coming in shallow, broken gasps. The blackened veins creeping from his wounds resisted at first, writhing like living things, curling against the edges of the light. But Aelina refused to let go, refused to let them win, refused to let the darkness take him.

She pushed harder.

The mark on her wrist blazed brighter, the heat burning through her body as if the magic had sunk its claws into her, too, tethering her to the fight for Elias's life. It wasn't just the corruption she was fighting—it was something deeper, something inside him that had never been meant to be touched.

And then—the resistance broke.

A sharp, guttural cry tore from Elias's throat as the darkness ripped free from his body, spilling upward in a burst of writhing shadow, twisting like smoke as it fought against being cast out. For a moment, it hovered between them, as if considering whether to latch onto something else, to bury itself in someone new.

It turned its attention to her.

Aelina felt it then. The pull, the weight, the whisper curling through the edges of her thoughts.

"You could take it."

The voice was not human. It was soft, insidious, full of promises she did not want to understand.

"You could wield it."

She clenched her jaw, forcing herself to focus, forcing herself to push the magic outward, to banish the remnants of the Shadowborn's corruption before it could find a new home in her flesh.

"You could be unstoppable."

No.

With a final burst of will, Aelina shoved the darkness away.

The twisted, writhing shadow let out a sound—**not quite a scream, not quite a wail, something hollow, something furious—**and then, it collapsed inward. The moment it hit the ground, it vanished, sucked into the cracks of the earth as if it had never been there at all.

And then—silence.

Aelina swayed, her vision blurring, the energy in her body plummeting.

She barely registered Dorian's hands gripping her shoulders, keeping her upright, his voice sharp and urgent.

"Aelina! Look at me."

She tried.

She barely saw him, barely felt anything except the raw emptiness that followed the magic's departure. It left her cold, hollow, shaking. She was losing herself, slipping too far into the void where her power lived.

Then, another voice.

Weaker. Hoarse.

"You—really know how to make a guy feel special, don't you?"

Aelina's head snapped down.

Elias was alive.

His silver-threaded eyes flickered weakly, his breath unsteady, shallow, but he was breathing. The blackened veins along his arms were gone, the wounds no longer pulsing with the Shadowborn's magic.

Aelina released a breath she hadn't realized she was holding.

Dorian, still holding her steady, muttered something that sounded like a curse before sighing heavily. "You're impossible," he told Elias, though there was a raw, undeniable relief in his voice. "You should be dead."

Elias smirked, or tried to. It was barely more than a twitch of his lips, and even that looked like it took too much effort. "Trust me," he rasped, "I was considering it."

Aelina's legs gave out.

She would have collapsed completely if Dorian hadn't been there to catch her. His arms locked around her waist, steady, warm, grounding, his breath ragged but solid.

Elias watched her carefully, his amusement dimming, his silver-threaded gaze flicking toward her hands. "What did you do?"

Aelina swallowed, her throat raw, her limbs trembling.

She knew what he was asking.

She also knew she didn't have an answer.

Before she could speak, a pulse of pain lanced through her skull, sharp and sudden. She barely had time to react before her vision tilted, her mind collapsing inward.

Not blacking out.

Falling.

A vision slammed into her, as vicious and unstoppable as a tidal wave.

She wasn't in the clearing anymore.

She was somewhere else.

Somewhere not meant to exist.

Aelina collapsed into the vision, her mind sinking beneath its weight before she had the chance to resist. The world around her fractured, split apart at the seams, until she was no longer standing in the clearing, no longer held steady by Dorian's grip or surrounded by the ruins of battle.

She was somewhere else.

The sky overhead was wrong—too vast, too shifting, a swirling storm of color and light that did not belong to the mortal realm. The ground beneath her was not earth, not stone, but something smooth, glasslike, reflecting the sky above in a perfect, endless mirror.

And then—the whispers came.

Not voices. Not words. Something deeper, something older. A pressure against her thoughts, a presence curling into her ribs, watching. Waiting.

Her pulse pounded against her ribs, her breathing too fast, too shallow. The weight of the vision pressed heavier, sinking into her bones, pulling her toward something she could not yet see.

Then, out of the shifting haze, a figure stepped forward.

She could not see its face. Could not fully comprehend its form. But she knew, in the marrow of her being—it knew her.

"You are beginning to understand."

Aelina's stomach turned to ice.

Because she did understand.

The power she had wielded tonight—the fire, the magic, the force that had burned away the Shadowborn like they were nothing but dry leaves in the wind—it had not been hers.

It had been borrowed.

No. It had been waiting.

And now, it had claimed her.

The figure tilted its head, considering. The whispers swelled, curling through the air, pressing against her like unseen hands.

"This is only the beginning."

Aelina's breath hitched.

The world shattered.

And she woke up gasping.

Dorian's voice cut through the haze first, sharp and worried. "Aelina!"

She blinked rapidly, her vision still tilting, her body cold, unsteady, shaking. Hands gripped her shoulders—warm, real. Dorian. She focused on his golden eyes, the tightness in his jaw, the unspoken fear written across his face.

Elias was sitting nearby, his silver-threaded gaze dark with understanding. He had seen it. Not the vision itself, but the aftershock of what it had done to her.

Aelina exhaled slowly, her chest aching with something deeper than exhaustion.

The words from the vision still echoed through her mind, curling into the spaces between her ribs, refusing to fade.

"This is only the beginning."

Her fingers trembled as she pressed a hand against her chest, as if she could keep whatever had been inside her from slipping free again.

She swallowed hard, lifting her gaze to Elias.

And for the first time, she did not ask for answers.

Because she already knew—there were no answers anymore.

Only the inevitable.

Chapter Ten:

The Gathering Storm

The night stretched wide around them, vast and endlessly silent. There was no wind, no rustling leaves, no distant calls of night creatures—only stillness, only waiting. The fire had burned low, its embers pulsing with a dull, red glow, barely enough to chase away the deep shadows curling along the edges of the clearing. Aelina sat close to its fading warmth, her arms wrapped around her knees, her thoughts a tangled mess of exhaustion and something far worse.

The vision still pressed against her skull, lingering like a brand burned into her thoughts, refusing to fade. She could still feel the presence of the figure she had seen, still hear the whispers curling into the edges of her mind, refusing to be ignored. The weight of it made her skin itch, made her mark throb with something deep and unsettled. This wasn't over—not by a long shot. Whatever she had awakened, whatever had stirred within her, it was waiting.

Dorian stood with his back to her, his arms crossed over his chest, his posture tense in a way that spoke of too many thoughts he wasn't ready to say aloud. His sword was still strapped to his side, though his hand hovered close to it, his fingers twitching every now and then, as if expecting another fight. He hadn't spoken much since she had woken up—just sharp glances, careful movements, unreadable silence.

Elias sat a few feet away, lounging as if he hadn't nearly died hours ago. His coat was draped over his shoulders, though she could see the fresh, ragged scars along his arms—a reminder of just how close the corruption had come to taking him. His silver-threaded eyes flickered in the dim light, watching the fire, watching her. He looked as if he was waiting for something, waiting for her to be the first to break the silence.

Aelina exhaled slowly, forcing herself to keep her hands still, to keep her breathing even. The power inside her had settled, but only just—a beast caught in its cage, waiting for the next time it would be let loose. She had never been afraid of her magic before, not truly. But after tonight, after seeing what it could do, what it was willing to take from her, she wasn't sure she could say that anymore.

The silence stretched, thick and suffocating.

Then, finally, Dorian spoke.

"What now?"

His voice was low, steady, but there was something else beneath it—something weighted, something carefully restrained. He wasn't asking for a plan. He was asking if she even had one.

Aelina lifted her gaze, meeting his golden eyes in the firelight. He didn't look angry. He didn't look afraid. But he looked at her as if he was waiting for her to decide which path they would take next.

She inhaled slowly, closing her fingers into a fist against her knee. "We leave."

Elias let out a soft chuckle, shaking his head. "Of course we do." His voice held its usual amusement, but his eyes were unreadable. "And where exactly are we going, oh wise and fearless leader?"

Aelina hesitated, only for a second.

Then, the answer came—not from her own thoughts, but from something deeper, something that had already been decided.

"To the city of the Forgotten."

Dorian frowned, tilting his head slightly. "You're serious?"

Aelina nodded once. "It's the only place left."

The fire crackled, spitting embers into the cold night air.

Elias sighed, rubbing the bridge of his nose. "Well, that sounds incredibly ominous. Why not."

Dorian ran a hand through his hair, muttering something under his breath. But he didn't argue.

Because, in the end, they all knew the truth.

There was no running anymore.

Only the road ahead.

The decision had been made, but the weight of it still hung thick in the air, settling over them like an unseen presence. The fire continued to smolder, its glow barely enough to illuminate their weary faces, their battle-worn bodies. Aelina knew there was no use lingering. Every second wasted gave the Shadowborn more time to regroup.

Dorian moved first, his body still taut with unspent energy, the kind that only a warrior fresh from battle carried. He crouched beside the fire, grabbing what little provisions they had left, tucking them into his pack with sharp, efficient movements. His golden gaze flicked toward Aelina only once, quick and assessing, before returning to his task. He had accepted her decision. Now, he was ready to act on it.

Elias, on the other hand, took his time. As always. He stretched his arms overhead, rolling his shoulders as if this were nothing more than an inconvenience rather than the next inevitable step into whatever ruin awaited them. His coat hung loosely from his frame, the remnants of his wounds still fresh beneath the fabric. But despite his nonchalance, he didn't argue, didn't hesitate.

"You do realize," he murmured, his silver-threaded gaze flicking toward Aelina, "the city of the Forgotten is called that for a reason." He pulled his gloves tighter over his fingers, an easy smirk playing at the edges of his mouth. "It doesn't exactly welcome visitors."

Aelina met his gaze, her body still aching, her thoughts still tangled from the vision that refused to fade. "Then it won't welcome what's following us either."

Elias's smirk deepened, but there was something else behind it—a flicker of understanding. He knew she was right.

Dorian tightened the strap on his pack before rising to his feet, casting a glance toward the darkened treeline. The battle had left the air heavy, tainted with the lingering scent of charred magic and distant decay. He could feel it as much as she could—they weren't safe here.

"How long until we reach it?" he asked, his voice even, measured.

Aelina adjusted the blade at her hip, her fingers tracing the hilt with a familiarity she didn't fully realize she'd developed. "Two days, maybe three if we're careful." She exhaled, scanning the edges of the clearing. "If we're not, we'll never make it."

Elias let out a low whistle. "Three days through cursed land. I do love a challenge."

Dorian shot him a look, sharp, impatient. "Pack your things, Elias."

Elias chuckled under his breath but did as he was told, grabbing his belongings with a lazy sort of ease. But Aelina knew better. He was watching her. He had been watching her since she woke up.

She ignored it.

Instead, she turned toward Dorian, lowering her voice. "Are you ready for this?"

His gaze snapped to hers, gold meeting steel, and for a moment, the sharp intensity of his eyes made her breath catch. "I should be asking you that," he said. "You're the one who nearly burned the entire battlefield to ash."

Aelina swallowed, glancing down at her wrist, where the mark still pulsed, still hummed with something she could no longer ignore. The weight of her magic still clung to her skin, a warning, a promise.

She flexed her fingers, testing the sensation, trying to push past the remnants of exhaustion, of the fear curling inside her chest. But fear had never served her before. She wouldn't let it now.

"I'm ready," she said.

Dorian didn't look convinced, but he nodded anyway. Because there was no other choice.

Elias swung his pack over his shoulder and clapped his hands together. "Right then. Onward to certain death, shall we?"

Dorian muttered something under his breath that sounded suspiciously like a threat.

Aelina let out a slow breath and stepped toward the trees.

The night was still waiting.

And so was whatever lay ahead.

The trees swallowed them whole.

The remnants of battle faded behind them, but the memory of it still clung to the air, thick with the acrid scent of scorched magic and Shadowborn decay. The path ahead was uneven, twisting through the gnarled roots of ancient trees, their bark slick with moss, their limbs tangled overhead like skeletal fingers gripping the night sky. The forest was alive—not with the sounds of birds or rustling leaves, but with something else.

Something watching.

Aelina kept her steps measured, her senses stretched thin, listening to every shift in the undergrowth, every whisper of wind curling through the dense foliage. The moon barely pierced through the thick canopy, leaving their surroundings in a state of half-darkness, painted in shadows and silver slashes of light.

Dorian moved ahead, silent, his body wound tight with tension that had no release. His golden eyes scanned the trees, his fingers twitching near the hilt of his sword, as if expecting something to lunge from the darkness at any moment. He was a soldier, a warrior built for war, but even he knew that some battles were fought on unseen fields.

Elias, for once, wasn't talking.

Aelina glanced at him briefly, noting the way his usual smirk had dimmed, how his silver-threaded gaze tracked something she couldn't see. He walked easily, fluidly, his coat barely shifting with his steps, but she knew him well enough now—he was listening.

So was she.

The first few miles passed in unspoken agreement. The road beneath them was narrow, uneven with jagged stones and old roots that twisted through the dirt like veins of something long buried. They moved quickly but carefully, avoiding the deeper parts of the undergrowth where the land was swallowed by thick fog, creeping low and slow, whispering across the forest floor like something searching.

It had been a long time since Aelina had felt hunted.

She didn't like the feeling.

A sharp snap—a branch breaking.

Aelina stopped instantly, her hand flying to the dagger at her hip, her breath frozen in her lungs.

Dorian halted a step ahead, his posture shifting into something more predatory, more controlled. Elias didn't move at all, only sighed.

"You might as well come out," he said, his voice almost bored. "We can hear you breathing."

For a long moment, nothing.

Then, the forest shifted.

The branches above trembled. The undergrowth shuddered, and from between the trees, figures emerged.

Aelina's grip tightened on her blade.

Not Shadowborn.

But not human, either.

The first figure stepped forward, its eyes black as the space between stars, its skin pale as bone beneath the moonlight. A mask of cloth covered the lower half of its face, embroidered with silver sigils that seemed to shift when Aelina tried to focus on them. Its hands were wrapped in strips of leather, dark with something that could have been ink—or dried blood.

Then more emerged. Five. Ten. Twelve.

All dressed the same. Silent. Still. Watching.

Dorian's voice was a low growl, barely more than a breath. "Who the hell are they?"

Aelina didn't answer.

Because she already knew.

She had seen the markings before, in the old texts buried beneath the archives.

Elias exhaled, shaking his head. "Well," he muttered, tilting his head as he studied the nearest figure, "this is unfortunate."

Aelina's jaw tightened.

"The Hollow."

The leader finally moved. Not much—just a shift of weight, a slight tilt of the head. Then, in a voice that sounded too smooth, too sharp, he spoke.

"A name remembered," he murmured, his gaze locking onto hers. "And yet, one that should have been forgotten."

Aelina's stomach turned.

Because she knew what they were.

Assassins. Shadows that moved between worlds, bound by no kingdom, sworn to no ruler but their own creed. The Hollow had not been seen in decades, not since their last massacre had turned their name into something whispered in fear.

And now, they were here.

Dorian shifted beside her, his stance widening, blade tilting slightly forward. "What do you want?"

The leader didn't blink. Didn't breathe.

Then, slowly, his eyes flicked back to Aelina.

"You."

Aelina's fingers tightened on the dagger hilt, the weight of it grounding her, her mind already calculating the distance between them, the likelihood of a fight. But the Hollow did not take prisoners. They did not waste words.

They killed.

Elias clicked his tongue. "See, now that's just rude," he murmured. "If you're going to demand something, at least pretend to be polite."

Aelina did not take her eyes off the Hollow.

"We don't have time for this," she said, voice steady, even though she could feel her pulse hammering beneath her ribs. "Either tell me why you're here, or get out of our way."

The Hollow leader took a slow step forward. Too smooth. Too sure.

And then, he smiled.

"Because, daughter of the Firstborn," he said, voice like the hush before a blade slips into flesh, "we were sent to bring you home."

Aelina's heart stopped.

For a moment, the entire world hung in the balance.

Then, the first blade flashed in the moonlight.

And the Hollow attacked.

The first blade sang through the air, slicing toward Aelina's throat with unnatural precision.

She barely had time to twist out of the way, the cold bite of steel grazing past her skin, close enough that she felt the whisper of death at her ear. She dropped low, one knee skimming the dirt as she yanked her dagger free, its edge glinting silver in the fractured moonlight. The Hollow didn't hesitate.

Another one lunged.

Dorian moved faster.

His blade clashed against the assassin's, the impact sending a bright arc of sparks into the darkness. He shoved forward, muscles straining, his stance unbreakable, forcing the Hollow backward with sheer strength. But they weren't fighting men of flesh and blood—these were shadows given form, honed by a lifetime of killing.

Aelina didn't have time to help him.

The next attacker was already on her.

She barely caught the strike in time, blocking with her dagger, the force of it vibrating up her arm. The Hollow was fast, too fast, moving with the grace of something that did not obey the same rules as mortals. Their movements were fluid, ghostlike, almost too perfect.

Aelina snarled, twisting beneath the weight of the attack, using the momentum to bring her own blade up, aiming for the weak spot beneath the Hollow's ribs. The assassin twisted at the last second, her blade missing by an inch.

Then, a hiss of pain.

Not hers.

The assassin staggered, dark liquid blooming at his side where her dagger had barely sliced through the layers of cloth. It wasn't deep, but it was enough. He had underestimated her.

Aelina would not give him a second chance.

She surged forward, shoving her dagger up toward his throat, but a hand closed around her wrist.

Cold. Unyielding. Stronger than she expected.

The Hollow leader.

His grip was iron, his black eyes glinting beneath the mask, and for the first time, she felt something beneath his expression—recognition.

Aelina kicked hard, catching him in the ribs, enough to loosen his grip just enough for her to tear away. She staggered back, chest heaving, pulse hammering.

Behind her, Dorian fought with the ferocity of a man who did not accept defeat. His blade was a blur, slicing through the air in lethal arcs, meeting every strike, every lunge with devastating force. Two assassins were already down, motionless in the dirt.

But more moved in, surrounding him, their steps too quiet, too measured.

Elias was nowhere to be seen.

Aelina barely had time to register his absence before the Hollow leader moved again. Fast—faster than before. He was no longer testing her.

He was trying to take her.

A blur of motion. A dagger flashing toward her side.

Aelina reacted without thinking.

The mark on her wrist seared white-hot, and suddenly, everything slowed.

The Hollow's blade froze mid-air.

Not physically. Not with force.

With power.

Aelina's breath caught. She hadn't meant to do it.

Hadn't called for it.

But the magic had answered anyway.

The Hollow leader's black eyes flickered in understanding.

Then, for the first time, they showed emotion.

Not fear.

Satisfaction.

"You are ready," he murmured.

Then, a piercing whistle split the air.

A signal.

Instantly, the Hollow disengaged.

Dorian cut down the last assassin closest to him, blood slicking the ground at his feet, but as soon as he turned, the others were already retreating, slipping into the shadows as if they had never been there at all.

Elias emerged from the trees, wiping blood from his dagger, his silver-threaded eyes narrowing. "That's not a good sign," he muttered.

Aelina couldn't breathe.

The leader hadn't fled. Not yet. He stood at the edge of the clearing, watching her, the shadows curling around him like living things. Then, without another word, he raised a hand to his chest in a motion that was almost reverent.

A farewell.

A promise.

Then—he was gone.

The Hollow had vanished.

The fight was over.

But Aelina knew—this was not a victory.

This had been a warning.

And they had only just begun to understand the war they were truly in.

The silence that followed the Hollow's departure was unnatural.

The forest, once alive with tension and the ringing clash of steel, now stood still and waiting. No wind stirred the trees. No animals rustled in the undergrowth. The very air felt tainted by the presence of what had just unfolded.

Aelina stood frozen, her pulse still hammering beneath her skin. Her hand ached from gripping her dagger too tightly. Her lungs burned, her body felt wrung out, but it was her mind that refused to settle. The leader's words echoed in the hollow space of her thoughts, curling through her ribs like a brand.

"You are ready."

She let out a slow, shuddering breath, willing herself to shake off the weight of those words, but they clung to her, coiled tight around the raw edges of her magic.

Dorian was the first to move.

His boots scuffed against the dirt as he took a slow, measured step forward, his golden gaze sweeping across the battlefield. It wasn't a victory. Not in the way it should have been. His jaw was clenched so tightly she thought he might crack his teeth, but his voice, when he spoke, was steady.

"You hurt?"

Aelina blinked. He was looking at her. His expression was hard, but there was something else beneath it. Something that almost resembled concern.

She forced herself to breathe past the coil of emotions in her throat. "Not badly."

Dorian's gaze flicked toward her wrist, toward the mark that still pulsed faintly in the darkness. His lips pressed into a thin line, but he didn't say anything.

She didn't need him to.

Elias exhaled a sharp breath, wiping his dagger clean on his sleeve before tucking it away. His silver-threaded eyes flickered with something unreadable, something that felt dangerously close to amusement, but Aelina could tell—he was unsettled.

"That could have gone worse," he murmured, rolling his shoulders like he was shaking off a weight only he could feel. "Could've gone better, too, but I suppose we take what we can get."

Dorian shot him a glare. "They weren't trying to kill us."

Elias smirked, but there was no real humor in it. "No. They weren't."

Aelina swallowed hard. That was what unsettled her the most.

The Hollow had no hesitation in cutting down their targets. They did not waste time. They did not leave loose ends. And yet, they had retreated, leaving them breathing, leaving her standing.

"Because they weren't here to kill me."

She gritted her teeth, her fingers tightening around the hilt of her dagger before she forced herself to release it.

Dorian turned sharply, his golden eyes locking onto hers with an intensity that left no room for avoidance. "What did he mean?"

Aelina blinked. "What?"

"You know what," Dorian said, stepping closer. Not in aggression, but in frustration. "He said you were ready. For what?"

She didn't have an answer.

Or, more truthfully—she didn't want to say it aloud.

The magic inside her stirred in quiet agreement.

Elias folded his arms across his chest, watching her carefully. "They knew you," he said. "Not just knew of you. They were expecting you." His lips quirked slightly. "And they didn't seem all that interested in me or our favorite golden boy over here."

Dorian ignored the nickname. His attention was still on Aelina, waiting.

She forced herself to meet his gaze.

"They called me 'Daughter of the Firstborn,'" she said, her voice quieter than she wanted it to be. "And they said they were sent to bring me home."

The weight of those words settled between them like a blade pressed against flesh.

Dorian's expression darkened. "That's not an answer."

Aelina's hands curled into fists at her sides, frustration rising. "I don't have an answer." The fire in her chest flared, reckless, unsettled. "I don't know what they want from me, I don't know why they were here, and I sure as hell don't know what I'm supposed to be 'ready' for."

Dorian exhaled slowly, dragging a hand through his hair, his frustration barely restrained. Not at her, she realized, but at the situation itself.

Elias, however, was watching her in a different way.

She could feel his gaze, sharp and knowing, like he had already pieced together something she had not.

"The Firstborn," he said. Not a question. A statement.

Aelina hesitated.

Dorian stiffened slightly. "The same Firstborn we just learned were responsible for the corruption?"

Aelina swallowed, nodding once.

Elias hummed thoughtfully, his silver-threaded gaze flicking toward the tree line, where the Hollow had vanished. "Well, that complicates things."

Dorian let out a short, humorless laugh. "You don't say."

Aelina inhaled deeply, forcing herself to steady. The answers wouldn't come here. Not tonight. But one thing was clear—she wasn't just running from the Shadowborn anymore.

There were other forces at work.

And whatever they wanted from her, they were getting closer.

She turned toward the dying fire, its embers still glowing faintly against the dark. They couldn't stay here.

"We need to move," she said finally, turning toward the path ahead.

Dorian nodded once, already adjusting the strap of his pack. Elias smirked, but he didn't argue.

No one did.

Because no one could deny the truth anymore.

This wasn't just a fight for survival.

This was a war waiting to begin.

And Aelina was standing at the heart of it.

The fire had burned to nothing but embers, a dull red glow against the night, but the heat of the battle still clung to Aelina's skin. The mark on her wrist pulsed, not painfully, but in reminder. A call she refused to answer.

Dorian was the first to move, stepping away from the clearing and toward the darkened road ahead, his movements sharp, precise, still wound tight with tension that had nowhere to go. He adjusted his sword on his hip, golden eyes flicking once more to the trees where the Hollow had vanished. He didn't trust the silence they had left behind, and neither did Aelina.

She took one last glance at the clearing before following, forcing herself to put distance between the ghosts of that fight and what came next. Elias, ever composed, fell into step beside her, his usual smirk subdued, his silver-threaded eyes flickering in the dim moonlight as if he could see something the rest of them could not.

The road ahead was treacherous in ways beyond terrain.

The land had once been well-traveled, a trade route carved through the spine of the forest, but now, it was nothing more than a broken, half-forgotten path, choked by twisted roots and the weight of centuries. Trees loomed overhead, their branches barely shifting despite the wind, gnarled and ancient in ways that did not feel natural.

The air was heavy.

Not thick with magic, not in warning of another attack—but expectant.

Aelina had spent years learning the subtleties of a land that had long since started to decay. She knew what normal stillness felt like. This was not it.

This was something else.

Dorian slowed ahead of her, casting a glance over his shoulder. "Are you feeling it too?"

Aelina nodded, her fingers hovering near the hilt of her dagger, more from instinct than immediate need. "We're not alone."

Elias let out a soft hum of agreement, his smirk returning, though it lacked its usual arrogance. "That's been true since the moment we stepped foot in this cursed forest." He gestured lazily to the overgrowth curling at their feet. "But this is different, isn't it?"

Dorian shot him a glare. "You say that like you know what it is."

Elias didn't answer immediately, and that was what made Aelina's skin prickle.

She glanced at him, studying the way his shoulders had stiffened, how his fingers flexed slightly, as if preparing to call on a power he never spoke of. Elias was rarely unsettled.

That he was now meant they had a problem.

Aelina slowed her pace, listening to the forest itself. The wind whispered through the trees in a hollow, almost unnatural way, curling through the branches like it was searching for something. The leaves underfoot were dry, but they crunched too loudly beneath their steps, as if the sound was stretching beyond itself, carrying farther than it should.

Then—a snap.

Not a natural one.

Not the movement of a harmless creature.

A branch broke in the distance, the sound sharp and deliberate.

Dorian reacted first, dropping into a stance that would allow him to strike fast if needed. Aelina mirrored him, her pulse steady, her breath even, the mark on her wrist thrumming like it was trying to tell her something she could not yet decipher.

Elias merely sighed, rubbing his temple. "I hate when I'm right."

Aelina ignored him. "What is it?"

For once, Elias didn't have a sharp remark. His silver-threaded gaze flickered between the trees, assessing, calculating. Then, he murmured, "Something old."

Dorian frowned. "Older than the Hollow?"

Elias tilted his head slightly, listening. "Older than us."

The words sent a sharp chill down Aelina's spine.

Something shifted ahead.

The trees did not rustle, the leaves did not stir—but the space between them seemed to bend, the darkness stretching, shifting, unraveling. Aelina felt it before she saw it, felt the same weight she had when she had stood in the chamber of the Firstborn, when the whispers of something older than time had brushed against the edges of her mind.

Dorian lifted his sword.

Elias, for once, didn't smirk. "This," he murmured, "is going to be a problem."

The shadows twisted.

Then—they took shape.

Aelina steadied her breath, keeping her stance loose but ready. The shadows ahead were not moving like living things, not yet, but they weren't idle either. They twisted along the trunks of the trees, stretching at unnatural angles, curling and unfurling as though they were searching for something—or someone.

Dorian adjusted his grip on his sword, shifting into a position that would allow him to strike in any direction at a moment's notice. His golden eyes flicked between the darkness and Aelina, reading her expression just as much as the battlefield ahead. "We don't even know what it is yet."

Elias exhaled slowly, rolling his shoulders as if unbothered, though Aelina could tell the tension was there, just beneath the surface. "Doesn't take a scholar to guess that whatever's coming isn't friendly." His silver-threaded gaze gleamed in the dim light as he flicked a hand toward the shifting void ahead. "Besides, I'd rather not wait until it decides to introduce itself."

Aelina's fingers hovered over her dagger, but she didn't reach for it yet. "If we attack blindly, we'll be playing by its rules." She exhaled slowly, pushing down the pulse of unease curling beneath her ribs. "We need to force it into ours."

Dorian's gaze sharpened. "You have an idea?"

Aelina nodded.

"The terrain isn't in our favor." She glanced to the thick forest hemming them in, the way the roots coiled around the earth like veins, the uneven ground littered with loose rocks and shifting shadows. There were too many places to be trapped, too many directions for an unseen enemy to strike from.

She turned toward Elias, watching him carefully. "Can you tell what it wants?"

His smirk returned, though it was sharper now, more controlled. "What makes you think it wants anything at all?"

Aelina clenched her jaw. "Everything wants something."

Elias tilted his head, watching the shifting void carefully. His expression was unreadable for a long moment before he exhaled through his nose. "It's... waiting."

Dorian stiffened. "Waiting for what?"

Elias flicked his gaze toward Aelina.

Her stomach turned.

It's waiting for me.

The realization slotted into place like a blade sliding home.

Her pulse spiked, but she didn't let it show. If this thing wanted her—**if it had been sent, just like the Hollow had—**then she needed to control how and when it got close.

She turned back toward Dorian, her voice steady. "You take the right flank. Don't let it box us in. We need to keep it moving."

Dorian gave a short nod, already shifting into position.

Aelina turned toward Elias next. "You—"

"Stay out of the way and look pretty? Got it."

Aelina narrowed her eyes. "No. I need you to figure out if it's bound to this place."

Elias raised a brow, genuine interest flickering across his features now. "You think it's tethered?"

Aelina swallowed. "I think if we don't figure it out fast, it won't matter."

Elias smirked but nodded, his silver-threaded eyes gleaming.

The shadows ahead stirred.

The air tightened.

And then—it moved.

The moment the shadows lurched forward, the entire forest seemed to breathe. The trees trembled, not from wind, but from something unseen shifting through them, twisting through the gnarled roots and curling against the bark like ink bleeding into parchment. The darkness itself moved—not like an animal, not like a man, but like something slipping between the layers of this world.

Aelina's pulse pounded.

Dorian was already in motion, stepping to the right, sword angled for an upward strike, his golden eyes tracking the movement of the shadows as if reading their intent before they even reached him. Elias remained back, his silver-threaded gaze flicking through the shifting dark, studying it, measuring it, waiting.

Then—the first shape emerged.

It wasn't a creature. Not exactly.

The void pulled itself forward, unraveling like a tattered cloak, the darkness writhing in slow, deliberate coils. It didn't walk, it didn't crawl—it flowed, gliding toward them in eerie silence.

And then it split.

From the single mass of shadow, two more broke away, mirroring the first. No faces. No form beneath the twisting void—just empty space, consuming everything around it.

Aelina's throat went dry. It wasn't bound by flesh.

Which meant—steel wouldn't stop it.

"Dorian, wait—"

Too late.

The first shadow struck, lunging faster than any mortal thing should move. Dorian's blade sliced clean through it, the silver edge cleaving the darkness in half—

And the creature did not falter.

The severed halves reformed instantly, closing around the gap like smoke curling back into itself.

Dorian barely had time to curse before it lunged again.

Aelina's body reacted before her mind could—her hand lifted, her magic surged outward.

A pulse of silver fire erupted from her palm, crashing into the shadow just before it reached Dorian. The moment the light touched it, the creature convulsed, the void twisting violently as if in agony.

It felt that.

Aelina's heart slammed against her ribs.

Magic could hurt it.

Before she could push another surge of energy forward, the second shadow surged toward Elias.

Aelina turned, breath catching—but Elias was already moving.

He didn't dodge. He didn't strike. He simply lifted a hand.

And the shadow stopped.

Aelina's breath caught.

Elias's silver-threaded gaze burned in the dim light, his fingers outstretched toward the writhing mass of darkness that had frozen in place before him. His usual smirk was gone.

"Interesting," he murmured.

Aelina's pulse roared in her ears. "Elias—"

The shadow shuddered.

And then—it spoke.

Not in sound.

Not in words.

But in her mind.

"You were meant for us."

Aelina's entire body went cold.

The third shadow lunged toward her.

And this time, she didn't have time to stop it.

It struck.

The moment the shadow struck her, Aelina fell.

Not in the way she expected—not physically, not into the cold grip of the earth, but into something deeper, something vast and inescapable. The world around her peeled away in an instant, the forest, the battle, the firelight of her magic—all of it swallowed into an endless, suffocating void. There was no sensation of movement, no air to breathe, no ground beneath her feet. Only a slow, terrible descent into nothingness.

The silence was absolute, but it was not empty.

Something was here with her.

Aelina clenched her hands, trying to summon her magic, trying to call on the fire that had burned through the Hollow, the light that had unraveled the Shadowborn—but there was nothing. No pulse of power beneath her skin, no response from the mark on her wrist. It was as though the force that had pulled her here had severed her from herself, stripping her of the one thing that had made her feel real.

Then, from the abyss, a whisper.

"You were never meant to be free."

Aelina turned sharply, searching for the voice, but there was nothing—only the vast, shifting dark, stretching beyond sight, beyond understanding. The voice was neither male nor female, neither human nor beast. It was inside her. A sensation curling in her bones, wrapping around her thoughts like a constricting hand.

"You have been wandering too long, child. It is time to return."

Aelina's pulse spiked, her throat tightening as something unseen pressed against her mind, wrapping around the edges of her thoughts like creeping vines. It wasn't an attack—not yet. It was probing, searching, peeling back the layers of her memories as if it had the right to own them.

She grit her teeth, forcing her voice through the suffocating weight. "I don't belong to you."

A soft chuckle, low and knowing.

"You do not yet understand what you are."

The darkness shifted, no longer just emptiness but something more—a presence, an awareness so vast it made her skin crawl. And then, from within the abyss, something stepped forward.

It was her.

Aelina stilled, her breath locking in her throat as she stared at the figure before her. It wasn't just a reflection—it wasn't just some imitation. It was her face, her posture, her very being, staring back at her with eyes that were not her own.

The eyes were black.

Not empty, not hollow, but filled with a depth so vast it felt like looking into the end of all things. They swallowed the light, swallowed the space between them, and when the figure smiled, Aelina's stomach twisted with something terrible and familiar.

"Do you see it now?" the voice asked, but it did not come from the figure's lips. It came from everywhere.

Aelina took a step back, her boots making no sound against the endless dark. Her chest tightened, her hands curling into fists, but still—her magic did not answer. It had been stripped from her, buried beneath whatever force had pulled her here.

Her own face tilted, watching her with patient amusement. "You've always known," the figure said, this time aloud, the voice a perfect mimicry of her own. "You've felt it beneath your skin. The power. The hunger."

Aelina shook her head, but the words slithered into her mind before she could push them away. She had felt it. The power inside her, the way it reacted, the way it wanted. How it had come when she needed it, how it had consumed whatever stood in its way.

The shadow-that-was-her smiled wider. "You think you can fight it?"

Aelina swallowed hard, but she did not look away. "I don't have to fight anything," she said, forcing her voice to steady. "Because I am not you."

The reflection chuckled, tilting its head in mock curiosity. "Aren't you?"

Then, it moved.

The space between them collapsed in an instant, and suddenly, she was no longer separate.

The darkness crashed into her like a breaking wave, curling into her ribs, pressing into her skull. It was no longer just a voice, no longer just something watching. It was inside her, weaving itself through the cracks, through the pieces of her she had never dared to name.

It knew her.

It had always known her.

Memories flashed before her eyes—not just her own, but memories that did not belong to her. War.

Fire. A battlefield soaked in magic so raw it burned the very air. And at the center of it—a woman.

No.

Not a woman.

A queen.

The Firstborn.

Aelina's lungs burned, her body trembling beneath the weight of what she was seeing. The figure in the vision lifted a hand, magic pouring from her like a living thing, silver fire twisting through the sky, shaping the very fabric of the world beneath her feet.

Aelina gasped.

She knew that power.

It was hers.

"You are only the beginning."

The words echoed through her skull, too loud, too real. The power surged through her veins, curling into her chest, and suddenly, she knew—this was what it wanted.

It wasn't trying to break her.

It was trying to claim her.

No.

No.

She clenched her jaw, forcing herself to push back, to sever whatever connection was wrapping itself around her like a noose. Her mind was not a battlefield. Her soul was not a prize to be taken.

With every ounce of will she had left, she shoved.

The darkness shuddered.

The voice hissed in frustration, the presence inside her recoiling. The weight pressing against her skull fractured, splitting apart like glass struck by a hammer. She did not belong to it.

And it would not take her.

The vision ripped apart.

Aelina fell.

And then—she woke up gasping.

Dorian was over her in an instant, his hands firm on her shoulders, his golden eyes wild with something dangerously close to panic. She barely had time to register the cold sweat clinging to her skin, the violent tremors wracking her body before she felt the ground beneath her again.

Elias crouched a few feet away, his silver-threaded gaze sharper than she had ever seen it. He wasn't smirking. He wasn't speaking. He was just watching.

Aelina's breath came in sharp, uneven gasps, her fingers digging into the dirt as if she needed to remind herself where she was, who she was.

She wasn't in the void anymore.

She wasn't alone in the dark.

She was here.

She was alive.

Dorian exhaled sharply, his grip still tight. "What the hell just happened?"

Aelina swallowed hard, her throat raw.

She didn't know how to answer him.

Because the truth was still lodged inside her chest, still burning, still waiting.

The past was not done with her.

And neither was the power inside her.

Aelina's breath came in uneven pulls, her body still trembling from the weight of what had just happened. Her skin felt too tight, too thin, like she was still caught somewhere between two realities, hovering at the edge of something vast and unknowable. The memory of the void, of herself staring back at her, black-eyed and smiling, was still clawing at the edges of her mind.

But she wasn't there anymore.

She was here.

Dorian's hands were still on her shoulders, firm, steady, grounding. His golden eyes were locked onto hers, searching, questioning, demanding. His expression was taut with frustration, but beneath that, something else lingered—concern.

"Aelina," he said, her name a sharp edge against the silence. "Tell me what just happened."

She tried to speak, but her throat was raw, like she had screamed for hours in a place where no sound could escape. She forced herself to swallow, forcing her fingers to unclench from the dirt beneath her. Her body still ached, the aftershocks of whatever had just tried to claim her leaving a dull, echoing thrum beneath her skin.

Elias moved before she could answer.

He crouched just beyond Dorian's reach, his usual smirk nowhere to be found. Instead, his silver-threaded gaze flickered over her, reading her in that infuriating way of his, like he could see past her ribs, past her bones, into whatever pieces of her had just been shattered.

"You weren't here," he murmured, not a question, but a fact. His voice was quieter than usual, more careful. "You weren't in your body."

Aelina stiffened.

Dorian's grip on her tightened slightly. "Where were you?"

She took a slow, shuddering breath. "The void."

Elias exhaled sharply, running a hand through his hair. "Well. That's an answer I really didn't want to hear."

Dorian's jaw clenched. "Explain."

Aelina's fingers curled into her palms, but this time, it wasn't fear that made them tremble. It was anger. Not at them, not at herself—at whatever had pulled her into that place, at whatever had made her see. She forced herself to look up, to meet Dorian's gaze first, then Elias's.

"It wasn't just the void," she said, her voice steadier than she expected. "It was something... older." She swallowed, forcing the words out before she could think better of it. "And it knew me."

Dorian's frown deepened, but Elias's eyes sharpened.

Knew.

The weight of that word settled between them like a blade balanced on the edge of a ledge, ready to fall.

Elias let out a slow breath, his fingers tapping absently against his knee. "I take it we're not talking about the casual, 'oh, I recognize you from that market one time' kind of knowing."

Aelina shook her head, her pulse hammering beneath her skin. "It called me something."

Dorian leaned in slightly, his focus unshakable. "What?"

Aelina hesitated.

The memory of the void pressed against her skull again, the whispers curling around her thoughts, trying to remind her of who she was, who she had been.

"You are the beginning."

Her stomach twisted.

Elias was watching her carefully, and for once, there was no amusement in his expression. No distance. "What did it say, Aelina?"

She took a slow breath.

"It said I was meant for them," she admitted, her voice quieter now. "That I was always supposed to belong to them."

Dorian's expression darkened.

Elias let out another sigh, rubbing the bridge of his nose. "Of course it did. Because life isn't complicated enough without eldritch horrors claiming dibs on you."

Aelina shot him a glare, but the heat behind it wasn't entirely real. She was too shaken, too exhausted, too furious with herself for how close she had come to losing control.

Dorian's hands finally dropped from her shoulders, but he didn't move far. His eyes, still sharp, still tense, locked onto hers. "And you got out?"

She nodded once. "I forced it back."

Elias let out a low whistle. "That's impressive. And, you know, probably not a good sign for whatever's in your blood."

Dorian's glare snapped to him, his frustration barely restrained. "This isn't a joke, Elias."

Elias raised his hands in mock surrender. "I'm aware." His voice lost its edge, settling into something closer to thoughtfulness. "This wasn't just some coincidence. This thing knew exactly how to reach her. And if Aelina's mark reacted when it happened, that means—"

"It'll happen again," Aelina finished, her voice tight.

Dorian exhaled sharply, running a hand through his hair. "Then we make sure it doesn't."

Elias arched a brow. "Unless you've figured out how to sever a magical tether between realms, I'd love to hear how you plan to do that."

Dorian ignored him, turning back to Aelina. "Did it take anything from you?"

She frowned, turning inward for a moment. The magic inside her still burned, but it wasn't weaker. If anything, it felt stronger, heavier beneath her skin, thrumming like it had been stirred, like it had been touched.

She shook her head. "No. But it tried."

Dorian nodded once, his jaw still tight. "Then we don't stop moving."

Elias huffed a quiet laugh, shaking his head. "Do you ever suggest anything that isn't physically exhausting?"

Dorian shot him a look. "If she stays in one place too long, it might happen again."

Aelina clenched her fingers into her palms, trying to ignore the truth in that statement. She didn't know how long she could resist something like that.

Elias sighed, finally pushing to his feet. "Fine. But let's not act like we know what we're doing. We don't even know what we're up against yet."

Dorian stood as well, but Aelina remained where she was for a moment longer, grounding herself. The dirt beneath her, the cool air curling through the trees, the distant crackle of the dying fire—all of it was real.

She was here.

She would stay here.

For now.

Aelina exhaled, then stood.

"Let's go."

Dorian nodded. Elias smirked.

And the road ahead waited.

The night pressed in around them, heavy and waiting. The wind had shifted, curling through the trees in slow, deliberate movements, whispering through the leaves like something that had heard their conversation, something that had been listening all along.

Aelina didn't let herself dwell on it.

The memory of the void still clung to her skin, still coiled tight around the edges of her mind like a presence that had not yet fully left. But she had made it back. She was still here. That had to mean something.

Dorian adjusted the strap of his pack, his golden eyes scanning the tree line with the same sharp focus he always carried after a fight. Elias dusted off his coat, rolling his shoulders with an exaggerated sigh as if shaking off the weight of something unseen. Neither of them spoke, but the air between them was thicker now, more charged.

No one said what they were all thinking.

This was only the beginning.

Aelina took the first step toward the darkened road ahead, the path winding through the ancient forest like a river of shadows. Dorian followed, close enough to catch her if she fell. Elias trailed behind, still watching, still listening to whatever unspoken things only he could hear.

And behind them, somewhere in the silence of the trees, the presence of something unseen lingered.

The road stretched forward.

And they did not look back.

Chapter Eleven:

The City of the Forgotten

The first thing Aelina noticed was the absence of sound.

The air was different here—thick, stagnant, carrying the weight of something lost to time. No birds called from the trees. No insects hummed in the undergrowth. Even the wind itself felt muted, as if it had learned long ago that this place was not meant to be disturbed.

Dorian slowed at her side, his golden eyes narrowing as he surveyed the land ahead. The trees had thinned, revealing a sprawling expanse of stone and shadow, the remnants of a forgotten city buried beneath the weight of centuries. Crumbling towers loomed like skeletal remains, their spires cracked and jagged against the sky. Faded sigils marred the broken walls, symbols that once held power now worn down to nothing but whispers of what they had been.

Aelina inhaled slowly, her fingers brushing against the mark on her wrist.

It thrummed.

Not in warning.

In recognition.

She swallowed hard.

"We're here."

Elias exhaled, his silver-threaded gaze flickering with something unreadable. "And now the fun begins."

Dorian didn't reply.

Because they all felt it now.

This city was not empty.

It was waiting.

The city yawned open before them, a sprawling corpse of stone and silence, half-swallowed by time itself. The remnants of its past—shattered archways, broken bridges, temples left to rot beneath the weight of forgotten gods—loomed like the bones of something once mighty, now ruined beyond recognition. The ground was cracked and uneven, veins of dead vines creeping through the gaps, their skeletal tendrils curling up the remains of fallen pillars. There was no life here. Only the crushing weight of absence, of something that had once been and was no longer.

Aelina stepped forward, the sound of her boots against the stone far too loud in the eerie stillness. The moment her foot touched the ruined road, something in the air shifted. Not physically, not in a way she could see, but in a way she could feel. A pressure. A hum just beneath her skin, inside her bones, in the very air curling around them. The city was watching.

Dorian's hand hovered near his sword, his golden eyes sweeping over the ruins, reading the landscape the way a warrior read the battlefield. Every archway, every half-standing wall, every collapsed tower could be a trap. He knew it. She knew it. The city was too still, too well-preserved in places, as if it had been waiting for someone to return.

Elias let out a low whistle, his silver-threaded gaze flickering between the remains of what had once been a grand courtyard. The stones beneath their feet were uneven, marked with the faintest traces of old blood, darkened smears long faded but never truly erased. A massacre had happened here. The kind that left echoes. The kind that did not forget.

"This place has stories," Elias murmured, his voice unusually careful, as if even he could sense the weight pressing in on them now. "And none of them ended well."

Aelina exhaled slowly, her fingers brushing against the dagger at her hip. She could feel it too. Something beneath the surface, something waiting. The closer they moved toward the city's heart, the stronger it became—like a pulse beneath stone, like a presence too old to be understood.

She turned her gaze toward a half-collapsed monument in the center of the square. What had once been a towering obelisk, carved with intricate sigils, now lay in jagged ruin, its inscriptions broken, shattered, erased by either time or intent. Aelina stepped closer, tilting her head, her fingers tracing the deep gouges where symbols had been forcibly removed.

Someone had tried to bury whatever had been written here.

Dorian stepped up beside her, his jaw tight. He didn't need to say it—he saw the same thing she did.

"This city wasn't abandoned," he said, his voice low, measured. "It was wiped out."

Aelina nodded, her throat tight. "And someone didn't want us to know why."

The wind curled through the ruins, cold despite the weight of the day, carrying something with it—not sound, but memory. Aelina closed her eyes for half a breath, letting herself listen, letting herself feel.

The mark on her wrist throbbed.

And then—the whispers began.

Not loud, not in words she could understand, but a susurration curling against the edges of her thoughts, seeping through the cracks of her mind like something had been waiting for her to step foot here, waiting for her to remember what had been forgotten.

Her heart slammed against her ribs.

She turned sharply, her breath catching—but there was nothing.

The city remained still. Watching. Waiting.

Elias arched a brow. "Aelina?"

She didn't answer immediately. She didn't know how.

Instead, she swallowed hard, forcing her voice to remain steady. "We're not alone."

Dorian's expression darkened further. His fingers flexed over the hilt of his sword, his stance shifting just slightly. "I don't see anything."

Aelina lifted her hand, pressing her fingers against the mark at her wrist. It burned like an ember beneath her skin. "You won't. Not yet."

Elias exhaled through his nose, watching her. "You're hearing something, aren't you?"

She nodded once.

Dorian cursed under his breath. "Then we move. We don't stand in the open."

Aelina barely had time to respond before a sharp crack split the silence.

It wasn't stone shifting. It wasn't the wind.

It was a voice.

Low. Ragged. Too close.

"You should not have come."

The shadows beneath the ruined archway at the edge of the square shifted.

Then, they moved.

The voice slithered through the silence, low and ragged, a whisper that did not belong to the living. The shadows beneath the ruined archway twisted, curling inward, then stretched into something almost human. Not quite. The figure that emerged was thin, too thin, wrapped in tattered robes that had once been regal but now hung in decay. Its face was hidden, obscured by a deep hood, but when it turned toward them, the air around it pulsed—alive with something ancient, something wrong.

Aelina's breath hitched as a cold pressure pressed against her chest, the same sensation she had felt in the void, the same unseen hand reaching through the barriers of the world to find her, to claim her. The mark on her wrist burned hot, pulsing in tandem with the presence before her, as if something inside her recognized it. Or worse—as if it recognized her.

Dorian moved first, his sword unsheathed in an instant, his stance already shifting to defend. But he did not strike. Even he knew this was something they could not cut down so easily. Steel had its limits. And this thing—whatever it was—was beyond them.

Elias, for once, was silent.

The figure did not step forward, but its presence expanded, filling the space between them. The air grew thick, the weight of the past curling through the ruins like unseen smoke. Aelina swallowed hard, forcing herself to speak, her voice steadier than she felt.

"What happened here?"

A low exhale, like a sigh from a body that had long forgotten breath. Then, the figure tilted its head, slow and deliberate.

"The same thing that will happen to you."

The words sank into her bones, deep and inevitable, spoken with the weight of someone who had seen the future and did not doubt it.

Dorian's grip on his sword tightened. "You're not helping."

Elias finally stirred, his silver-threaded gaze locked onto the figure with something close to calculated curiosity. "Let's not pretend you're just here to haunt the place. You know who we are." He tilted his head, smirking slightly. "More importantly, you know who she is."

Aelina felt the shift immediately.

The figure stilled.

The air turned frigid.

Then, the city spoke.

Not in words. Not in whispers.

But in a memory.

The ground trembled beneath them, the ruins shuddering as if exhaling their final breath. The darkness stretched long and deep, and suddenly, Aelina was no longer standing in the present.

She was standing in the past.

A city alive, whole, untouched by time. Towers of white marble stretched toward the sky, their spires reflecting the golden light of a sun that no longer existed. Banners embroidered with sigils she could not read fluttered in a wind she could not feel. People filled the streets, their voices rising in a melody of life, traders calling, children laughing, the steady rhythm of a kingdom thriving.

But beneath it, the rot had already begun.

Aelina turned, drawn toward the heart of the city, where a great temple loomed. A temple she recognized, though she had never seen it before. The steps leading to its entrance were worn smooth by centuries of worship, its doors carved with the same sigils she had seen in the ruins, the ones that had been forcibly removed.

This was what they had tried to erase.

She climbed the steps, her footsteps soundless, her breath caught somewhere between the present and whatever this was. She wasn't just watching. She was remembering.

Inside, the temple was vast—impossibly vast. Pillars lined the halls, stretching high into a ceiling veiled in shadows. Figures stood gathered at the altar, their robes pooling at their feet, their hands raised toward the dark.

A ritual.

Aelina's stomach twisted.

They were speaking in a tongue she did not understand, but the magic in their voices resonated with something inside her, something buried deep and old and waiting.

Then, the doors behind her slammed open.

A woman entered, her presence commanding, undeniable. She strode down the aisle like she owned the air itself, like the world was hers to shape.

Aelina's breath stopped.

She knew this woman.

Or rather—she had seen her before.

Not in dreams. Not in nightmares.

In the void.

The woman who had stood at the center of the battlefield in Aelina's vision, the one who had wielded power like it was an extension of herself. The Firstborn.

And this—this was her city.

Aelina turned toward the altar, toward the gathered figures. The ritual was reaching its peak, the air thick with magic, the shadows above them stirring, responding.

Then, all at once, the light shattered.

Aelina gasped, lurching backward—and suddenly, she was no longer in the past.

She was back in the ruins.

Back in the present.

The figure still stood before her, watching, waiting. But now, Aelina understood.

This city had not just been destroyed.

It had been sacrificed.

The figure exhaled again, that same tired, hollow sound.

"Now you see."

Aelina's pulse roared in her ears. The city had been wiped from history, not by war, not by conquest—but by its own people. Something had been unleashed here, something that could not be controlled, something that had forced the Firstborn to make the ultimate choice.

She had destroyed her own kingdom.

And Aelina could feel, deep in her bones, why the memory had come to her now.

Because whatever had been locked away here—it wasn't gone.

It was waiting.

And it was calling to her.

Aelina's body shook with the weight of the vision, her breath coming in sharp, uneven gasps as she staggered backward. The cold from the ruins had sunk into her bones, wrapping around her like a shroud, like the hands of the past refusing to let go. Her mind still reeled, still trapped in that place of blinding light and whispering shadows, in the moment when a queen—the Firstborn—had sacrificed everything. The knowledge was still burning through her, raw and fresh, searing into the marrow of her existence.

Dorian was beside her in an instant, his grip firm but not forceful, steadying without restraining. His golden eyes burned as they searched hers, his voice low but demanding. "What did you see?" There was no room for hesitation in his tone, no space for lies. He had felt something shift when she collapsed into that memory, had watched as the ruins themselves seemed to react to her presence. He knew this was more than just a hallucination. This was a revelation.

Aelina swallowed hard, forcing herself to steady, to breathe, but the weight of what she had seen threatened to crush her beneath its enormity. She turned toward the ruins, toward the shattered remnants of what had once been a kingdom, and she understood now why it had been erased. "The Firstborn," she murmured, her voice barely above a whisper. "She did this." The words felt foreign on her tongue, like speaking them aloud gave the truth more power than she was ready to accept.

Elias, still crouched near the edge of the ruins, let out a slow exhale, his silver-threaded gaze sharp with something close to expectation. "I had a feeling we'd get to that part eventually," he muttered, tilting his head. "Care to elaborate, or should I start making dramatic assumptions?" His usual smirk was absent, though, and that unnerved her more than anything.

Aelina turned to face them both fully, her hands curling into fists at her sides, as if gripping the reality of what she had seen might make it easier to bear. "This city wasn't destroyed by war," she said, each word a blade carving into the cold night air. "It wasn't conquered. It wasn't abandoned. It was sacrificed." The weight of those words settled between them like a stone dropped into dark water, the ripples stretching outward, touching something far greater than just this place.

Dorian's jaw tightened, his grip shifting on the hilt of his sword. "Sacrificed to what?"

Aelina hesitated, but the truth had already rooted itself in her mind. "To something she couldn't control." Her voice wavered, but she pushed forward. "There was a ritual—a ritual so powerful that even now, its remnants are still here, buried beneath these ruins. They weren't trying to build something. They were trying to seal something away." She turned her gaze back to the cracked foundation of the temple she had seen in her vision, the place where the sigils had been erased, and understood why they had tried so hard to erase them.

Elias rubbed his temple, exhaling through his nose. "And let me guess," he said, voice dry but heavy, "it didn't work."

Aelina met his gaze, and for the first time since she had known him, there was no humor between them. "It worked," she said. "But not forever."

Dorian cursed under his breath, stepping away, running a hand through his hair as if that might physically tear through the frustration now settling over him. "So we're standing on top of a grave," he muttered. "A grave that's waiting to open."

Aelina forced herself to keep her breathing steady, even as the mark on her wrist pulsed again. "Not just a grave." She turned back to face them fully, forcing them to see the truth in her eyes, the undeniable connection between the past and the moment they stood in now. "A prison."

Elias let out a quiet chuckle, but there was no amusement in it. Only understanding. "I hate how much sense that makes."

Dorian straightened, his golden gaze sharp as steel. "And the Firstborn?" His voice carried a weight that made her chest tighten. "What happened to her?"

Aelina didn't answer immediately, because she wasn't sure she could.

The last image of her vision still burned in her mind—the great queen, standing alone in the temple, surrounded by magic so fierce it had nearly ripped through time itself. The shadows had curled around her, waiting, thirsting for more. She had been powerful, unstoppable—but she had known. Known that her power alone was not enough. Known that the thing she had sealed away would not stay there forever.

"She paid the price," Aelina said finally, her voice hollow. "She used her own power to seal the city, to lock whatever it was away. But it cost her everything." She swallowed hard, her throat tight. "The power in my blood—it comes from her. She didn't just bind the darkness to this place. She bound it to her own line."

Elias let out a slow, quiet whistle. "Well," he muttered, "that's inconvenient for you, isn't it?"

Dorian shot him a look, but Aelina barely noticed.

Because she understood now.

The Hollow had been right when they said she was meant for this. The mark on her wrist was not just some fragment of magic, not just a curse or a blessing—it was a tether. A direct link to whatever had been left behind in this place.

And now, standing in the ruins of the city that had been sacrificed to hold it back, she could feel it.

It had been waiting.

And it knew she was here.

Aelina turned back toward the ruins, her breath slow and controlled, her hands curling once more into fists. "We need to leave," she said. "Now."

Dorian didn't argue. Elias, for once, didn't push back with some glib remark. They both knew.

Because the air had changed.

The city was no longer just waiting.

Something had awakened.

The moment Aelina uttered the words "We need to leave," the air around them shifted. It was a small thing at first, subtle, like the moment before a storm breaks the sky. The stillness they had walked through—the unbearable, suffocating silence—was gone.

Something breathed.

Not air. Not wind.

But something old, slow, patient.

Dorian moved before she could tell him to. His sword was drawn in a single, fluid motion, the blade gleaming in the dim, unnatural light. Elias straightened, his posture changing—still loose, still casual, but his silver-threaded gaze was no longer amused. Aelina didn't need to see his hands twitch at his daggers to know he was ready.

Then, from the broken temple ruins, the shadows moved.

Not like before—not a flicker of natural darkness, not the slow crawl of evening across the stones. This was deliberate. It spilled from the cracks, oozing from the broken pillars like ink bleeding through paper, thick and hungry, curling toward them as if tasting the air. The prison had been stirred.

And something was looking back.

Aelina felt it in her ribs, in her spine—an unblinking awareness pressing down on them from all sides. It wasn't a simple presence. It was many. Countless eyes in the dark, watching, waiting, considering whether to strike.

Dorian's voice was low, even. "Run."

Aelina's breath hitched—but she obeyed.

She turned, pushing off the broken stones, her boots pounding against the uneven ground as she sprinted away from the ruins. The broken towers, the cracked foundations, the remnants of a city that had been sacrificed and sealed away—it was all unraveling now. The shadows followed, racing along the edges of the ruins, slipping through the cracks like living veins spreading through a dying body.

Elias was close behind her, his coat snapping in the wind as he matched her pace, his expression unreadable. Dorian kept to her side, his steps deliberate, his golden eyes flicking between the treetops and the creeping shadows, calculating every possible ambush before it could happen.

The trees ahead loomed, black silhouettes against a bruised sky, their branches stretched like skeletal hands waiting to pull them deeper into the night. But they were no longer the most dangerous thing in this forest. The thing behind them was.

Aelina risked a glance back.

The ruins had changed.

What had once been a silent city of the dead now pulsed with something unnatural, something waking up. Thin, elongated figures moved through the ruins—shifting like ink, their limbs stretching and contorting as they pulled themselves free from the places they had been buried in time. The prison had not broken yet, but the presence inside it had stirred, and whatever was guarding it—**whatever had been left behind to make sure it never escaped—was awake.

"Faster!" Dorian snarled, grabbing Aelina's wrist and yanking her forward just as the first of the creatures—if they could be called creatures—detached from the ruins and took its first step into the world.

The air turned to ice.

Aelina's breath hitched as a whisper curled through her thoughts, soft, insidious, ancient.

"You should not have come."

She clenched her jaw, pushing harder, forcing her legs to move, forcing her mind to stay hers.

The treeline was close now. Too close and too far at the same time. The moment they crossed it, she felt the change immediately—the city's reach stopped here. The magic that had been pressed against her skin like unseen hands eased, pulling back into the ruins, retreating into its tomb.

But the knowledge of what it had wanted did not leave her.

They did not stop running. Not until the ruins had disappeared behind them, swallowed by the dense thicket of trees and underbrush, their presence now nothing more than a hollow ache beneath her skin.

Finally, they slowed.

Aelina's lungs burned, her fingers shaking as she braced herself against the nearest tree, trying to catch her breath. The silence had returned, but it was different now. Before, the air had been heavy with something watching. Now, it felt like the world itself was holding its breath.

Dorian was pacing, his sword still drawn, the muscles in his jaw twitching with restrained frustration. Elias was watching her, sharp-eyed, his usual smirk still absent.

Aelina pushed away from the tree, forcing herself to stand taller.

She felt wrong.

Not sick, not weakened, but changed. Like something from the ruins had brushed against her mind and left something behind. The mark on her wrist was still pulsing, slow and steady, as if answering an unseen call.

Dorian was the first to break the silence. "What the hell was that?"

Aelina licked her lips, her mouth too dry. "The city isn't just a grave. It's still alive."

Elias exhaled slowly, rubbing the back of his neck. "I hate how much that makes sense." He looked back toward the ruins, now just a mass of black beyond the trees. "We didn't wake it up completely, but we sure as hell knocked on its door."

Dorian stopped pacing, turning to face Aelina fully. His golden eyes were still sharp, but beneath them, concern coiled tight. "Did it touch you?" His gaze flickered to her wrist, to the mark, and his jaw tightened. "Did it take anything?"

Aelina hesitated.

She didn't want to answer.

Because the truth was, she wasn't sure.

Something had changed.

Something had seen her.

Something had recognized her.

"I'm fine," she said finally, but her voice felt like a lie.

Dorian studied her for a moment longer, then exhaled sharply, rubbing a hand down his face. "We need to keep moving."

Aelina nodded, but she knew the road ahead was different now.

This journey had begun as a means of survival. A means of escape. But now—

Now it was a hunt.

She just didn't know if she was the hunter or the prey.

As they set off down the road, the weight of the city followed them.

Not in sound, not in whispers.

But in the knowing.

The ruins had not forgotten them.

And neither had what was inside them

The road ahead stretched long and unforgiving, a winding path of uneven earth and half-buried roots, swallowed on both sides by the dense, towering forest. Night clung to the world like a second skin, the pale light of the moon fractured through the tangled canopy above, casting jagged shadows across their path. The air remained too still, too heavy, like the world itself had yet to decide if it was letting them go or merely giving them a head start.

Aelina walked slightly behind Dorian and Elias, her steps measured, her breathing controlled, but the weight in her chest had not lessened. The ruins were behind them, but not gone. She could feel them, not in the way one remembers a place after leaving it, but in a way that felt too much like being followed. Like something from the city had slipped into her skin, into her thoughts, settling inside her like a presence waiting to make itself known.

She flexed her fingers, watching the way they trembled slightly. It wasn't exhaustion. It wasn't fear. It was something else. A pulse beneath her skin, a whisper curled into the marrow of her bones. Her magic had changed. She could feel it, even now, sitting just beneath the surface, humming like a live wire, no longer something she had to reach for—but something pressing against the edges of her mind, waiting to be used.

That was what terrified her the most.

Ahead of her, Dorian slowed, glancing toward Elias before muttering, "We need to decide where we're going next." His voice was low, edged with frustration, but not directed at anyone in particular. He wasn't one to be rattled easily, but this was different. The ruins had shaken something in him too, just in a way he didn't show outright.

Elias let out a slow breath, running a hand through his already-ruffled hair. "You say that like we have a long list of comfortable options." His voice carried its usual ease, but the sharpness in his silver-threaded gaze said otherwise. Even he was unsettled.

Dorian ignored him, turning slightly, casting a glance back toward Aelina. She felt his gaze before she saw it. A sharp, assessing thing, skimming over her like he was looking for something different about her. She didn't like that it made her stomach twist.

"You felt something back there," he said, not a question, but a statement. "More than just the memory."

Aelina kept her gaze forward, refusing to meet his eyes. "I saw the past," she said carefully. "I saw the Firstborn. I saw what she did."

Dorian's lips pressed into a thin line. He knew she was avoiding something. But he didn't push.

Elias, on the other hand, tilted his head, his silver eyes flickering in the dark. "That's not all, though, is it?" He gestured loosely, as if tracing the edges of her shape in the air. "Something in you changed."

Aelina inhaled slowly, resisting the urge to close her hands into fists. He wasn't wrong.

Dorian shifted closer, his tone turning quieter but no less firm. "What did it do to you?"

Aelina hesitated. The truth lodged itself in her throat, heavy and unwelcome.

Because the answer wasn't simple.

She could still feel the mark on her wrist pulsing faintly, the memory of the ruins pressing into her like a second heartbeat. The magic inside her no longer waited in stillness—it watched, it listened, it stirred beneath her skin like something awakening.

"It didn't take anything from me," she said finally, but the words felt like a lie.

Elias hummed, unconvinced. "That's an interesting way of saying it left something behind."

Aelina exhaled sharply, dragging her gaze up to meet his. "Does it matter?"

Elias smirked slightly, but it lacked its usual arrogance. "It might. You don't just walk into a cursed ruin, wake up the echoes of a lost city, and walk away unchanged."

Dorian's voice was quieter, but it held an edge of warning. "Especially when that city was built on something waiting to break free."

Aelina clenched her jaw. They were right. She knew they were right.

But knowing it and admitting it were two different things.

She turned her gaze back toward the path ahead, the darkness pressing in on either side, and focused on breathing. The world felt different now, slightly off-balance, like the road beneath them wasn't quite real.

She was still herself.

Wasn't she?

Aelina pushed the thought aside. "We need to move," she said, not waiting for an argument.

Dorian studied her for a long moment, then nodded once. He didn't press further—not yet. Elias gave her a knowing look but let it slide.

And so they walked, deeper into the night, deeper into whatever waited for them next.

But Aelina knew, deep in her bones—

She had not left the ruins entirely.

And they had not left her.

The night had deepened, pressing in around them with an almost unnatural density, the thick canopy overhead blocking out all but the faintest slivers of moonlight. The road beneath their feet was uneven, cracked with the slow decay of time, roots snaking through the dirt like veins in flesh. Each step felt heavier, like the very air was thickening, weighing them down with something unseen, something unspoken. Aelina kept her breathing steady, but her body was on edge, her nerves singing with an awareness she didn't yet understand. The presence from the ruins was fading, but not gone—never gone.

Dorian must have felt it too, because he slowed, his golden eyes flickering toward the treeline, his fingers tensing near the hilt of his sword. He was always attuned to danger, his instincts sharpened by years of battle, but this was different. This was patience. The kind of stillness that came when a predator was waiting for the right moment to strike. He didn't say anything, didn't need to—his posture alone told them enough. Elias caught the shift as well, though his reaction was more measured, a single arch of his brow before his smirk faded into something too careful.

The wind changed.

Not a normal breeze, not the kind that moved the trees or carried the scent of earth and damp leaves. This was a current of air that felt directed, purposeful, sliding through the forest like something unseen was exhaling. Aelina froze mid-step, her pulse hammering as the first whisper of sound reached her ears—not speech, not an animal's cry, but a soft clicking, sharp and deliberate. It came from the trees to their left, followed by a second, from somewhere farther ahead, and then a third, echoing behind them. Encircled.

Dorian moved first, blade unsheathing with a whisper of steel, his stance shifting into something ready to strike. His breath was measured, but his jaw was set, his expression a cold, unreadable thing beneath the moonlight. Elias didn't go for his weapons immediately—he was listening. His silver-threaded gaze flickered between the shadows, his body loose, but his fingers twitched in anticipation. He was waiting, calculating.

Aelina swallowed, her magic already stirring inside her, curling like a living thing beneath her skin. Whatever was out there, it wasn't human. The energy in the air told her that much—it was wrong, twisted, something that did not belong here. The mark on her wrist pulsed, an echo of what it had done back at the ruins, and she knew, with horrible certainty, that whatever had stirred beneath that city had not been the only thing watching them.

The clicking sound came again, closer now, followed by the faintest shuffle of movement against dead leaves. Then—silence. Aelina's fingers curled into fists, tension winding up her spine as she turned slowly, her gaze sweeping the darkened treeline. The quiet was worse than the sound. It was the moment before a storm, the inhale before a scream.

Then, all at once, the forest erupted.

A blur of movement, too fast, too fluid, and then something leapt from the darkness. It landed in the center of the road with a sickening, wet sound, its limbs moving in an unnatural, skittering motion, bent at angles that should not have been possible. Pale, elongated fingers pressed into the dirt, blackened nails scraping across the ground, and when it lifted its head—Aelina's stomach twisted violently.

It had no face.

No eyes. No mouth. Just a smooth, stretched expanse of pale flesh, marred only by a thin, black slit running vertically where its face should have been. The slit quivered slightly, opening just enough to reveal something slick, glistening, breathing. Aelina didn't want to know what was inside.

The second one landed to their right. The third to their left.

Dorian didn't hesitate. His blade was already in motion, swinging in a brutal arc toward the closest creature, but the thing moved before steel could touch it, its body snapping backward in a contorted, impossibly fast retreat. The motion was wrong, unnatural, like it didn't fully understand how to mimic human movement. The sound it made—**not a scream, not a growl, but a wet, gurgling click—**sent ice down Aelina's spine.

Elias had drawn his daggers, but he wasn't attacking. He was watching. Studying. His lips curled back slightly, his silver eyes flickering with an unreadable emotion. "You don't belong here, do you?" he murmured, almost amused, but Aelina could hear the tension coiling beneath his voice.

The creatures didn't answer.

They lunged.

Aelina barely dodged, twisting back as one of them sliced a clawed hand through the space where she had been standing. Dorian was already in motion, meeting the second one with a brutal downward strike, but again—it moved too fast, its body contorting out of the way like a puppet with its strings cut. They weren't just attacking. They were testing.

Aelina didn't give them the chance.

She reached for the power inside her, and for the first time since leaving the ruins, it responded instantly. The magic didn't need to be pulled forward—it was already there, waiting, humming beneath her skin like a presence at her back. She didn't hesitate. Silver fire erupted from her palm, twisting toward the closest creature in a violent, searing arc.

It screamed.

Not in sound—not in anything human—but in pure, mind-breaking agony. Its entire body convulsed violently, the black slit in its face splitting open in a hideous, writhing movement. It tried to retreat, but the fire had already taken hold, licking across its too-thin limbs, eating away at whatever held it together.

Dorian's golden eyes flickered toward her, brief but telling.

He saw it too.

This was the only thing that hurt them.

Elias clicked his tongue, flipping one of his daggers in his hand. "Good to know," he muttered, then whirled, throwing the blade toward the nearest creature. It hit its mark, burying deep into the thing's shoulder, but it barely reacted—until Aelina twisted her wrist, sending another burst of silver fire arcing toward it.

This time, it screamed.

And it fled.

All three of them retreated at once, vanishing into the trees like shadows dissolving in water, their movements jerking, twitching, unnatural. The forest swallowed them whole, leaving only the faintest echoes of their clicking behind, curling through the night like an aftertaste of something foul.

Aelina didn't lower her hand immediately.

Her heart was still pounding, still trying to decide if they had actually survived.

Dorian exhaled sharply, running a hand down his face before sheathing his sword. "We need to move."

Elias retrieved his dagger from the ground, his smirk returning, but it was thin, forced. "I'd say that went well."

Aelina shot him a sharp look, but she didn't argue. Because he was right.

They were still alive.

But something had changed.

The things from the ruins weren't the only ones watching them now.

And Aelina was starting to realize—they were being hunted.

They didn't stop moving until the trees thinned, until the oppressive weight of the watching dark eased just enough to let them breathe. The wind picked up again, whispering through the tall grass and brushing past their faces like a quiet reassurance that the world beyond the ruins was still real. The scent of damp earth replaced the metallic tang of battle, but the air was still too thick, too charged with what had just happened. Aelina's muscles ached, her body thrumming with the lingering energy of her magic, but her mind—her mind was louder than all of it. She could still see the creatures, the way they had moved, the way her fire had burned them, and the way they had retreated like they hadn't expected her to fight back.

Dorian came to a stop near a sloping embankment, his breathing measured but deep, as if he was forcing himself to calm. He didn't sheathe his sword this time—he just held it loosely at his side, fingers flexing against the hilt, golden eyes scanning the horizon. He was still waiting for something, still listening for a threat that had not fully passed. The lines of his face were sharper now, his usual controlled expression marred by something tighter, something edged in a frustration that had no clear target. When he turned to Aelina, his gaze was unreadable, but it held the weight of a thousand unspoken thoughts.

Elias, unlike him, immediately collapsed onto a fallen log with an exaggerated sigh, rubbing a hand over his face. His silver-threaded eyes flickered briefly toward Aelina before rolling skyward, his smirk returning—but it was thin, hollow. "I'd like to formally declare that we have officially been through too much," he drawled, stretching his legs out before him. "A cursed city, faceless horrors, and now what?

An entire forest that wants to eat us alive?" He rubbed his temple, his voice dipping just slightly. "It's almost like something wants us dead."

Aelina sat down slowly, pressing her back against the rough bark of a tree, trying to ignore the ache deep in her bones. The magic inside her still hummed, still waited, still felt like something foreign and familiar all at once. She wasn't shaking, not outwardly, but she could feel it beneath her skin—the reality of what had just happened sinking in, pressing against her ribs like something she had yet to fully grasp. Her pulse still hadn't settled, but neither had her thoughts, and when she finally spoke, her voice felt too steady for the storm in her head. "They weren't trying to kill us."

Dorian turned to her sharply, his golden gaze darkening. "They attacked you." His grip on his sword tightened just slightly, his stance still rigid, still poised for a fight he knew wasn't over. "They were testing you," he continued, his voice quieter now, but edged in something she couldn't quite name. "You felt it too." It wasn't a question.

Aelina swallowed hard, her fingers tightening around the hilt of her dagger, not for comfort, but for control. She could still hear the clicking, still see the way those creatures had moved, the way they had studied them before attacking. She had felt it the moment her fire had burned them—not just pain, but recognition. "They weren't just attacking," she admitted, finally meeting his gaze. "They were learning."

Elias let out a slow breath, tilting his head back to stare at the sky, the false humor in his expression finally slipping away. "Well," he muttered, voice quieter now, more thoughtful, "that's deeply unsettling." His fingers tapped absently against his knee, as if working through something he didn't want to say aloud. "It means they weren't just mindless things wandering in the dark." He turned his gaze toward her, serious now, sharp in a way she rarely saw from him. "They knew what you were."

Aelina's throat tightened.

Because she knew he was right.

Dorian exhaled sharply, running a hand through his hair before turning away, his shoulders tense with a frustration that had nowhere to go. "Then we don't stop moving," he muttered, as if the answer was that simple, as if putting more distance between them and whatever had been watching would be enough. But Aelina knew better. Whatever had been lurking in the ruins, whatever had followed them into the forest—it wasn't finished with them.

She could still feel it.

Still waiting.

Still watching.

And it had already learned too much.

The fire they built was small, muted, barely more than glowing embers cradled by a loose ring of stones. It wasn't for warmth. None of them were cold. The adrenaline from the attack still thrummed beneath their skin, keeping them wound too tight, their bodies unable to fully settle. The fire was simply there to remind them that light still existed in this world—that the shadows pressing in from the trees could only come so close before being burned away.

Aelina sat with her knees drawn up, watching the way the flames licked at the wood, their glow reflecting in the golden thread woven into Elias's eyes, in the sharp edges of Dorian's unreadable expression. They were all quiet now, the tension between them thick, but not heavy in the way of unspoken anger. It was something else. Something fragile. A silence held together by the weight of too much knowledge, too many near-deaths, and the unshakable feeling that they had just stumbled into a war much older than themselves.

Dorian sat apart from them, his back against a boulder, his sword resting across his lap, his fingers tracing absently over the worn leather grip. He wasn't asleep, wasn't even close. He wouldn't be. His mind was still with the creatures in the trees, with the way they had studied Aelina, the way they had learned. His eyes flickered toward her briefly, scanning, assessing, then shifted back to the darkened forest, still as vigilant as ever.

Elias, for all his usual sarcasm, was quiet as well. He lounged near the fire, legs stretched out, but his fingers tapped absently against his knee, the only sign that his mind was not at rest. His silver-threaded gaze flickered toward Aelina now and then, but he didn't say anything, not yet. He was waiting. Waiting for her to be the first to break the silence.

But she wouldn't.

Because she didn't know what to say.

The mark on her wrist still pulsed faintly beneath her skin, a rhythmic, steady beat, almost like a second heart. She could still feel the ruins, the weight of them stretching across the miles, the memory of that faceless thing in the dark pressing against her like a whisper that had not yet fully left.

Something had changed in her back there. Something had awakened.

And she didn't know if it was hers.

Or if it belonged to something else.

The fire popped, sending a small ember flickering into the night, and Elias finally exhaled, shaking his head. "Well, that was fun." His voice was lighter than the moment deserved, but the edge beneath it made it clear that even he wasn't buying his own humor. "What do you think? Should we take bets on how long before the next horror tries to kill us?"

Dorian didn't respond.

Aelina simply stared at the fire, unblinking.

Elias sighed, dragging a hand down his face. "Fine. Be brooding warriors. I'll just entertain myself."

Silence settled again. Longer, deeper this time.

The wind picked up, carrying with it the distant scent of rain.

A storm was coming.

Aelina inhaled deeply, slowly, letting her lungs fill with the heavy night air. Whatever had followed them from the ruins, whatever had watched them from the trees—it had left them alone. For now. But she knew this wasn't over.

This wasn't even close.

She shifted slightly, leaning back against the tree behind her, letting her body settle, if not relax. The weight of exhaustion was finally creeping in, slow but insistent. Tomorrow, they would decide what came next. Tomorrow, they would move forward.

But tonight, they would keep the fire burning.

And they would wait.

Chapter Twelve:

The Stirring Veil

Aelina woke to the soft hush of rain, a slow, rhythmic pattering against the leaves overhead, collecting in heavy droplets before slipping down to the damp earth below. The fire had burned to little more than a bed of embers, faint glows of red and orange buried beneath a layer of cooling ash. The air was thick with petrichor, the scent of damp earth and moss curling into her lungs as she blinked against the early morning light filtering through the trees. Her limbs ached, weighted with exhaustion, but the heaviness in her body was not what made her pulse spike. It was something else—a shift, a presence, something crawling just beneath her skin.

She sat up too fast, her breath catching as a sudden wave of energy rippled through her chest, down her arms, curling into the tips of her fingers. It wasn't painful, but it was foreign—like something inside her had stirred during the night, stretching, reaching outward without her command. Aelina swallowed hard, lifting her hand, watching as silver light shimmered faintly across her palm, a residual glow that flickered and pulsed like a slow heartbeat. The mark on her wrist was quiet now, but the power beneath it was not. It felt like it had settled deeper, woven itself into her bones while she slept, no longer waiting to be pulled forward—but ready, present, lingering.

Dorian was already awake, standing a few feet away, his golden eyes fixed on the treeline, scanning for movement. His sword was still in hand, though relaxed, the blade's edge gleaming with the dampness of the morning mist. He had been awake for a while. Probably hadn't slept at all. The tension in his shoulders, the stiffness in his stance—he was still on edge, still waiting for the next threat to show itself. But when Aelina shifted, when her breath hitched, his gaze flickered toward her, and his brow furrowed immediately.

"You felt it," he said, not a question, but a fact.

Aelina nodded slowly, curling her fingers into a loose fist, testing the sensation still humming beneath her skin. "Something's different," she admitted, her voice quieter than she wanted it to be. "It's not just...power anymore." She glanced down at her palm again, watching the faint shimmer of energy that had not been there before. "It's awake."

Elias stirred from where he had been sprawled against a fallen log, stretching lazily before rubbing a hand over his face. He didn't look as tense as Dorian, but there was an alertness to him that hadn't been there before. His silver-threaded gaze flickered toward Aelina's hand, narrowing slightly before he let out a low whistle. "Well, that's unsettling." He smirked, but there was no real humor in it. "And here I was hoping we could have at least one morning without a revelation that could potentially kill us."

Aelina ignored him, turning back to Dorian. "This isn't normal," she said, her throat tightening slightly. "Magic doesn't just...shift like this. It doesn't change overnight." She flexed her fingers again, feeling the way the energy responded to her movements, not forced, not reluctant, but—waiting. "This feels like something was unlocked."

Dorian didn't respond immediately. He watched her, his gaze sharp, assessing, before exhaling through his nose and turning toward the dwindling embers of their fire. "We need answers."

Elias huffed a quiet laugh, shaking his head. "You say that like answers are just waiting for us on the side of the road." His gaze flicked toward Aelina again, sharper now. "You don't recognize it, do you? This change?"

Aelina clenched her jaw. "No." But that wasn't entirely true. Something about this power, this shift, felt familiar in a way she didn't want to name. Like an echo of something she had felt before, something buried deep in her memory.

Dorian sighed, rubbing a hand down his face before stepping toward her. "Then we find out what it is before it finds out for us." He glanced at Elias before tilting his head toward the road. "Pack up. We're moving."

Elias groaned dramatically but didn't argue, already gathering his things with a resigned sigh. Aelina forced herself to her feet, her body still adjusting to the strange hum beneath her skin. This wasn't just a result of the ruins. This was something else. Something deeper.

And for the first time, she wasn't sure if it had come from within her—or if it had been waiting for her all along.

The road ahead was slick with rain, the damp earth swallowing the sound of their footsteps as they moved through the thinning trees. Mist clung to the ground in slow, curling tendrils, weaving through the underbrush like something half-alive, shifting and twisting as though it had a mind of its own. The morning light was weak, filtering through the heavy clouds in a dull, gray wash that did little to lift the weight pressing against them. It felt wrong—like the world had not quite woken up. The air held a quiet charge, something unseen pressing against Aelina's skin, a current of energy that she couldn't shake.

Dorian led the way, his posture tense, his golden eyes scanning the path ahead with the sharp focus of a man waiting for an attack that hadn't come yet. His sword was still in hand, the blade resting against his side, loose but ready. He wasn't speaking, but he didn't need to. Every movement, every measured breath told Aelina that he was just as unsettled as she was. Elias walked slightly behind her, his usual lazy stride more deliberate now, his silver-threaded gaze flicking toward her with quiet curiosity. He had noticed the way she kept flexing her fingers, the way her breath hitched every time the pulse of magic beneath her skin shifted on its own.

Because it was shifting. She could feel it.

The magic had settled beneath her ribs like an ember still smoldering, waiting, whispering in the back of her mind. It was different from before—not something she needed to call forward, but something that was already there, moving with her, breathing with her. The weight of it was unfamiliar, not heavy but present, like a shadow just at the edge of her thoughts. And for the first time, she realized that it wasn't just waiting.

It was listening.

She clenched her hands at her sides, trying to ignore the way her skin prickled, the way the mist curling at her feet seemed to shift as she passed, reacting to her presence. It wasn't real, it couldn't be—just a trick of the light, just a lingering effect of the ruins. She told herself that, but the magic beneath her skin hummed in quiet disagreement.

Dorian slowed slightly, casting her a glance over his shoulder. His gaze flickered down to her hands, then back up, his expression unreadable. "You're quiet."

Aelina exhaled, forcing her fingers to still. "Thinking."

Elias made a quiet sound behind her, something close to amusement. "Dangerous habit."

She ignored him, her attention still focused on the sensation creeping through her limbs, the way her body felt off balance, like she was walking a path she couldn't quite see. The magic pulsed again, a slow, steady rhythm, matching the beat of her heart. She tried to push it back, to bury it the way she always had before, but this time—it pushed back.

A flicker of silver light danced across her fingertips.

She sucked in a sharp breath.

Dorian saw it.

His steps halted immediately, turning fully to face her, his expression sharpening like a blade drawn too fast from its sheath. Elias stopped as well, tilting his head slightly, the usual ease in his posture vanishing beneath a quiet, assessing stillness.

"Aelina," Dorian said carefully, his voice controlled, but his grip on his sword tightened. "What was that?"

She stared at her hands, her pulse thudding painfully against her ribs. The light had already faded, but the sensation remained—a lingering warmth beneath her skin, a presence that refused to be ignored. She swallowed hard, flexing her fingers again, half-expecting the glow to return. It didn't.

Elias whistled low, stepping closer, his silver-threaded eyes gleaming with something between interest and wariness. "That wasn't normal," he mused, rubbing his jaw. "And considering what we've been through, that's saying something."

Aelina's throat felt tight. "I don't know what's happening."

Dorian studied her for a long moment, his golden gaze sharp but not unkind. "It's changing," he said simply. "You're changing."

She shivered, despite the humidity in the air. "It doesn't feel like mine."

Elias hummed thoughtfully, rocking back on his heels. "No, I don't think it does." His gaze flickered to Dorian before returning to her. "But it recognizes you."

The weight of that truth settled heavily in the space between them.

Dorian exhaled, looking past her toward the road ahead, his jaw clenching. "Then we figure out what it wants before it takes something you can't get back."

Aelina bit the inside of her cheek, nodding slowly. Because she knew, deep in her bones, that this was only the beginning.

The magic wasn't going to wait for her to understand it.

It was going to move forward—with or without her.

Aelina barely had time to process the weight of Dorian's words before the forest shifted.

The air thickened, the mist curling in tighter, pressing against her skin like unseen hands. The silence stretched, no longer natural but calculated, waiting. The wind had died completely, the damp leaves hanging limp, heavy with the unnatural stillness that had settled over them. It was the kind of quiet that came before something terrible.

Then, the ground trembled.

It wasn't violent, not at first—just a pulse beneath her feet, a slow, rhythmic beat that sent ripples through the earth. The trees shuddered, their branches creaking in protest as if something had disturbed the roots beneath them. Dorian's sword was in his hand before Aelina could blink, his body shifting instantly into a defensive stance. Elias straightened, his usual ease vanishing entirely, his fingers twitching toward his daggers, his silver-threaded gaze flicking through the mist like he was searching for the source of something only he could see.

Aelina's pulse spiked.

Because the energy that had been humming beneath her skin flared, responding to something beyond her control. The mark on her wrist burned, not with pain, but with recognition.

Something was calling to it.

A low, guttural sound rolled through the mist—not quite a growl, not quite a whisper. The trees around them groaned, their roots cracking beneath the shifting ground as something massive moved through the fog. Aelina took an instinctive step back, her breath catching in her throat as she saw it—a shape looming just beyond the mist, its body shifting with the unnatural fluidity of something that did not belong to this world.

It was ancient. Not just in size, not just in presence, but in the way it moved, slow and deliberate, as if time did not exist for it. Its body was part shadow, part flesh, a towering form with too many limbs and not enough logic, its silhouette shifting with the mist as though reality could not quite hold its shape. And its eyes—its eyes burned like molten gold, deep and knowing, locked onto Aelina with an intelligence that sent ice lancing through her veins.

"You were meant to awaken."

The words slammed into her skull, not spoken aloud, but pressed directly into her mind, curling around her thoughts like a noose. The weight of them was unbearable, the kind of knowing that did not allow room for denial.

The creature moved.

Dorian was already stepping between her and it, his blade raised, his body taut with the promise of a fight he knew they were unprepared for. "Aelina," he said, not looking at her, his voice tight, controlled only by sheer force of will. "Tell me you know what that is."

Aelina's mouth was dry. Because she did know.

She didn't know how, didn't know why, but some part of her remembered.

It had been waiting for her.

The mist thickened again, coiling around them, dragging against their limbs, slowing their movements. Elias cursed, his fingers tightening around the hilts of his daggers. "Whatever it is, it doesn't feel like the things from the ruins." His voice was too calm. Too careful. "It's stronger."

Aelina clenched her fists, her pulse roaring in her ears. The energy inside her had never felt like this before—alive, burning, aching to be used. It wasn't just waiting anymore.

It was demanding.

The creature took another step forward, and the earth beneath them shuddered, the mist parting slightly, revealing the jagged length of its form.

"Come, child of the Firstborn."

Aelina staggered back, the force of the voice in her mind sending sharp, white-hot pain splintering through her skull. Her hands flew to her temples, but it was inside her, deeper than anything she could pull free.

She had no choice.

She had to fight.

She reached for the power—

And this time, it did not resist.

Silver light exploded from her skin, pouring from her hands, her chest, her very breath. The mist around her ignited, burning away in an instant as the force of the magic lashed outward. The creature recoiled, its massive form shuddering as the light struck it, carving through the shadows clinging to its limbs.

Dorian shielded his eyes, his stance bracing against the shockwave. Elias swore, stumbling back as the energy twisted through the air like wildfire, unrestrained, untamed, nothing like the measured flickers of power Aelina had wielded before.

It was too much.

The creature lunged.

Aelina threw everything she had at it.

The world erupted in light.

And then—nothing.

Aelina collapsed to her knees. The force of the magic that had ripped through her body left her gasping, trembling, her limbs useless against the sheer weight of it. The world was slow to return—sound muffled, the scent of scorched earth thick in the damp air, her vision blurred with the remnants of silver light still burned into the back of her eyelids. The air was different now, hollowed, cracked, as if something had been taken from it—or something had been added. The weight of what she had done pressed against her ribs, curling into the spaces between her bones.

The creature was gone.

Not dead. Not destroyed. But... banished. The air still trembled with its absence, the mist curling into broken wisps where its massive form had stood, as if the world was trying to seal the wound it had left behind. But Aelina knew better. Whatever it had been—**whatever it had wanted—**it was still waiting. She had not won.

Dorian's voice cut through the ringing in her ears. Sharp. Rough. "Aelina."

She barely had the strength to lift her head, but she did. And when she met his gaze, she saw it. The wariness. The disbelief. The realization. Dorian had always been guarded, but now he looked at her like she was something he wasn't sure he could trust.

Elias was watching her too, his silver-threaded eyes flickering over her with an unreadable expression. Not fear. Not quite. But something close to it. Not because she had failed. But because she hadn't.

The ground beneath her still tingled, the magic within it altered, reshaped. She had not simply called on power—she had changed something fundamental in the space around her. And the world had felt it.

She swallowed hard, forcing herself to her feet. Her legs barely held her, but she ignored the weakness, ignored the way the magic inside her still hummed, still ached, still felt like it was adjusting to a body that was not meant to contain it.

Dorian's jaw was tight, but his voice was steady. "What the hell just happened?"

Aelina didn't know how to answer.

Because the truth was too big, too dangerous, too impossible.

She had wielded something that was never meant to be hers.

And she had done it with frightening ease.

She turned her hands over, staring at her palms, half expecting them to still glow with the silver fire that had erupted from her skin. The same fire she had seen before. The same fire she had seen in the ruins.

And in the vision.

The Firstborn's fire.

Dorian exhaled sharply, dragging a hand down his face, his frustration barely contained. "That thing spoke to you. It knew you." His gaze flickered toward the space where the creature had stood, his fingers tightening around his sword. "What was it?"

Aelina's throat felt tight. She had heard its voice, not just in her ears, but in her mind, the weight of its words still pressing against her thoughts like a bruise that wouldn't fade. She licked her lips, forcing the answer past her lips. "It was a Guardian."

Elias let out a low whistle, rocking back on his heels. "A Guardian of what, exactly?"

Aelina already knew.

A prison.

One that was breaking.

One that had been sealed by the Firstborn.

Her chest tightened. This wasn't just about her, wasn't just about whatever was happening to her magic. This had started long before she was born. Before the ruins. Before the prophecy.

Before Anira.

Her breath hitched, the realization striking like a blade to the ribs.

Anira.

She had been another piece of this. Another thread in the tangled history they had been forced into. The prophecy, the Hollow, the Shadowborn—it was all connected. The war that had begun in the Firstborn's time wasn't over.

And it wouldn't end until the final battle was won.

Elias must have noticed the shift in her expression, because his smirk faded slightly. "You're thinking something dangerous," he mused.

Aelina inhaled sharply, shoving the pieces of her thoughts into place. She couldn't tell them everything. Not yet. But she could tell them this.

"This is bigger than us," she said, her voice steadier now.

Dorian arched a brow. "We knew that already."

Aelina shook her head. "No. Bigger than just the prophecy. Bigger than just us." She met his gaze, her pulse pounding with the weight of what she was about to say. "Whatever the Firstborn sealed away—it's waking up."

Silence.

Elias let out a slow breath, rubbing the back of his neck. "Well, that's inconvenient."

Dorian didn't move. Didn't blink. But his grip on his sword tightened.

Because he understood.

They all did.

This wasn't just about what had happened in the ruins. It wasn't just about what had followed them through the forest.

The weight of what had just happened hung between them like the charged air before a storm, thick with questions none of them had the courage to ask. The world had shifted. Not in a way they could see, but in a way they could feel—a fracture in something too old to name, a tremor beneath reality's surface that would only grow wider. Aelina stood, staring at the space where the creature had been, at the scorched ground where her magic had torn through it, at the undeniable truth that had settled deep in her bones.

Nothing would be the same now.

Dorian sheathed his sword slowly, but his posture did not relax. His shoulders were still tense, his breath still measured, as if he had not yet convinced himself that the fight was over. His golden gaze flickered toward her, unreadable, but she knew what he was thinking. He had spent years fighting battles he could see, wars he could prepare for. This was different. How did a warrior fight something that could not be cut down with steel? How did he fight something that was already inside her?

Elias was the first to break the silence, running a hand down his face before letting out a slow, deliberate breath. "Well," he muttered, "that was entirely more dramatic than I was hoping for." His smirk was half-formed, forced, his usual ease undercut by the tension lingering in his silver-threaded gaze. "So. Just to be clear—things are officially worse now, aren't they?"

Aelina inhaled deeply, forcing the answer past the tightness in her throat. "Yes."

Elias clicked his tongue. "Fantastic."

Dorian exhaled sharply, rubbing the bridge of his nose. "It's not just the Guardian," he said, more to himself than anyone else. "It's the prophecy. The Firstborn. The war." He turned to Aelina fully now, his golden eyes sharp and unwavering. "You said it's waking up."

She nodded once, her fingers flexing at her sides as she stared at the ground, as if the answer might be buried beneath the scorched earth. "The Firstborn sealed something away," she said, her voice quiet but steady. "But she didn't destroy it. She couldn't." She swallowed, the memory of her vision still clawing at the edges of her mind. The silver fire, the weight of that final spell, the knowledge that even as she cast it, the Firstborn had known it would not last. "And now it's stirring."

Elias let out a slow breath, his silver-threaded gaze scanning the blackened grass, his expression calculating in a way that sent unease curling through Aelina's ribs. "If it's been waiting all this time, why now?" he asked, tilting his head. "What changed?"

Aelina hesitated.

She already knew the answer.

She lifted her wrist slightly, staring at the mark that had burned hot with recognition, the mark that tied her to the past, to the Firstborn, to whatever magic had been sealed away centuries ago.

She had changed.

She looked up at them both, her breath unsteady. "It's reacting to me."

Dorian's expression darkened, but he didn't speak. Elias exhaled through his nose, shaking his head. "Great," he muttered. "So, that means wherever we go next, we're carrying a war inside you." His voice wasn't accusing, but it wasn't light, either.

Aelina clenched her jaw. "I didn't ask for this."

Elias met her gaze evenly, his silver eyes unreadable. "I know."

Silence stretched between them again, but this time, it was heavier, filled with too many things left unsaid.

Dorian finally spoke, his voice quieter now, but no less certain. "Then we prepare." He turned, scanning the horizon, his fingers twitching at his sides like he was already planning for a battle that had not yet begun. "We find out what's coming. What it wants. How to stop it before it reaches full strength."

Elias huffed a quiet laugh, shaking his head. "Is that what we do? Just get ahead of something we don't understand?"

Dorian's golden gaze snapped back to him, sharp. "That's what we have to do."

Aelina shifted, the pulse beneath her skin still humming, still waiting.

She wasn't ready. None of them were. But it didn't matter. The war wasn't going to wait for them to be ready.

Aelina ran her fingers along her wrist, tracing the mark that had been there since she could remember. It no longer felt like a part of her. It had been hers once, something she had learned to live with, but now—it was something else entirely. The energy beneath her skin still thrummed, steady and patient, like an unseen presence watching from the depths of her own body. She had wielded something impossible. And it had not left her.

Dorian had moved slightly away from them, his eyes still scanning the road ahead, his fingers twitching at his sides. He did that when he was thinking, planning—trying to control something he could not yet hold in his hands. He had spent his whole life in battle, had fought things with flesh and blood, things he could strike down, break, defeat. But this—this was different.

Elias had settled into his usual stance, his weight leaned onto one hip, his arms crossed, but there was no amusement in his expression. No teasing remark to make light of what had happened. That unsettled Aelina more than anything.

"I need to understand it." The words left her lips before she fully processed them.

Dorian turned toward her immediately, his golden gaze sharpening. "Understand what?"

She exhaled, curling her fingers into her palms. "This—" She gestured to herself, to the space around them, to the lingering energy that still crackled faintly in the air. "My magic. The change. The things that are waking up because of me." Her throat felt tight. "The war we are walking into."

Elias let out a quiet breath, tilting his head slightly. "And where exactly do we find that kind of knowledge? Because I don't think this is something we can just ask the nearest scholar about." His silver-threaded eyes flickered to Dorian. "Unless you happen to know of some long-lost texts about what happens when the world decides to bind its ancient horrors to one person?"

Dorian's expression darkened. "There might be something," he admitted, running a hand through his hair. "Not texts, but people."

Aelina frowned. "People?"

Dorian hesitated, which was unlike him. He never hesitated.

"There are those who study the Firstborn's legacy," he said carefully, watching her reaction. "They are scattered, hidden, but they exist. They might know something about what was sealed away, what your magic is becoming."

Aelina narrowed her gaze. "And why do I get the feeling you know exactly where to find them?"

Dorian's jaw clenched. He did.

Elias let out a low whistle, shaking his head. "Of course you do," he muttered. "You have a secret cult contact, don't you?"

Dorian shot him a look. "They are not a cult."

Elias arched a brow. "You hesitated again."

Aelina didn't let them fall into their usual bickering. She took a step toward Dorian, her pulse steady but insistent. "Where are they?"

Dorian met her gaze, unreadable for a moment, then exhaled. "I never said it would be safe."

Elias scoffed. "Since when has anything we've done been safe?"

Dorian sighed through his nose. "They are not allies. They do not trust easily. But if they know something—" He paused, his golden gaze locking onto Aelina's. "If they know what's happening to you, we need to find them before it's too late."

Aelina's stomach twisted. Too late for what?

She didn't ask.

Because she already knew the answer.

Whatever was coming—it had already begun.

And if they didn't move now, they would never be able to stop it.

The road stretched ahead, swallowed by mist, curling low over the earth like something waiting to rise, to claim. The trees on either side loomed, their skeletal branches clawing toward the sky, their roots buried deep in secrets that had long since been forgotten. The air had changed—not just in temperature, not just in weight. There was something beneath it now, a presence, an awareness that had not been there before. Aelina felt it with every step, her pulse slow but heavy, the energy inside her no longer dormant but awake.

Dorian moved first, his strides steady, purposeful, his golden eyes scanning the path ahead like a soldier already calculating the battle before it had begun. He was leading them toward something none of them understood, toward people he had not seen in years, toward knowledge that could break them as easily as it could save them. He said nothing as he walked, his grip loose on his sword, but his body rigid with control.

Elias followed beside Aelina, his pace unhurried but measured, thoughtful. His usual smirk was absent, his silver-threaded gaze flickering between the mist and the distant treeline as if expecting something to emerge at any moment. There was no ease in his movements now. No glib remarks to chase away the tension coiling around them. That, more than anything, made Aelina's unease grow sharper.

The quiet between them was not empty. It was full of the things they had not said.

They had made a choice. To go forward, to seek answers, to step willingly into the unknown. But there was no turning back now, no second path winding beside this one, no escape from the road they had placed themselves upon. They were walking toward something far greater than themselves. And something was waiting for them to arrive.

Aelina exhaled slowly, her breath curling into the cool air. She didn't know what they would find. She didn't know if the people Dorian spoke of would give them the answers they sought—or if those answers would be worse than the uncertainty. But she knew one thing.

The deeper they walked into this, the closer they came to something that had been waiting for them.

And it had waited long enough.

The mist moved.

Not in the way mist should—not carried by wind, not shifting naturally. It curled in deliberate patterns, stretching, pulling away, parting to reveal the road ahead as if something unseen was clearing the way. Aelina's fingers tensed at her sides, her wrist burning faintly, a pulse that matched her own.

She knew what this was.

The same force that had called to her in the ruins.

The same presence that had followed her through the forest.

Elias hummed low in his throat, tilting his head. "I don't like that."

Dorian didn't respond. Because he didn't like it either.

They kept moving.

Aelina forced herself to breathe. The magic within her pulsed, shifting beneath her skin, adjusting to something she could not see but could feel. There was something ahead—not a person, not a creature, but a knowing, a presence.

They were being expected.

And whatever waited at the end of this road had already prepared for their arrival.

The mist did not clear. It stretched ahead of them, thick and knowing, swallowing the road like a great, yawning mouth waiting to consume. The deeper they walked, the heavier the air became, pressing against their skin like something unseen was watching, waiting, remembering. Aelina felt it beneath her ribs, in the marrow of her bones—this path was not just theirs. It had been walked before. And it would be walked again.

The war they had stepped into was not new. It had begun long before them, long before the Firstborn's fire burned the sky, long before the magic in Aelina's blood had awakened. It had been written into history, etched into the bones of the world itself. A cycle. A battle never truly won, only delayed. A sacrifice never enough to end it, only to hold it at bay.

Dorian strode ahead, his golden eyes fixed on the road, a soldier walking toward a war that had been waiting for him since the moment he first lifted a blade. Elias was quieter than usual, his silver-threaded gaze flickering toward Aelina every so often, like he could see something she could not. Like he knew—this was only the beginning.

And Aelina... Aelina knew that she would not be the last.

The power inside her, the way it had changed, the way it had responded to the Guardian, to the ruins, to the whispers buried in the mist—it was not just hers. It had been passed down, carried through bloodlines, through stories, through the choices of those who had come before her. And it would not end with her.

The war would not be decided in one lifetime.

It would stretch across the centuries, through battles not yet fought, through names not yet spoken. It would weave through the bloodlines of those who had yet to be born—until the final battle brought them together.

Until the ones meant to end it were found.

Aelina inhaled sharply, her fingers twitching at her sides. She could feel them. Not as faces, not as names, but as threads in the great, tangled weave of fate. They were out there. Future warriors, future kings, future sacrifices. Bound to this magic. Bound to this war. Bound to one another.

And they did not yet know what was waiting for them.

The road stretched ahead.

And Aelina walked forward, knowing that one day, others would follow.

Epilogue:

Echoes of the Future

The wind stirred over the ruins of a forgotten city, weaving through crumbling towers and shattered archways, carrying with it the whispers of voices long lost to time. The air was thick with memory, with the weight of battles fought and fates unwritten. The past had not been buried here. It had been sealed. And now, something within it had begun to stir.

A figure stood at the edge of the ruins, cloaked in deep gray, the folds of their hood pulled low over their face. The mist curled around their feet, hesitant, like even the air itself was afraid to touch them. They did not move. They only listened.

And the world whispered back.

"It has begun again."

The voice came from nowhere and everywhere, rippling through the stones, through the empty streets where once, a kingdom had stood. The figure did not flinch. They had expected this. They had known it would come.

"The magic has awakened."

A pause. A slow exhale.

"Yes," the figure murmured, their voice neither young nor old, neither male nor female. They were something between. Something beyond. "And so have the players."

A silence stretched, thick and knowing. The shadows trembled, the mist curling toward something unseen.

"She has stepped onto the path."

The figure's lips curved, just slightly.

"Then the cycle continues."

They turned, their cloak billowing slightly as they strode deeper into the ruins, their steps sure, deliberate, knowing. They passed crumbling statues, worn by centuries of time, their faces lost to erosion and neglect. But the symbols carved into their stone remained.

A serpent. A flame. A crown broken in two.

The figure ran their fingers over the worn sigils, their touch slow, reverent. "Not yet," they murmured, their gaze shifting toward the horizon. "But soon."

In the distance, storm clouds gathered, dark and swollen with promise. Lightning cracked through the sky, illuminating the ruins for a fleeting moment. And in that instant, the past and the future became one.

Because this had happened before. And it would happen again.

The ones who had been chosen were moving into place.

And when the time came, they would all stand together.

Or they would fall alone.

The wind shifted. The whispers faded.

And the figure disappeared into the mist.

A Heartfelt Thank You to the Reader

To you, the reader, the dreamer, the seeker of stories—thank you.

Thank you for choosing The Serpent Prince's Heart, for walking this path alongside Aelina, Dorian, and Elias, for stepping into the mist, for feeling the weight of destiny in every word. This journey is only possible because of you. You are the reason these stories live, the reason their struggles and triumphs matter. Every page turned, every moment felt, every breath held in anticipation—we share this journey together.

I want to take a moment to sincerely apologize for not including a thank you in the e-book version of Thorns of the Eternal Rose. It was never my intention to leave you without gratitude. The print version carries my appreciation, and it should have been in both. You are part of this world, this story, this series, and I am endlessly grateful for you.

This is more than just a series—it is a tale woven across time, a legacy of love, sacrifice, and the unbreakable bonds that shape fate itself. And you, dear reader, are part of that legacy.

So, from the depths of my heart—thank you for believing in these words, in these characters, in the magic that binds them together. Thank you for being here, for reading, for feeling.

This is not the end. There is more ahead. And I cannot wait for you to walk that path with me.

With Gratitude,

Everett Vale